# LAUREN DANE

# BACK TO
# YOU

ISBN-13: 978-0-373-77958-1

Back to You

Recycling programs
for this product may
not exist in your area.

As ever, I am humbled and grateful for the people in my life who have gone above and beyond to help me in some way. I would not be where I am in my life without all that kindness.

That I was able to actually get through 2014 is in a huge part due to all that generosity and love.

Thank you.

# CHAPTER ONE

KELLY'S FIRST INSTINCT was to pretend she wasn't sure she heard Ross right. But it would have been a lie and she hated lying. Regardless, she didn't know how to answer.

She was thirty-three years old. She had two great kids, a successful professional life, and this man, whom she could see building a life with, had just asked her to marry him. Only less romantically, it was more of a *we've been sleeping over at one another's houses for a year now. We should just get married because it's good for everyone and it would be more cost-efficient, don't you think?*

What else could she do but say yes? It didn't matter that Ross wasn't Vaughan. Or, actually, it *did* matter that he wasn't the man who'd broken her heart into so many pieces she'd been uncertain she could ever get over it.

Kelly was pretty sure by that point that she wouldn't. So it was more like trying to figure out how to have a happy life even though she still ached for someone who didn't love her.

Eight years. She'd walked out on her ex-husband and the father of her children eight years before. And she'd waited. Waited for him to figure out she was amazing and that together they could have such a wonderful, loving family. If he just got his shit together.

Plenty of tears and lots of lonely nights later, all she'd gotten was the lesson that no matter how much she wished it wasn't true, Vaughan Hurley wasn't a stable, reliable bet.

Worse, Kelly wasn't sure he ever would be. Whether he'd ever grow the hell up and be a man worth her love wasn't something she could bet on anymore. What was she supposed to do? Be single forever? Wait for something that might *never* come to pass? Kelly didn't want to be alone anymore. She wanted to be married. Wanted to come home to someone every day.

Ross was a good man. He'd be a good husband. She had no right to expect superhot chemistry every single moment. She loved him. They could have a good life. He was exactly what she needed.

She had to stop waiting around and start living her future. She focused on Ross's warm, brown eyes. He was *safe*. "All right. Yes," a stranger seemed to say, though Kelly didn't take the words back or argue with them.

Ross smiled and hugged her tight.

VAUGHAN HURLEY WAS finally home after being away for the past three months touring with his band, Sweet Hollow Ranch. Even before that, he'd been hard at work on their new album. It'd been a good move on his part, as his career and the band's sales and tour had done exceptionally well. But there'd been no denying he'd put pretty much his entire focus on work.

He was done with that for now. He had things to do.
Things he'd avoided doing for years. Maybe too long.

And it had taken his ex-wife's being proposed to,
to finally get him to admit it.

*"I thought I should let you know Ross asked me to
marry him and I accepted."*

*His heart lurched as he struggled to keep his com-
posure. "When are you getting married?"*

*"We haven't set a date yet, but not for another year
or so." She waited. He needed to beg her not to do it.*

*"Oh. Congratulations."*

*She'd nodded. "Thanks. Have a good tour." She'd
turned and left him there on her porch, and he'd
driven back home on autopilot.*

Vaughan'd been thinking of little else over the past
three months. Not just her engagement, but his ridiculous silence and the way she'd waited for him to say
something, and when he didn't she'd walked away.

And here he was, after a show, amped up and missing something he hadn't realized he'd been blessed to
have until he'd lost it.

They shared two beautiful daughters he adored like
crazy, though. After three months on the road and not
being able to kiss or hug them, he missed them. As
they got older it was harder and harder to leave them
each time. Because the next time he saw them, even
if it was just a few weeks later, they'd have grown and
lived and he'd missed all those moments.

Despite that, he was blessed that they loved him
back. His little girls, smelling of that strawberry sham-
poo they loved, snuggling and kissing him good-night.
When they looked at him with so much trust and love,

it broke him apart and put him together anew every damned time.

He drove the short distance, waiting until he was parked at the curb in front of the house his ex-wife raised their children in. *Their* home. A place he had to ask to visit.

All his goddamned choice. His divorce had been the epitome of being sorry you got what you wished for.

The lights appeared to be on upstairs so he had hope that he could at least poke his head in on the girls if they were asleep and drop presents off.

And see her.

He pulled his phone out and texted her that he was outside. But she didn't text him a reply. Instead Kelly appeared on the porch and waved him inside. He moved to obey and that's when he noted her urgency.

Fear seized his heart as he rushed to her. "What is it?"

"It's Maddie. She's got a really high fever and abdominal pain that when it happens is so bad she can't stand through it. I'm just about to take her to the emergency room. Can you come?"

Vaughan looked at her, truly looked at her for the first time in a while. She still made his heart skip a beat but right then, it was totally clear she needed him. He shook himself loose and focused on the problem. "Yes, yes, of course. Tell me what you need."

Kelly paused. Just a slight one, and drew a quick breath. She licked her lips and then pointed him upstairs. "I just finished getting her dressed. I have her shoes in my purse. Can you bring her down? I'm going to get the car unlocked and ready. Take her out the front door." Her delivery was clipped and very precise, and that moment of intimacy between them passed. He took some comfort in her apparent self-control and got his shit together, too.

Halfway up the stairs, he remembered their younger daughter. "Kensey?"

"She's spending the night with a friend. Hurry, Vaughan."

He did, jogging to the bedroom at the end of the hall. His baby smiled up at him briefly. "Daddy? You're here. I'm glad. I have a fever."

Vaughan bent, picking her up, the heat of her burning against his skin. Panic licked at the edges of his consciousness. He dug deep and got it under control. His child needed him. "I heard. Come on, baby. Your mom is getting the car ready."

She nodded sleepily, her pale green eyes glossy with fever.

Kelly was at the door and she led him to the car where he loaded Maddie in, sliding next to her.

"Settle in, noodle. We're going to the doctor now. Lean on Daddy." Kelly met his gaze in the rearview mirror. He noted her fear. Thank God he'd been there, and she and Maddie hadn't had to go through this alone.

No one spoke much as they hurried to the hospital not too very far from Kelly's place. Once during the ride Maddie tightened up with a hiss as the pain shot through her abdomen, but it was fleeting.

When she pulled up under the awning outside the ER, Kelly came around to his door. "I'm going to take her inside. I have all her medical info and they know me here. So I need you to park the car and join me inside afterward. Can you do that?"

Her tone was exactly what he needed to hear. No nonsense. In charge and efficient. He got out, transferred Maddie to Kelly's arms and she went inside.

Vaughan didn't waste any more time looking longingly at her. He jumped back into her SUV and found a place to park as quickly as possible. His phone to his ear as he called his parents, he also managed to grab his hoodie and Maddie's stuffed pig before hurrying back toward the double doors leading to the emergency room.

VAUGHAN STOOD ACROSS from Kelly, on the other side of the gurney their daughter lay on. They were preparing to roll her into the operating room, and Kelly paused to press a kiss to Maddie's forehead after brushing the hair away from her eyes, already heavy with the first step of sedation.

She looked so small, so vulnerable. Fear sent Kelly's heart pounding fast, but she worked to keep her tone upbeat. To hold it together because that was her job. "I love you. I'll be waiting right here when you get out."

That her daughter already knew that meant everything to Kelly. And when Maddie murmured, "Love you, Mommy," that was enough to get through and be the person her children could always depend on.

Vaughan whispered that he loved Maddie and would see her soon before he stepped back, standing next to Kelly as the hospital staff wheeled the gurney down the hall and through another set of double doors.

She kept her gaze on the spot Maddie had been. A sob tried to escape the pit of her stomach and she wrestled it back. But not before Vaughan heard it. He took her hand then, squeezing it. "She's going to be aces, Kel. You know it."

That made it a lot harder to wrestle tears away, but finally, Kelly nodded, hearing the fear in his tone, adjusting her tone to soothe. He needed her, too. She'd dealt with stitches and middle-of-the-night croup-driven sessions in a foggy bathroom with the hot water running. That kind of parenting had taught Kelly just how amazing and resilient kids could be. Maddie would be just fine and she needed to keep her focus on that.

Vaughan hadn't had to deal with an emergency in the middle of the night, she reminded herself. Empathy was something she could give him freely and it wouldn't harm her. Kelly smiled at her ridiculously beautiful ex-husband. "Thanks."

They headed out to the small waiting room and she slumped into one of the chairs with a sigh. It was nearly one in the morning and the adrenaline was beginning to wear off, leaving her exhausted and jittery at the same time.

Thank God Kensey was safely elsewhere so she wouldn't need to be disturbed and Kelly could be there at the hospital without worry. She ticked off her mental checklist, making sure she hadn't missed anything important.

Vaughan looked her over critically, looking a little more settled. "How long has it been since you've eaten?"

It flustered her when he was like this. It was easier when he was gone from her life for long periods of time. She could *not* love the man who'd chosen to let go of his family so he could keep from growing up. Kelly had two children; she didn't need a third. Didn't need to chase after the fleeting moments of true connection when she had something good with Ross.

*Her fiancé*, she reminded herself when she started to think about the way it sounded when Vaughan said her name. Eight years after her heart had been broken and she finally had the chance to make a family with someone else.

"I made Maddie dinner at five. She hadn't been feeling well so I made her tomato soup with a grilled cheese sandwich. She didn't eat much."

"My mom used to make me that when I was sick." He smiled and her stomach did a little flippy thing. Probably just because she was worried. "I noticed you told me when Maddie ate, but not if you did."

"I had soup and a sandwich, too. Did you eat? You just got off stage. I remember what you were like." She colored, though she tried not to. After a show he'd be starving. For food and for sex. No one had ever made her feel like Vaughan had. She'd wait for him in his dressing room and he'd head straight to her. It would be raw, hard. He left bite marks on places only he would see. It had been overwhelmingly hot. So sexy and intensely pleasurable she'd gotten lost in it. And in the end it hadn't been a good thing. She shook her head to release her memories. Because it had never been more than that to him, while for her it had been part of the *everything* he'd been.

"You can go if you want to. I'll keep you updated on her status. You've got to be exhausted."

Vaughan looked at her for a really long time. Long enough she'd started to squirm. Finally, he said, "I'm done going."

She knew he meant something other than just Maddie. She forced herself to ask, though she wasn't entirely sure she was ready for whatever he might answer. "What?"

He shook his head. "I'm not going anywhere, Kelly. I'm just glad I stopped at your place. I'm here. This is our child. We can do this together."

Maybe she was projecting and he hadn't meant anything more than that. She was too tired to push. Her eyes burned. Her stomach hurt and she was jittery and emotional.

He was Maddie's dad. And Kelly always encouraged the girls' relationship with their dad and his family. Here was Vaughan trying and she decided to let him and be grateful. "Okay. I'm glad you're here, too."

"I have a proposal. There's a twenty-four-hour joint not too far away. Nothing fancy, but I stop there with the girls sometimes before I bring them home. How about I go and pick some food up and bring it back?"

Her hands had started to shake a little so she balled them into fists a few times before shoving them into her pockets. Food would be good, especially since they'd be up hours more.

She also needed some time alone to get herself together and make some calls.

"Yeah, that'd be great. Thanks."

"I'll call it in so it's ready when I get there. I should

be back in half an hour or less." Vaughan smiled for a second. "I said this already, but I'll say it again. I'm glad I stopped by tonight." He handed her his sweatshirt. "Here, you look a little chilly."

He left quickly and she leaned her head back, closing her eyes.

She'd given up on Vaughan being there when she'd needed him at all a long time ago. Wished it didn't matter that he'd been there that night.

It made a difference. And she was a fool to let it.

It seemed as if she'd been trying to get over Vaughan Hurley since before they divorced. Of all the people she'd sought attention and affection from in her life, only Vaughan still had a hold on her heart and it made her so stupid, but love did that.

With a groan, Kelly sat up and pulled out her phone to text her best friend. Stacey was across the country in Manhattan. She was attending some conference where she was presenting a paper. As much as Kelly wished Stacey could be there with her right then, this paper was a big deal.

So she kept her text pretty light. Gave the basic details and urged her to stay in New York. There really was nothing Stacey could do at that point, but Kelly would keep her updated.

That done, she texted Ross. He didn't like Vaughan, though he never showed that in front of the girls. He was resentful of any time Kelly spent with him, even for family events, and jealous that Vaughan had a connection to Kelly through their children. She filled him in about the situation with Maddie and said she'd talk to him when he got up.

All that done, Kelly stood, stretching. She pulled on Vaughan's sweatshirt, as it was indeed chilly in the waiting room. It had been years since her skin had been this close to his scent and it sent her reeling.

An ache that she'd grown accustomed to many years ago throbbed at the memories of what it had been for a brief, shining time. She slammed that shut by remembering the Hurleys would be showing up soon enough.

Of this she had zero doubt. They'd drop whatever they were doing and rush over because Vaughan needed them, and every damned one of them would show up to support him and Maddie.

Mostly she was grateful her children had that support and love in their lives. *Mostly.* Her former mother-in-law might hate Kelly, but she loved her grandchildren and her sons.

Kelly had no room to judge. Especially because she had absolutely no plans to call *her* mother. Rebecca Larsen was in the Hamptons for the summer—at the house Kelly's money had bought—and Kelly liked it that way.

Kelly had grown up in an angry, turbulent household. At twelve, when she'd walked a show for the first time, she'd recognized it as her means to get away from Rebecca.

When she'd given birth to Maddie and they'd gotten home from the hospital, Kelly had been alone with her daughter and she'd made a promise right then and there to make a family with that tiny creature. To keep her safe and loved and to do her all to empower and raise a child who knew every moment of every day that she was worthy.

With a sigh, Kelly focused on the prerequisite black-and-white nature photo on a far wall as she sank into a chair. Letting herself go blank, a meditation technique she'd learned from an old roommate back in her modeling days, Kelly let go of everything that wasn't Maddie.

Being a mother hadn't made Kelly into a woman or anything like that. But it had dug roots into Kelly's life in a way she'd never really experienced before. This was a toss-yourself-in-front-of-a-speeding-car-to-save-someone love, and it had revolutionized her entire existence.

She'd been strong in a way she could look herself in the mirror every morning and not flinch. Sometimes the only thing that gave her the ability to keep going was to always be a good example to her kids. Maddie would be fine because Kelly would rip the world apart to make it so.

THEY MOVED DOWN to the main waiting room once Vaughan had returned with the food. Only he and Kelly had been allowed in the one just outside the pediatric surgery, but they could see through to those doors from where they were seated now.

"Not the first time we've eaten diner food after one in the morning." He grinned at her. She wore his sweatshirt and though it had been so long, he wasn't surprised that it still made him greedy for her. Or that it made him remember the way she'd looked in nothing but one of his T-shirts after a show.

She balled up her napkin after wiping her mouth. "I'm not as young as I was then. I'm going to have to take an antacid. As far as a meal in a hospital this late at night goes? It's top-notch. Thanks for going to pick it up."

"It gave me something to do and like I said, I was hungry, too."

"I hadn't really had the chance to ask how the tour went." There was a caution in her tone that he rarely heard from her on other subjects.

This topic was full of briars and hidden traps between them. Had been. And maybe, just maybe, it was his fault.

Before he could answer, though, Kelly stood, a smile on her face. "Why are you here? I told you to stay home."

Vaughan withheld his growl of annoyance at the sight of Kelly's *boyfriend* Ross strolling into the waiting room and enfolding Vaughan's *wife* into a hug she clearly needed. One Vaughan hadn't offered. Because he had no right to anymore.

Ross kissed her forehead and Vaughan wanted to punch the guy. The guy who said, "I decided you could be forgiven for such a ridiculous request since you were under duress. Of course I'm here. Where else would I be?"

All Ross's attention had been on Kelly but Vaughan knew very well the other man hadn't missed Vaughan in the room. Especially when Ross's gaze focused on Vaughan for long moments before he released Kelly and held a hand Vaughan's way.

"Hey, Vaughan. Good to see you. Sorry about the circumstances."

Ross may not have liked Vaughan, but he had good manners. He also clearly loved Kelly. And why shouldn't he? Kelly was gorgeous. She had her own businesses, she was a great mom and she was smart. And funny. Her skin was really soft and she smelled really good.

"Good to see you, too." Which was a total lie. Vaughan would be happy if he never saw the other dude's mug again.

Ross turned back to Kelly. "What's happening with Maddie?" He brushed her hair away from her face. "Let's sit." He led her back to where they'd been sitting, settling next to Kelly.

Vaughan used that opportunity to check in with his brothers but even with his back turned, he could see their reflection in the window he stood before.

KELLY LEANED INTO ROSS. Relieved that he'd come. Soothed by the stability he always brought into her life. "Who's with the girls?" Ross had two daughters roughly the same age as her own.

"My mom came over. I wouldn't even have seen your text until the morning but I got up to go to the bathroom and I saw my phone as I passed back to bed."

He kissed her temple and spoke into her ear. "Did you think I wouldn't come? With all his family most likely moments from descending on this hospital?"

Of *course* he would have thought about how it would feel for Kelly to be the only non-Hurley in that room. She knitted her fingers with his. Ross was what she needed. Steady. He would carry his weight. He was what she'd been missing most of her life.

Though it had been something she found herself having to repeat over and over like a mantra, and she was pretty sure it wasn't because it made her so happy to think about.

Halfway through her telling, Sharon and Michael Hurley came in, heading straight to Vaughan, hugging him and speaking quietly before they all returned to settle in to wait for news.

THE DOCTOR CAME in shortly after that to let them know Maddie was out of surgery and that things had gone well. Vaughan stood at her side and squeezed her hand at the news.

They went back to recovery where they were allowed to kiss Maddie and tell her they loved her. Kelly pulled Pete from the pocket of her hoodie and tucked him in against Maddie's side. "Daddy brought Pete to keep you company."

Maddie's smile was goofy as her eyes slowly closed.

"So glad you brought him," Kelly murmured as they left.

"Yeah?"

He looked so eager for her approval it made Kelly feel guilty.

"Yeah."

"They're buds." He shrugged, blushing a little.

He may have never taken his kids to a dental appointment, but he knew that. He didn't know their friends, either, but he knew how much his daughter loved that stuffed animal and that it would comfort her. He paid attention when it mattered. At least when it came to his children. Which in the big picture was important. She chided herself to always remember. Especially when she started to get bitter. Things could always be worse.

"Hang on a second. I need to stop by the nurses' station."

He stood at her side as she made sure they had her daughter's allergies noted. She also got the times they could come back to see Maddie.

In the long hallway, before they hit the swinging doors leading back to the waiting room, Vaughan stopped her. "Hey, thank you for letting me be here. It means a lot to me."

"It means a lot to her, too."

His smile was lopsided. The one she'd dropped her panties for way back when. It still made her happy and sad all at once.

"What's next? What can I do?" Vaughan asked, looking a little lost.

"I'll hang out here awhile longer and then head home. You should go and get rest. You have a tour-ending show tonight."

He stopped her with a hand at her shoulder. "This is a million times more important."

It was, of course, but it was nice to hear *him* say it. Even if she didn't believe him all the way. He'd chosen music over his family more than once. She understood that this tour meant they were employing the crew, filling seats with fans who loved Sweet Hollow

Ranch and who'd be disappointed if they didn't play. So many livelihoods to be responsible for.

"Look, I'm not going to be upset if you do. If she keeps improving over the day, there's no reason you should cancel," Kelly said. Which was true, of course.

Vaughan looked as if he was arguing with himself but finally shook his head. "Ezra and Paddy hooked me and my parents up with hotel rooms for today. We also talked about tonight and the show and we're all agreed that we're waiting to see how Maddie is today. *I'm not going anywhere*, Kel."

Kelly nodded. Even though she knew he hadn't been before. She'd needed him and he just hadn't been there. She nodded, even though she knew he could easily rip her trust to shreds if she gave it to him, so she wasn't going to risk her trust. Especially not when it came to her daughters. And yet what point would there be in saying all that? Why call him out and start something when they were both on edge and stressed?

Vaughan loved his daughters. They adored him right back. That was important. That was what she always had to remember.

This was about Maddie, who would undoubtedly benefit from having her dad around. And Kensey, too, because she'd be worried about her big sister, and her daddy would be around to make her feel better.

"All right."

"Thank you."

# CHAPTER TWO

THE FOLLOWING DAY, Kelly really wondered just what the hell she'd been thinking when she'd invited all these people over. Her house nearly groaned at the seams with Hurleys. All Vaughan's brothers were there and each of them had a woman along. Mary, Damien's wife, was hugely pregnant and yet she'd moved through Kelly's kitchen with ease, continuing to produce food at a rate that made Kelly begin to wonder if the other woman didn't have one of those magic bags that Hermione had in the Harry Potter books.

They all happily bustled through Kelly's house, comfortable with one another. Even just a year before it would have made her feel lonely. So *alone*. But this place was hers. At one time she'd been far more comfortable on the *other* side of the camera, but in the years since she'd retired from the runway, she'd made herself at home taking photographs. The walls were covered in memories.

Every pillow, picture, plate and towel existed as a sort of talisman for Kelly. A bit of magic that made her feel safe. This was *her* home, her heart. Even Sharon Hurley being in her kitchen wasn't enough to shake that.

Though it stung to see how warm Sharon Hurley

was with everyone else's women. Not once had the woman showed even a sliver of that toward her.

A knife shaped like jealousy and doubt sliced through her, and Kelly ruthlessly pushed it aside. It didn't matter. She left and that was that.

Ross had recently left, taking his daughters along with him. His oldest had a piano lesson and after that, they had their weekly family dinner. At his ex-in-laws' house. Yeah, that was sort of annoying. He still hung out with his ex-wife and her family weekly, but what could she say when her house was full of Hurleys?

So, Kelly had urged him to keep their schedules. Things needed to get back to normal. And to be honest, she really needed to think about how much hostility Ross had shown—in private, of course—over Vaughan and his family being around so much. He thought their *lifestyle* was bad for the girls to be around.

But that lifestyle was their world. Their dad was a musician. There was no getting around that. She didn't want the girls to be ashamed or conflicted about it. It wasn't Ross's place and she pushed back but he didn't like it much.

Blended families could work. They did work. But if he continued to attempt to get between the girls and their father, it made success impossible.

And damn if Vaughan wasn't making it worse. He kept *looking* at her. Not in a *where's the food* sense, like most people looked to one another in these situations. But an *I like your boobs* way.

Their sexual chemistry had never dimmed. Ever. Years ago Kelly had accepted she would always burn

for Vaughan. But aside from his general flirty behavior—he had always been like that—he tried to
keep it light. He certainly didn't stare at her as if he
wanted to rub on her the way she'd caught him at a
few times that day.

When it was time to eat, he'd tried some monkey
business, placing Kelly at the opposite end of the table
from Ross but next to Vaughan. He'd put her in a corner and she didn't like it one bit.

So Kelly had picked up her things and headed down
to sit with Ross and his girls. Vaughan was up to something and she had no idea what the hell it was. But she
was *not* pleased that he'd manipulate her like that.

But like so many things with Vaughan, she couldn't
call him out. Not in a crowded house. Not with his
daughter around. There were always reasons and it
normally just made her sad. But now? She was mad.
And she'd take mad over sad. Yes, she would.

Anyway, it was easier to resist him when she was
mad.

Kelly headed out a side door, into the backyard. She
needed some alone time for just a few minutes so she
sought the privacy, and chocolate, of the tree house.

She'd made a nice little nest up here after the girls
had gotten bored with the custom play space they'd
begged for. Predictable, she knew. Why not make lem-
onade out of those lemons?

Kelly settled in the low folding chair and pulled
the pretty blue mason jar from the little built-in table.

Inside, a sensual rainbow of delight. Chocolate bars
of every type, wrapped in a variety of colors and tex-
tures. Pale lavender with silver writing, midnight blue

with gold stars, the saffron yellow with bold green. All her favorites.

Kelly looked to the tick marks on the inside of the lid and allowed herself to select the lavender. Salted caramel with almond. She made a quick note and closed the lid. Settling in with a sigh as she kicked off her sandals.

She slid a fingertip down the seam, baring the glossy dark chocolate inside. Six squares.

Snapping off two, she broke that in half again and that's when Vaughan's head popped in through the open hatch.

He started, clearly surprised to see her there. "Oh! Sorry." He started to go. And she *should* have let him but instead, she called him back.

"Is everything all right?"

He popped in again. "Yes. I just…"

"Needed some quiet?" Kelly asked.

Relief flooded his face. "Yes."

She held the candy bar his way. "Come on, then. I have chocolate."

He gave her a look and settled in, criss-cross-applesauce style. He probably did yoga to move with such ease.

She handed over a square of chocolate and popped the other into her mouth, not letting his presence ruin the luxury of that first taste. Yum.

"Thanks for inviting my family over here. I know my mom can be…"

Kelly held a hand up to stop him. "Nope. Not going there with you. We're not married anymore and your children are nowhere in sight. I don't have to be nice so whatever. I don't want to talk about her. You were all worried about Maddie. You all got hungry. My house is here. Kensey is delighted to have her uncles and grandparents here. That's all I need to care about."

"You've changed your tune."

Seriously, her chocolate Zen was really getting messed up by this. "Not really, Vaughan. This thing with your mom isn't about me at all. It's about *you* and I'm not paying for your sins. Not anymore." She broke off two more squares, handing him one.

"I guess that's fair."

"You guess." She snorted.

He gave her a lopsided grin. "Did you take medication and sneak some wine?"

"I wish. I'm drunk on indignation, I think. It's the only kind of libation I can have until the only Hurleys in this house are me and Kensey."

"Why? No one is going to care."

"I can't get sloppy when your mother is around. I never know when she might attack." She hadn't meant to say it, but once the words came out, she was glad she had.

"I'm sorry. For…a lot."

*For a lot.* Kelly sighed, exhausted and utterly fed up. The trickle of anger she'd been dealing with all day began to flow a lot more freely. Eight years and he still couldn't just say it out loud.

"You're not saying anything," Vaughan said.

Kelly stared at him, blinking. She couldn't have imagined anything worse for him to say at that moment. "*You're* going to take that tone with me? Where the fuck have you been, Vaughan? Huh? Are you kidding me with this?"

He jerked back a little. In the past, this would have been the place *she'd* have apologized, even though she wasn't at fault for anything. An ingrained response to keep her mother calm that she'd taken with her from childhood like a tic.

But she closed her mouth and refused to say she was sorry when she was most definitely not. Anger had sharpened parts of the pain of their breakup she thought she'd left in the past.

And instead of running from it, she let it slice through her. She needed to never forget what loving this man had cost her. Though she'd never trade the pleasure they'd shared to erase the pain, she couldn't allow herself to pretend it was safe to trust him without cost.

She wasn't willing to pay it. Not again. Not even with a lot more years and experience under her belt. She was completely beyond her ability and she couldn't once again be in a relationship where she was far more deeply committed and invested than her partner was.

"So, okay, then. You don't accept my apology. And I understand."

For real? The man avoided all of this stuff for years and years and suddenly he decided to talk about it? And she was supposed to simply accept it and jump in where he was without protest?

Without even her input on whether or not she even wanted to do this right then? Ugh, his ego was insufferable. And hot, but right then insufferable. "Oh, you do?"

His eyes widened. "You're mad." He said it with surprise. As if he hadn't even considered that as one of her reactions. Kelly really wished she'd have tucked a bottle of gin out here. Chocolate wasn't enough for this.

"Yes, I'm mad!"

"That I finally apologized?"

Years later and this was how he decided to say he was sorry? No, worse, this was what he thought saying he was sorry looked like. Maybe it was that she had terrible taste in men. She needed to use one of those matchmakers. They'd do the choosing and she could avoid everyone who made her want to punch them in the junk.

But at the moment, the audacity fueled her and she gave it free rein. "I should have known that when you finally got around to it—eight years later—you'd be pissed off that someone told you to own your shit."

She took a few moments to find the right way to say the next bit. "*I'm sorry for a lot* means everything and nothing at all. You should be sorry for both, I guess. But you're here in my house and you're acting weird and apologizing for nothing and everything and I want to know what is wrong with you?"

"I want to know what's wrong with you," he countered.

It would be easy to let her anger turn her into her mother. To give over to an existence that was a torrent of negativity. It was why she rarely let herself get mad. Anger was a drug. It messed up everything in your life and for everyone in it. It was a cancer. And even in small doses it was a luxury she hadn't been able to afford.

Carefully now, though, she was ready to let some of it free. It wasn't overwhelming, it was…real. Real enough to not get swayed by his looks, or the way she loved him still, so very much.

Pissed off was a good defense against his charm and it wasn't junk punching, so it was a good compromise.

"You haven't changed at all." Which made her tired and sad. She moved to the hatch but he intercepted her, a hand at her wrist. The cramped space was usually comfortable, but right then it was confining.

"How can you say that?" He'd shifted so that he remained between her and the hatch to leave.

"Shouldn't you be off to your show soon?" Kelly looked at a spot just over his right shoulder, telling herself it didn't matter that he was either blind to what was happening or that he was willing to let her walk away because he couldn't be frank.

"Not until we talk. How can you say I haven't changed? That's unfair, Kelly."

She shifted her attention from that spot over his shoulder to his eyes. "This entire conversation is making me really cranky."

Kelly spun the ring she wore on her middle finger. The familiarity of the movement enabled her to get her words together. She hoped he really listened.

"If I recall correctly, we had a version of this non-conversation conversation complete with a non-apology apology years ago. You didn't have the balls to say what you did out loud then, either. Still getting pissy that someone other than your mother was calling you on it. Lucky for you, she's still your number one girl and she's just inside. Save your bullshit for her."

Yeah, it was harsh, but no less truthful for it.

"That's mean," Vaughan said.

"*Mean?* Fuck you, Vaughan. That woman called me a whore. Because her precious son fucked his marriage up and then never had the decency to tell her the whole truth. She's in *my* house, after eating at *my* table. For that matter, *you're* in my house, too, and I haven't set either one of you on fire yet. I'm not mean. But I'm not a doormat. Not anymore. You may not have changed, but I have."

He paused. "I'm sorry I brought this up right now. Sorry because I have to leave shortly for the arena, like you said. Sorry because I want to talk to you honestly but now isn't the time."

"It never is." She pushed against his restraining hand and he let go, moving aside so she could get out of there. Once her feet hit the grass, she hurried back inside, leaving him to do whatever it was he needed to do.

That little discussion up in the tree house had been some sort of epiphany. For years she'd told herself it didn't matter. That it was over and done. That she had to focus on her children and building her business. And she did need to do those things. To do them still.

But this…*mad* bubbling up from her belly was cathartic. Invigorating. She had to call Stacey to give her the news. Her best friend had been telling Kelly for years to get mad. Now that she had, it made a difference.

Stacey would say *I told you so*, but it was cool. Kelly would have in her friend's place, as well.

## CHAPTER THREE

"BEFORE WE GO out there and kick ass with this last show, you want to tell me what you're up to?" Ezra, Vaughan's oldest brother and someone he trusted implicitly, didn't look up from his case where he'd just pulled out his guitar and handed it off to his guitar tech. They were backstage, just minutes out from showtime. Ez had some sort of meditation-type thing he did now instead of being fucked up so he radiated solid calm. Utter confidence and capability.

Just being around Ezra made Vaughan feel better. More focused. Everyone seemed to react that way around the oldest Hurley son.

Though Ezra had stumbled into the pit of addiction, he'd fought his way back. He was stronger than anyone Vaughan knew. Protective of those he loved. Vaughan had already gone to him just that afternoon for some advice, but it helped to bounce his thoughts off his brother's brain.

"I've been thinking about what you said earlier today. After you and I talked, she and I had this... It was a fight."

Ezra shifted his attention then, turning to look directly at Vaughan. "A good one or a bad one?"

"There are good ones? Oh, you mean the ones with

sex after? No, definitely not that. But she didn't stab me with broken glass, either. I said I was sorry. About before. Sort of. She didn't think it was a good apology. Oooh boy, did she get pissed. Told me off."

Vaughan told Ezra about how he'd stumbled into Kelly's tree house hideaway and their argument. "She gets annoyed with the same stupid crap everyone else does. But she only very rarely gets *angry.*"

He'd never revealed to anyone what Kelly had grown up with. At first he'd told himself it was to respect her privacy. Her story was her business and he had no right to share it.

While that had been true in part, it was also because he'd known what she'd been raised by and he'd hurt her anyway.

"She can't stand to be around truly angry people. Her mother, well, you've met her."

Rebecca was unpredictable. Kelly'd built her entire life around keeping her mother on the other side of the country. Or, if they had to be in the same place, managing her to keep Rebecca from making a scene.

Her mother had an impressive variety of ways to create drama. Vaughan had been in the woman's presence just three times and each time it had been a master class on how to wreak the most destruction.

Just three times and that was his impression. Vaughan really couldn't imagine what it had been like for Kelly to have grown up with a raging inferno of a stage mother who was the most narcissistic human being he'd ever dealt with.

Vaughan blew out a breath. "Understandably, she isn't prone to showing that sort of extreme emotion."

He pinched his bottom lip as he thought about how to explain it all. "I can't lie to you, Ez. For years I thought it was a simple case of a bad breakup." And it had been. He'd delayed things without ever coming out and saying he wanted her to stay. And then he'd told so many pretty lies to himself he didn't know what was true anymore.

In retrospect, those things brought him shame. He'd been young and selfish and shitty. He'd wanted her to break and tell him she wanted him back. Because he was too weak to say it first.

"I hurt her. Made her sad. Broke her heart. I did those things. But today when she got really angry it was like a big giant buzzer sounded. She peeled all that calm back and showed me stuff I've never seen from her. Until she walked away from me, fuming like some gorgeous creature of vengeance, I thought she was totally done."

Vaughan paced as the noises of a rock-and-roll concert getting ready to start sounded all around them. Strange as it was, he found the hum and chaos of it to be soothing.

"I made so many mistakes. I didn't apologize right. Not eight years ago and not today. She called me out and I deserved it."

"You're not that guy anymore, Vaughan," Ezra said. "You were a spoiled kid when you two got married. Still a spoiled kid when you got divorced. You're a man now. They're your family. Don't let fear keep you from doing the right thing because Ross won't."

It had been Vaughan who hadn't wanted to be married, not Kelly. She'd served him the papers first, but he'd been the one to toss a divorce at her to make her leave a subject alone.

He'd thought—at the time—that she'd cool off and back down. He meant to make it up to her once he'd gotten off tour. But he never got the chance. He'd said it one too many times and much to his surprise, she'd taken him at his word and filed for divorce.

Then pride had taken over. If she wanted to end their marriage, fine. He'd still have a great life. He'd told himself that for years as he'd driven the road from Hood River to Gresham where Kelly had offered to settle so he could be close to the girls.

He'd told himself being single was better anyway. That his life was too fucking fabulously full of women to bang for him to go tying himself down forever.

And every time she opened her door he knew everything he said had been a lie. But pride was a fucking killer and he'd let himself hide behind it for way too long.

This engagement had tripped him up. For the past three months it had rattled around in his head. Kelly being someone else's wife. Kelly sleeping next to another man. His kids waking up to another dad on Christmas morning. And Ross didn't like him. While he'd never done or said anything in front of their daughters, Vaughan couldn't help but wonder if and when that might change.

"I'm scared I can't do it. That I don't have what she needs. For me, there's no one else. It's just her. But she's got a software engineer with a big house in the burbs already. This guy wants to marry her and erase me from her life. I can feel it. He wants to take my place."

"I have to be honest and say I think you're right. Ross hates your guts. He hates the way you look at Kelly. Hates the way she looks at you. Bummer. But if it's you or him, make it you. This is love."

It was long past time to finally just admit that he was thirty-four years old and in all his adult life there had been *one* woman he'd loved and it was Kelly. He'd *already* found the right woman to settle down with and, whether Ross liked it or not, Vaughan planned to do everything he could to get Kelly to give him a second chance.

"She's not going to let you get away with avoiding responsibility, though. If you can't own your shit and say exactly what you're sorry for and how you plan to make it up to her, why should she let you? Comfort is great and all. Reality isn't nearly as fun when things are hard. You can be comfortable and alone, or banging chicks you barely know and don't care about. Or you can do some hard, painful work and have a family with the woman you love. I know what I'd choose."

He missed how it felt to have Kelly belong to him.

He needed to be a real, daily part of Maddie and Kensey's life. He'd base himself in Portland and then come back and forth as he needed to. He'd be away from the ranch awhile, which was also necessary, as well.

The gong sounded, indicating it was time to head toward the stage. Vaughan tipped his chin at Ezra. "Thanks. Tell me what's going on with Tuesday."

Ezra's smile went sort of predatory for a moment

as he thought about the gorgeous woman he was so clearly gone for.

"That one we're taking step-by-step. Let's go kick some ass."

As they headed out to the roar of a hometown crowd, Vaughan wasn't tied in knots. He'd made a choice. One he needed to make. Now he just needed to see it all through.

STACEY PUSHED A cup of coffee toward Kelly as she opened the door to admit her best friend. Who Kelly'd specifically told to stay in Manhattan where she'd been attending a conference.

"It's gonna be a long day. I brought sustenance."

"I know you heard me tell you to stay at your conference."

"Please, as if I listen to nonsense like that." Stacey tossed her bag on the couch and kept on until they reached the kitchen. "What's for breakfast?"

"There's like forty-five pounds of food in the fridge. Vaughan's sister-in-law brought over a boatload of stuff yesterday and fed people for hours. There's actually more left. I had some mu shu pork stuff. I shouldn't have mentioned it, though, as I ate it all and there's none for you. Why did you come back? I thought you were presenting your paper today?"

"I told them I'd had a family emergency so they let me present it yesterday. I was on a plane back here a few hours later," Stacey explained.

Kelly hugged her. "I'm so glad you're here. So much has happened since I spoke to you last."

"Get to drinking that coffee while I go through your food like a hungry bear."

Now that Stacey stood there in her kitchen, Kelly allowed herself to be relieved and then thrilled. "I'm so glad you're a disobedient nag."

Stacey moved back to her, hugging her once more. "She's going to be all right."

"I know." Kelly drank her coffee while she watched Stacey fill a plate. "It's not even that. I mean, I was freaked when it first happened. But Maddie's going to be fine. It's…Vaughan."

Stacey slid up onto the stool across the island from Kelly. "Please tell me you didn't sleep with him."

"I didn't sleep with him!" She kept her tone low, not wanting to wake Kensey just yet. All this stuff had been bubbling up and she'd had no one to say it to. Thank goodness for her friend.

Stacey arched a perfectly shaped brow. "You wanted to."

Kelly had met Stacey eight years before when Stacey had been her divorce attorney. After the divorce had been final she'd been minus a husband but up a friend.

An unlikely pairing, but the two of them clicked. Stacey was the sister of Kelly's heart and a big part of the way Kelly had been able to stand up and claim a safe place for herself and her kids.

The moment Kelly had fully fallen in love with her friend was when Kelly overheard Stacey giving a stern lecture to Vaughan's attorney about not underestimating Kelly's intelligence simply because she happened to be beautiful. No one had ever defended her like that before. It usually tended to be double-edged. In her modeling days she'd had friends, but they'd all been wrapped up in the track to the top. She did have people she kept contact with since she'd left, but Stacey had become the closest friend Kelly ever made.

Which also meant Kelly couldn't lie to her. She put her head down, resting on her arms and groaned. "I *always* want to. That's not a secret. I feel like I need one of those 'days without a workplace accident' signs only with 'X days since I last boned my hot-as-shit ex-husband.'"

Stacey fanned her face a second. "He *is* hot as shit. No denying it. One of the most superior male specimens I've ever seen. And yet, he's a thirtysomething man-boy who lives with his mom. Don't forget that."

Kelly burst into laughter. "He has his own house. He doesn't live with them."

Stacey snorted. "Oh, I see, he lives in the carriage house with his own entrance! Please. Same difference, Kelly. You can't have a life with a man who lets anyone else have that much say in his decisions concerning *your* family."

"I hate it when I can't just say, *you're jaded because you're a divorce attorney.*"

"And why is that?" Stacey had no problem making Kelly come out and say it.

"Because you're right. *In part.* He's suddenly in my space. Sure, I see him often enough when he's not recording, writing or on tour. He sees the girls regularly, is what I mean. Which is good," Kelly added.

"Get to the real point and stop giving the man a gold star for doing what is a necessary and normal thing. It's not a special achievement to be there for your children. Nor should you have to note it every time like a credit he gets paid for. Ugh. He's *supposed* to be a good parent."

When Kelly thought about her own upbringing, she couldn't help but give Vaughan credit because she'd grown up without anyone who loved her the way he loved their children.

"What about Vaughan and Kelly? Don't get side-tracked by your obsessive need to be nice. Not when we're talking about sex and stuff. He's reacting to your engagement."

Kelly thought so, too. "Maybe. When I told him about the engagement he was surprised."

"But the tool held his tongue to the point of pretty much rolling with it A-OK."

Kelly shook her head, disagreeing with that. "It felt more like he ran from it. Not acceptance. Avoidance." The distinction shouldn't be important, but it was. "It's recent and stupid and it doesn't say anything. Not really. But it feels like he's trying to get close to me. Like a deliberate step into my life."

She told Stacey about the thing he'd done at the table the day before and the support he'd shown her at the hospital and even after. And about the argument in the tree house.

"You got mad at him? Like to his face?" Stacey put some potato salad on her sandwich and topped it with a slice of bread. Kelly shook her head. Who was she to judge? She'd eaten mu shu pork before six in the morning.

"Suddenly I just… I wasn't able to keep it back.

So I got mad as hell and said all sorts of stuff. I don't regret any of it. I thought about being sorry but then, you know what? It felt good to finally let the anger out. The problem is that now it's like a switch has been flipped or something. I can't stop thinking about him or why he's evading my questions."

Stacey pointed with her fork for extra emphasis. "He's evading your questions because he wants you back. I actually thought he never would get off his ass to fight for you. Bold move, if he's committed to it. Maybe he can pull it off. Neither of you are the same people you were when you divorced."

Kelly blinked, beyond words for long seconds. "And what should Ross think about that?"

Stacey kept eating her sandwich.

"So, let me get this straight. You're not going to tell me to lock the door and keep an aspirin between my knees?" Kelly asked.

Stacey laughed. "It wouldn't do any good. I love you and want you to be with a man who loves you and deserves you. Ross is nice, though he's way more connected to his ex-wife's family than I think is normal. You let them eat here when your kid was in the hospital. That's not weekly dinners at your ex-in-laws' like he does. Regardless, Ross would be a *proficient* spouse. He's a good provider—not that you need it, but it's a good indicator of character—and he enjoys your girls. The ones on your chest and the ones you gave birth to. But he doesn't *adore* you. He doesn't cherish you. He wants you. Plus? You don't love him."

Denial sprang to her lips automatically. "I do *so* love him." Kelly sighed as she searched for something she was more certain of. "He's everything I've been missing. He's *stable*. He came to the hospital because he knew the Hurleys were going to show up and I'd be there alone. I said yes to his proposal. I should have said yes." Kelly added a sharp nod of her head to underline that. Stacey kept looking at her. "What? I'm sorry, but it's true. It was a logical choice. His girls and mine get along. We share the same general parenting philosophy. He's a good choice."

Kelly winced at how empty the words sounded. Though maybe there was a slight flavor of desperation, a need to believe it. If she just said it all over and over again she'd believe it.

"Jeez. Yes, yes, Ross is a great guy. And he'll make the right woman a great husband. You're not that woman. He can't handle you. He doesn't even know it yet, but he will sooner or later. And resent you for it. Right now, though, he wants more than you can give so he's accepting that you're settling. Which will leave you both unhappy. I think marrying Ross would be a terrible mistake. No matter what you decide with Vaughan," Stacey added. "The world is full of nice people who make good choices and floss. But those things, in and of themselves, aren't enough to get married to someone over."

"Why didn't you tell me this earlier?"

Stacey peeked in a few containers she'd brought out from the fridge, sniffed a few, putting most back but bringing the rest to the table. "It's not like I've hidden my general feelings about Ross."

That much was true. But Stacey was really good at seeing past the emotional but not necessarily important stuff to get to the heart of the matter. She gave great advice, even if she herself didn't always follow it.

"Well, but whether or not he's bland, that's not going to color your perception as to my *marrying him*. You're too single-minded and Borg-like for that. It would be irrelevant unless you had a good reason," Kelly said.

"Borg-like?" Stacey snickered. "That's a good one. Also, correct. Because even if I hated him, if you loved him and I thought he'd make you happy I'd suck it up and hold my tongue. I've been waiting until you asked."

"You're good at this friend thing. I'm just saying."

"Right?" Stacey winked. "Back to Ross. He's nice. So what? Nice?" She blew raspberries. "Fuck nice. I don't even want nice shoes much less a nice partner." She put her sandwich down and after a judicious wiping of any potato salad remnants, Stacey grabbed Kelly's hand for emphasis. "Does he make your heart beat faster? When he says your name, does it feel like your skin can't hold in the intensity of what you feel? Because if not, don't get married. Every day I see the end of one marriage after the next and while yes, it does make me jaded, it also convinces me that successful marriages are a mix of things, but they have an essential spark between the couple. Ross would be sure your car got detailed. The guy you should marry? He'd know you get up at four thirty so you can work out an hour before you start your day. He'd accept that you do it because you were raised by a sociopath but that you work quite hard to not let it go into more obsessive behavior."

"It's weird that you feel no hesitation bringing up the state of my mental health," Kelly said.

"Whatever. I'm socially awkward and useless when it comes to being subtle anywhere but in my job. I say what I think. You need that. You ignore that I'm weird in my own ways."

Kelly giggled quietly. "You're my weirdo soul mate."

"My point is, being *known* by someone else—understood—that's worth everything. Nice is one thing. But true connection? That's a universe away from nice. It's *necessary*. Kelly, you don't have that with Ross. And I don't think you ever will."

Kelly frowned. "I am totally done being single. I want a partner. I want someone to have long talks with, late into the night. I want someone to come home to. Other than the girls, obviously, but you know what I mean. I want to be with someone. Ross isn't exciting like Vaughan, no. But he's a good choice."

"There are men from sea to shining sea. Especially when you're tall, blonde, blue-eyed and gorgeous. You don't have to settle and marry someone you don't love." Stacey indicated Kelly with another fork point.

"None of this matters anyway. Vaughan hasn't said anything specific. When I asked him directly about it he avoided answering. I'm off balance. He'll go back to the ranch tomorrow or maybe even tonight and it'll all be over." It'd be easier to think about marriage to Ross once Vaughan had disappeared from her life again.

"I don't know, Kel. I mean, look at you. You're flushed. He's got you flustered."

"I didn't say the situation would be over. Just his part in it. I have to think about the engagement. I've had second thoughts over the last few weeks." Upstairs she heard Kensey moving around. Walking down the hall from Kelly's bedroom to her own. They probably had about five minutes before she came down, so Kelly needed to wrap this up before they had an audience.

Stacey shrugged. "You know my opinion of the engagement. If you want more from me, tell me. I'm just trying to keep my mouth shut and support you after this."

Kelly laughed some more. "You butt out? Ha!"

"I didn't say I was going to butt out. I said I told you how I felt but that you're my friend and I want you to be happy so I'll support you in that."

"Fair enough. Thanks again for coming home."

"Not a thing. Tell me what you need. I can stay here with Kensey while you go pick Maddie up. I can bring her with me to the hospital, take her to my place for a while. I can run interference with the Hurleys. Whatever."

"Thank you. I called the hospital already to check in. She's awake and doing well. They said I could come over there after eight. The doctor told us last night that if everything kept on the way it was that we could bring Maddie home sometime late morning today."

"When's Shurley arriving?"

Kelly couldn't stop her snicker. Shurley was what

they called Sharon Hurley so no one knew they were talking about Vaughan's mother.

"Vaughan should be here within the next fifteen minutes. I imagine his parents will be arriving either with him, or sometime soon after. I hope after. I don't have enough coffee in me yet for before. The rest of the brood I expect will show up at some point once we get Maddie home and settled."

"How was it yesterday? Aside from the argument you had with Vaughan?"

"It was all right. Everyone was friendly, especially everyone who wasn't a certain mother-in-law. Ezra has a new girlfriend. She's pretty cool. Makes jewelry so I'm all over looking at what she does. Maybe for the shop."

Kelly co-owned two clothing boutiques. One in Portland and the sister store in Manhattan. She and her business partner had decided to start carrying more accessories like jewelry and bags recently. As they liked to feature women artists and designers and also support locals, she'd been thrilled to meet Tuesday and get along with her so well from the start.

"It could have been dreadful and it was only uncomfortable. So, yay, I guess. But there won't be as big a houseful today so that means I may have more one-on-one time with Shurley. Maddie's in raptures that her dad and grandparents will be here. I'm trying to hold on to that. If you could just be here to run interference if I need that, I'd appreciate it."

"Got it."

## CHAPTER FOUR

KENSEY, SINGING AT the top of her lungs "Me and Bobby McGee"—the kid had taste—came downstairs and when she caught sight of Stacey, she stopped singing to shriek Stacey's name as she launched herself at their visitor.

Stacey, laughing, hugged Kensey tight, kissing each cheek before putting her back down. "Good to see you, peaches."

"Did you hear that Maddie's appendix got bursted? She got surgery and Daddy promised her a new bike. But then she made him promise to get me one, too. Which I thought was pretty nice of her to share."

Stacey's gaze met Kelly's for a brief moment. Amusement lit her eyes.

By the time Kelly slid a plate of eggs and toast to Kensey, Vaughan had arrived, also bringing coffee, along with a box of doughnuts.

He came up short at the sight of Stacey at the island, seated next to Kensey.

"Morning, Kelly." He turned to Stacey and lifted a hand in greeting. "Stacey."

At first it had been weird, becoming such close friends with the attorney who handled her divorce. But it had been years since then and it wasn't so odd anymore.

Vaughan bent to hug Kensey, who grinned at her dad. "Auntie Stacey came over to have potato salad sandwiches for breakfast. She's been in Manhattan at our other house. I told her she could have my room but she likes Mom's room best."

"Her bed is bigger. My feet hang off the end of your bed." Stacey stood, clearing away some dishes as she did. "I do wear your clothes when I'm there, though, baby." She winked.

Kensey put her hands over her mouth and laughed.

"Have you eaten? The fridge is full of stuff left over from yesterday but I can scramble you a few eggs if you'd rather," Kelly asked him.

His wariness eased away as his smile deepened, took root and made her slightly dizzy. "I'm going to have a doughnut with some coffee and see where I go from there. My parents went home last night but they called me twenty minutes ago and said they were leaving the ranch."

"They're welcome here after we handle Maddie's discharge." Hopefully for a short period of time. Maddie would need rest and quiet, not a house full of her relatives.

"Much appreciated. I figure everyone can come by here, see that Maddie is safely tucked in and happy and then they'll all go. I asked my brothers to stay home today. They'd like to visit her this week sometime, but I'll coordinate that with you first."

Kelly eyed him carefully. That was pretty thoughtful of him, and of them. "Of course. She loves to see her uncles, you know that. She can't stop talking about

Mary and Damien's baby and how they'll have a new cousin to play with."

Kensey cleared her dishes and danced past her parents. About 70 percent of the time, their youngest child didn't bother to walk or skip or run to get around; she pranced and leaped; she shimmied and pirouetted. Kensey had been a dancer even before she could walk. "Auntie Stacey, will you fix my hair?"

Stacey nodded. "Yes, that would be awesome." Hand in hand, the two headed back upstairs, leaving Vaughan and Kelly alone.

"How do you want to do this?" Vaughan asked her. "I'd like it if it could be just you and me at the hospital. Okay?"

"No Sharon and Michael?"

He shook his head. "No Ross, either."

She gave him a look, suspicion at the edges. "Why?"

"I want to be a little selfish, okay? I want to be the one who carries her in from the car. The one to bring her to her bed so you can tuck her in." He paused. "Please?" Vaughan knew Ross spent more time with his daughters than he did. But he'd decided the night before to end that. To not only win his family back, but to deserve them, too.

Kelly blew out a breath. "All right. It's a fair request. As long as it's *just* you and I."

Licking his lips, Vaughan searched for the right words. "I'm sorry about a lot of things. I wasn't specific yesterday and I can't really be right now. But I'm working on it. I made so many mistakes. I promise you my mother will behave. But she'll do it from here. They already promised they wouldn't stay a long time. They appreciate your being so welcoming to them."

The rift between his mother and the mother of his children had come from him. It had grown to epic proportions and then settled into painfully precise civility.

He hated knowing Kelly had to be wary of an attack from his mother. Sharon Hurley wanted to protect her family so she'd reacted defensively from the start.

She'd never given Kelly a chance, and their split had only made things worse.

Kelly shook her head. "I don't want to go into that right now. I have enough to manage at the moment."

"Fair enough." Vaughan finished the second doughnut and dusted the sugar from his hands. "One more thing. I know it's going to take a week to two weeks for Maddie to recover totally. I'd like to be around as she recuperates. I want to be with them both more. I've missed a lot. I don't want to… I'm here and this is what dads should be for. I'll stay in my place in Portland and commute here. Help with school and stuff. I know you work at your store while the girls are in school so I can be here while you do that. I want, very much, to be a better, more involved father. I want them both to count on me to make things better."

He wanted her to have that, too.

Vaughan took in the way the sun hit her back, the gold in her hair gleaming in the light. She wore it up in a ponytail. Not wearing much makeup, she was casual in jeans and a bright blue shirt and sandals. And yet she made it elegant. Something about her always made him think about expensive champagne. She seemed to sizzle on his tongue and then wisp away.

He knew she smelled of the same perfume she'd worn since he met her. Chanel No. 5.

Their daughters had her tall, blonde looks. Blue eyes, though closer to the green of Vaughan's than their mother's deep ocean blue. They had the same grace Kelly carried herself with.

Kelly spoke again, catching his attention. "Maddie would really love that. Both girls would love having you around more. But your condo is nearly as far away—given traffic—as your place at the ranch is." She twisted her ring a moment. "If you really want to do this, I have a guest room with a bathroom attached. You can stay there for the next few weeks."

"Really?" Being here would put him close to them. He wouldn't go to bed every night in another place, hoping for a phone call to update him. He'd be *there* for them. All three of them. He could help and get to know Kelly all over again and hopefully prove that he'd changed while he was at it.

"Yeah, of course." She nodded.

"That would be great. Thank you so much. Really. This means a lot."

He hugged her and stepped back after he sniffed her hair.

"I can cook fairly well so I can help with breakfast, too."

"Baby steps, Vaughan. Let's just go bit by bit."

"Don't you trust me?"

She cocked her head and looked him over. "Depends on the issue."

He frowned. He wanted to argue, but he couldn't. He had no ground to stand on because he *had* failed her. He'd have to prove himself.

"Fair enough."

"WELL, LOOKS LIKE I've missed some stuff," Ross said as he came into the kitchen. His tone had a lot of anger and tension in it, which meant what? That he was mad about Vaughan in general or that he'd eavesdropped?

"Good morning to you, too. What stuff?"

"You have a new lodger, I see." Ross gave a jerk of his head, indicating Vaughan.

This was a sort of angry she hadn't seen in Ross before. Terse. Clearly agitated. It wasn't as if he'd walked in on them doing anything untoward at all.

"We do. Vaughan is going to stay in the guest room while Maddie recovers." Kelly decided to just ignore his snit and move on.

Everyone shifted, uncomfortable, and Kelly stood there, staring at them both. Her life used to be a lot more simple.

"Is there a problem?" Vaughan asked Ross.

Kelly hit her *enough* point. "Why are you asking *him*? This is my house."

Both men looked to her, surprised. As if they were shocked she had an opinion about something happening in her own damned kitchen.

Kensey and Stacey came downstairs before anything else broke out.

Kelly dried her hands. "I'm going upstairs to finish getting ready. We can ride to the hospital together,

Vaughan." She bent to kiss Kensey, who had already caught sight of her dad and headed his way.

Ross followed her up the stairs and into her room. Ross was nearly perfect, but his anger tended to be passive-aggressive and she realized she had no energy to play along. This was extra annoying and she wasn't interested. If he wanted to say something he needed to do it without some big pouty game.

He sighed dramatically a few times but she pretended he was one of the girls and ignored it while she changed into a nicer shirt.

Ruthlessly, she only allowed herself enough time at the mirror to make sure the ponytail she'd redone was neat.

Finally, Ross met her as she came back into the bedroom from her closet. "He's here too much."

"Vaughan? The guy whose kid is in the hospital?"

"He doesn't give a *shit* about them. He wants to use them to get close to you. They're tools to him." It was such a hateful, wrong thing to say she physically took a step back. Ross noted her reaction and sighed, agitation in the sound.

"That sort of thing demeans you, me and Vaughan, too. Whatever his faults, he absolutely does care about them. He's supposed to be here when they need him, and the things you just said really piss me off."

"You didn't even ask me if he could stay here."

"Uh. No, I didn't. Mainly because I didn't know about it until this morning. He told me he was going to stay in Portland while Maddie was healing up and that he wanted to be helpful with the girls. Am I supposed to say no? That's a haul for him. I have a big

house. His children live here. It made sense to offer."
And she didn't need to run it by him! He hung out
with his ex and her family all the time.

"I'm uncomfortable with him being here."

Kelly didn't want him uncomfortable. Or upset or
sad or any of that. "Why?" She sat on the edge of
the bed.

"He's your ex-husband."

"You sleep at your ex-wife's house at least four
times a year. You hang out with her and her family
every weekend."

"That's different."

"Why is that?" She hated to keep asking why, but
she just wasn't getting his deal when he did the same
thing.

"My kids are there!"

"And mine are here."

"I don't want him staying here. And you do." He
said it like he'd never imagined such a thing.

"Well, we aren't going to agree on everything."
She needed to break the engagement. She should say
it right then. It wasn't fair to either of them. But she
had enough drama right then. She just wanted to get
her kid home from the hospital. And as annoyed as
she was, there was no call to be hurtful. When she
broke it off it didn't need to happen in a house where
Vaughan was.

"If you let him stay here we can't be together. It's
me or him." Ross couldn't have known it, but he'd
tossed the ultimatum out in a way nearly identical to
Vaughan, when he'd tossed out his *go ahead and divorce me then if you're so unhappy* eight years ago.

Well, that just made her mad all over again. "You had your ex-wife stay at your house for three weeks when she got a nose job. And she has family in town. I never said a single thing about that." Though, boy, she'd wanted to a few times. His ex-wife was one of those superhelpless types. He was constantly fixing things at her house. If her internet went down she called him about it. For three weeks she'd camped in Ross's bedroom while Ross slept in the guest room and paid for daytime help when for heaven's sake she'd had a nose job, not a liver transplant.

But this was the mother of his children, and Kelly had trusted him to make the choices he thought were best for his kids. And he wasn't doing that for her.

"That was different. She needed me. He doesn't need you. You don't need him. You and the girls are better off without him and his influence anyway."

"What the hell are you talking about? Influence?" Kelly asked.

"He's not good for the girls. They need to spend less time with him, not more. Inviting him into your home doesn't fit those goals."

"Whose *goals* are those?"

"Naturally, when we marry, I'll adopt the girls. Once he can't have you anymore he'll lose interest anyway."

Kelly went very cold. "You know my story and you'd actually suggest I hold my children away from their dad? Are you kidding me?"

"I'll be their father. That's for the best. Can't you see that? I'll take Kensey for the day and you can tell him he can't stay here when he goes to the hospital with you. I'm not like your father. I'll take care of them. I'll protect them from harm. He will only bring pain."

She tried to find words but ended up looking like a goldfish as she kept opening and closing her mouth. "You can't possibly be serious. Where is all this coming from?" It was absurd.

"Don't you think I can see how he watches you? He lives the kind of life that's wrong for you. He cheated on you. He doesn't value you."

She blew out a breath, trying to find patience but she was nearing the end of her rope. "Ross, I didn't know you felt this way."

"Well, you do now. I'm sorry I have to insist, but that's how it is. I'll tell him if you feel uncomfortable doing it." He crossed his arms over his chest as if the matter was settled.

"That's not going to happen. *You're* going to get hold of yourself and realize you're being ridiculous and saying things you don't mean. Saying things you can't take back," she added. "I invited him to stay and I'm not rescinding that invitation. It would be rude. It'd give the girls a bad message. I want him to be an involved father. The girls love him. He loves them. End of story. Imagine yourself in his place. If one of your children had been in the hospital. You'd never leave their side. Which is how it's supposed to work. Show some empathy."

"I don't want him here. He's trying to take my place. If I can't be around during this time, he'll get all the time with Maddie. Building trust with her. I could be doing that. Experiences like that are important in creating long-term bonds in blended families."

"I don't think I can marry you." In her head, it had sounded like a panicked blurted wail. Surprisingly, her voice remained calm. Once she said the words she had to fight the overwhelming urge to fall face-first on the bed with relief.

"What?" Ross paused, surprise on his handsome features.

"You'll make someone a good husband, but I'm not for you. You're not for me. Not in a let's-get-married-and-merge-our-lives way."

"I don't understand," he said.

"You demanded that I choose you or Vaughan. This doesn't have anything to do with him. I'm choosing *me* and my children."

"You don't mean that. We're good together." Ross still didn't get it.

Honestly, she wanted to go to the hospital, pick Maddie up and grab Kensey, running away from everyone who wanted to make all her choices.

It wasn't that they'd been bad together. Just two days before he'd been lovely to her by showing up at the hospital. Only now she realized it was some sort of territory marking with Vaughan.

"I think we were good together, too. But not in a forever way. I'm not going to make you happy. This is going to come up over and over in our marriage. You're not going to adopt them! They have parents and neither of us would sign away our rights to Maddie and Kensey like that. I'm frankly really disgusted that you'd ever think I'd want such a thing. Or that *you'd* want it. What would it do to my children to have their father sign them away as if they were property?"

She pulled off the beautiful engagement ring he'd given her three months before and put it in his palm.

"I'd have treated you like a queen. He's going to hurt you again. That's what men like him do. And then what will happen to your children? I hope to God they don't take after their mother when it comes to picking losers to love."

She knew he was hurt and striking out, but she'd had enough.

"You need to leave now before either of us says anything more. I'll go through everything over the next two days and whatever is here I'll bring to your house. I wish you the best and I hope after a while that we can remain friends."

She led the way to the door, opening it and heading downstairs. She wanted him out of her house before he came out of his stupor and decided to make a scene.

Laughter came from the family room where Stacey and Kensey were playing Go Fish for probably the nineteenth time. Kelly unlocked the door to the garage and then opened the bay, letting the door to the house close behind them.

"Here." Kelly pulled the keys to his house—for emergencies as she still always knocked when she came over to visit him—from her key ring and handed them his way. "It's easier for you to give mine back, too. Since we're already here and all."

She stared at him until he handed her keys over. Near the open door to the driveway, Kelly spotted the air pump she'd borrowed for the basketball and handed it over, stepping into the open of the drive-way. "This is yours."

"You can't just dump me like this." He kept his voice low and Kelly wanted to keep it that way.

"I'm not dumping you. I'm ending our engagement. You clearly have some major issues with things that I'm not willing to change. You and me, that's one thing. But this is way more than that. This is something we can't get past and so we'll only keep hurting one another, and that's not what marriage should be." It was as if someone else had taken control of her speech center. As angry and upset as she was, her daughter was inside and she couldn't allow it to spill over into their lives.

"When you come to your senses you know where to find me. I'm sorry if I was overzealous. But I feel quite strongly. We're all better off without Vaughan Hurley in our lives."

"Please. Leave. I can't believe I have to tell you this, but I won't ever choose anyone over Madeline and Kensey. You'd expect me to put their needs and emotional well-being behind your feelings? That's not how it works."

Ross started to speak again but shook his head, turned and stalked to his car. She went back into the garage once he'd driven away and headed into the house.

# CHAPTER FIVE

ALL DAY VAUGHAN had managed not to comment on the way Ross had come and gone that morning. They hadn't had much time alone anyway. His parents had arrived and had stayed at the house with Kensey and Stacey while Vaughan and Kelly had gone to pick Maddie up.

And then his mom and dad had stayed for several hours. Kelly had been friendly enough, though reserved, but everyone was tired and it was time for guests to go.

Yesterday Vaughan would have been considered a guest like that, too. But now he could step in and start showing Kelly he was serious about being around.

Finally, he got his dad alone and asked nicely for them to go. "I'll bring Maddie by to see you guys when she's better. Or you can come back later in the week. She needs it to be quiet now."

His father smiled and clapped his shoulder. "I've been waiting a long time for you to step up for them. Before we go, take a walk with me."

Vaughan and his father headed outside. "You have a tool kit here, or know where one is? I noticed this step is a little loose." His dad pointed to the wooden swing set and climbing wall.

LAUREN DANE                               63

"Garage probably."

Kelly, as it turned out, did have a pretty adequate set of tools so he and his dad were able to fix the step relatively easily.

"What are you doing here, son?" his father asked as they put the tools back.

"I want this." Vaughan indicated the land, the house, all it represented. "I want it with them. With Kelly and our daughters."

"How does she feel about that?"

"I haven't said anything to her about the wanting-her-back part. Not yet. But I said I wanted to be around as Maddie recovered. I have felt like a visitor in my daughter's life. It was Kelly who handled this whole thing. She made the decisions. She kept herself together the whole time. I had all of you. She had no one and she did it and pretty much took care of me, too. I should have been there for her to lean on. For the girls to lean on. But I wasn't."

The shame of it crawled over his skin.

"You were, but not in the way you could have been. Or should have been. You love them, they love you. So what did Kelly say when you told her you wanted to be around for Maddie as she recovered?"

His dad was clearly going to be blunt.

"She offered to let me stay in her guest room for a few weeks. She didn't seem to take it seriously when I said I wanted to pitch in and help with the girls. But I'm going to prove her wrong."

"That's a good sign. What's going to happen with the fiancé? I notice he wasn't here today."

"He came into the room right after she'd invited

me to stay. He wasn't pleased. They went upstairs for several minutes and then she led him outside to the garage. I heard her tell him to leave. I heard a bunch of stuff. She broke the engagement but hasn't told me yet." He didn't need to tell his dad exactly what Ross had said about him. It was enough that Kelly had reacted the way she had.

"This is your second chance. It's going to require every last bit of your attention, commitment and concentration and then three hundred percent more than that for you to be worthy of that. Don't give up. I know you can do this," his father said.

"I made mistakes. A lot of them."

"You did. She did, too, I imagine."

Vaughan shrugged. "We probably could have gotten through her mistakes. I crashed us into a ditch and walked away."

Michael leaned back against the wall after they'd put the tools back. "I've learned a thing or two over my life. You can't undo what you did. You can't go back and erase it. That damage is done, boy. You made it. It hurts and it should. You fucked up."

A bubble of inappropriate laughter snuck from Vaughan's belly. Their dad was the calm one in the family. *Fuck* wasn't a word he used very often.

"I did. God help me, I did." Vaughan scrubbed his hands over his face. "I didn't know what I had. I didn't... I thought it would be easy to find it again someday. When I was ready. But it wasn't easy because what I had was special and I don't think I was ready to truly understand how special until now. And it might be too late, which sounds like some messed-up curse or something."

"Being a man means standing up when you've done wrong. It's not easy, but it's what you do. For your children and the woman you're trying to win back. We raised you right. All four of you boys have had your challenges, but your mother and I expect nothing less from you than success."

"Thanks for the advice and for the ear."

"I'm your dad. It's my job and my privilege to help when I can. You know where I am the next time you need me."

They went back inside where his mother had gathered their things and was ready to get back on the road to Hood River. His mom had been pretty cordial to Kelly, who continued to keep Sharon Hurley at arm's length.

She didn't come out with him when his parents left, but his mom thanked Kelly for letting them be around, and Kelly thanked them for coming over.

It was a small start. Something he could work with.

Stacey and Kensey came downstairs, Kensey's hand tucked in Stacey's before she dashed over to Vaughan. "I like it that you're here!"

"Hey, darlin', I like it, too."

"I'm going to head home." Stacey hugged Kelly. "Call me later to check in. If you need anything and I find out you didn't ask me for it we're going to rumble."

Kensey giggled madly at that.

"I promise. Thank you for coming back." Kelly hugged her friend one last time before she headed out and then it was just the four of them. Vaughan and his women.

"What's next?" Vaughan asked.

"Kensey needs to finish her book report and I need to do laundry."

"I have to go to school tomorrow? Maddie will be home and she'll have Daddy all to herself and that's not fair. I won't miss anything important. Let me stay home, too."

In the face of so much adorable he was hard-pressed to say no and he nearly relented, but Kelly knelt in front of their youngest. "We all have jobs in the family, remember? Right now your most important job is to go to school and train your brain. Your sister's job is to get better first. Your dad and I need to do our jobs, which is taking care of you two. Everyone's going to be all right, but we need to cooperate and do our jobs."

Kensey nodded and hugged Kelly before she scampered off to finish her homework.

"Nicely done. I'm the baby, too. It's hard sometimes."

"She's good at it, though." Kelly's smile belied the annoyance in her tone.

"She is. It's hard to say no to her."

"I want them to be resourceful and independent. Those things will serve them far better than big eyes."

"True. And it's good to teach them their brains are more important than their looks."

Kelly shrugged. "Also an important life lesson. I was going to give you a set of keys, but the locksmith is going to be here in about twenty minutes to change all the locks. We'll get you a set then."

He put a hand on her arm. "Is everything all right?"

"It's fine. I might as well tell you that I broke my engagement with Ross today."

"Did he hurt you or scare you?" Vaughan was the least punch happy of his brothers but the need to hurt someone to defend Kelly surged through him.

"Oh, no. Not like that." She shook her head firmly. "He's unhappy. He gave me my keys back, but I thought it would be easier if I stopped wondering if he had another set and just changed the locks."

Vaughan didn't think it sounded easier at all. But if that's what she needed to have happen, it would. And he'd be extra sure to keep an eye out for Ross.

"Was it about me? You breaking the engagement I mean," Vaughan asked her.

"It was about him and me."

He wanted to say more, but Kensey was just around the corner so it wasn't the time. "All right. Well, I've got some stuff to put away in the guest room. Maybe tonight after dinner you could go over the schedule with me. I meant it when I said I wanted to help. I'm trying to be a better dad."

"We'll talk about it later. Settle in. I'll get you the network password. If you need a space to work, there's a desk in the guest room, and my office has a printer in it if you need one."

He nodded as she spoke and followed her as she showed him where everything was before telling him to make himself at home and disappearing into the laundry room.

Alone, he headed to the guest room and began to unpack his things.

"Hi, Daddy!" Kensey bounded into the room and hopped onto the bed. "I can't believe you're going to be my neighbor! You have your own bathroom, though. That's good because now Maddie takes too much time in there so when I have to pee Mom lets me use hers if I'm upstairs."

Vaughan let the steady stream of talk from his youngest smooth around him, tucking him in. She never told a story without a great deal of dramatic emphasis that he found himself at turns charmed and exhausted by.

"Will you walk me to the bus tomorrow? Mom usually walks us both but you never have. I would like for the other girls to see what my dad looks like. You already made my teacher last year ask about you all the time."

He wrestled back a smile. "That so?"

"I finished my book report. Want to see it and make sure my penmanship is nice?"

He opened his arms and she leaped into them as he hugged her tight, kissing the top of her head before he set her on her feet.

"WE WATCHED MOVIES and read books and she napped a few times. Maddie can't eat solids, but she's awake and lonely. Would it be cool with you if we all ate together up in her room?" Vaughan stood very close to Kelly and she felt like a horrible person because this morning she was going to marry someone else but right then, Vaughan looked so good her hormones did a slow roll. Like onto their back, belly and all the good parts exposed.

"That's a great idea. I'd considered bringing her down here, but keeping her in bed is better. Kensey, can you get the trays out? I made shrimp pasta salad for you."

Kensey pumped her fist with a shouted *"yes!"* as she brought out the trays they used when they had snacks in the family room and watched movies together.

Kelly put some warm chicken broth in one of her to-go coffee cups and slid a lid on. "She can have broth, they said. I had some in the freezer. I hope you like shrimp pasta salad. I should have asked. If you don't, there are still leftovers from yesterday in the fridge."

"Shrimp pasta salad sounds great." Vaughan's agreeable smile was handsome and she realized this had been the longest it had been just the four of them in her house. No Hurleys. No Ross or Stacey. Just Kelly, Vaughan and their daughters.

A long time ago she'd dreamed of normal moments like this one. And she'd given up on them. Or so she'd thought.

Hope was a tiny ember in her belly. Fear lived there, too. Because he'd broken her heart. That had sucked and it had taken a long time to get over. But hope wasn't backing down and Kelly thought maybe it wasn't such a bad thing to let it stay as long as she kept her expectations low.

Right?

Kelly instructed Kensey and Vaughan as they loaded their dinner up on the trays and headed up to Maddie's room.

"We should listen to music, Momma," Maddie murmured sleepily. Kelly pressed a hand to her belly for a moment, attempting to massage away the bittersweet ache.

Maddie had been calling Kelly "Mom" for a year or so by that point. Every once in a while when she got sick or was upset or tired she'd revert to the days where she'd hug Kelly's neck and let Momma fix everything with kisses and a cup of hot chocolate.

Kelly pulled her phone from a pocket. "What do you want to hear?"

"Star Is Born!" Kensey chimed in.

"Yes. Guess which one I want."

They'd watched the edited-for-television version of *A Star Is Born* with Kristofferson and Streisand at least three times that winter and spring so the soundtrack had become a favorite around the house.

"I think I might know." Kelly connected to the wireless system in the house and found the song. She went to her knees to kiss Maddie's forehead before settling on the floor again.

As the piano began Vaughan grinned. "'Everything.' I love this song."

Maddie sang along softly. Normally she could belt this one out but as the kid had just been sliced open the day before yesterday, Kelly thought it could be excused.

Kensey joined in and Vaughan came along, harmonizing, and Kelly sat back, watching these incredibly talented creatures, singing together because they were all born for such things. And because they all had that basic joy they took into most situations.

She was still smiling as she turned off the light in Kensey's room after tucking her into bed. Maddie was fast asleep already. Vaughan stood a few feet away at the top of the stairs.

"She's waiting for you to come in to kiss her good-night," Kelly said on her way past.

"Awesome." He headed down the hall, a smile he wore just for his youngest daughter on his face.

## CHAPTER SIX

KELLY OPENED THE door to her bedroom to find him there. He'd changed into sleep pants and a T-shirt.

"Hi."

She gave him a look. "Hi." And then she let him in. Like an idiot.

"Can we talk awhile?"

"I was thinking about having a glass of wine. Do I need one for this conversation?"

His grin was slow and sexually charged. "Maybe."

Being alone and in close quarters with Vaughan was an iffy proposition. But as she was already taking the express train to bad-decision town, she may as well relax on the trip.

"Okay, then, I'll be right back. You want a glass?"

He nodded.

"I'll be right back." She waved at the room in her wake. "Make yourself comfortable."

In just a few minutes she'd returned to her room with a bottle of wine and two glasses.

Avoiding the bed and anything bed-related, she settled on the love seat and poured two glasses of red before settling in.

"How are you feeling?" Vaughan asked at last, after draining half his glass.

"Tired. Like I could sleep three weeks."

"And the broken engagement?"

She blew out a breath. "How do *you* feel about it?"

"I'm sorry his feelings got hurt, but I'm not sorry the engagement is broken. Is this…? You changed the locks. It's for sure, then?"

"He and I had some elemental differences in parenting styles. It wasn't a sacrifice I was willing to make. He was upset today, but I believe in time he'll see my point and know I was right. I'll miss his daughters." Probably more than she'd miss Ross.

"He didn't like me much."

Kelly snorted. "You didn't like him much."

"We both wanted the same thing."

She slammed her lips against the first reply she'd thought of giving. And then the second. By the third she was better able to get her thoughts together.

"And what was that?"

He smiled and her toes curled.

He was a human churro. He smelled good and she knew for damn sure he tasted good. She'd gorge herself on him and in both cases, she'd end up sorry later that she'd lost her control.

But she never missed a chance to attend an event where churros would be available.

And there he sat, in her bedroom, with a boner. Oh, holy shit he had a hard-on.

She blushed and looked down to her wine.

"He and I wanted *you*."

Still blushing, avoiding looking anywhere but his face, Kelly waited for the rest.

"I'd like for you to give me a chance to prove my-self. And once I do, I want you back."

Kelly waited for more. This was a good start, but it wasn't anywhere near enough.

He put his glass down, leaning forward, elbows on his knees. "I let you go before. I shouldn't have. And then I waited too long to come to my senses and get you back. But I'm here now and ready to prove how much I've changed. I never stopped loving you."

"Is that it? Because if it is, my next words are going to be *fuck you*."

Surprise and then pleasure slid over his features. "You're pissed."

"Why does that make you happy? Did you hit your head on something?" She did such a bad job of pick-ing men. Jeez.

"You're sexy when you're pissed. Course, you're sexy when you're not pissed, too."

"Keep it up. See where cute gets you." She frowned. "You've been gone nearly eight years by this point. A lot has changed. *I've* changed. Just because I'm not with Ross anymore doesn't mean anything as far as you and I are concerned." Which was a lie. At least she didn't feel guilty when she'd thought about lick-ing sugar and cinnamon off his abs just now, though.

He did have the good sense to be chagrined. "I know you've changed. I've changed, too. I'm not the same young, cocky asshole who let his whole life slip through his fingers."

"And what does all that bullshit mean?"

"You've gotten hard." He tried for saucy and she wanted to flick him in the nose for it.

"You haven't said anything much more than that you still loved me and wanted a chance to get me back. What does that mean to you? *Why* should I give you a chance? You haven't even articulated an actual apology for any of what you did."

"I said I made mistakes. And I did. I let you go too easy."

She'd been right about one thing. Just because she'd broken things off with Ross didn't mean she had to run to Vaughan. Even if he was living in her house. Even if for years she'd wanted to hear the sincerity in his tone that night.

But it wasn't enough. Kelly couldn't begin to trust him enough at that point. He not only had a lot of proving himself to do, he also had to make some genuine apologies for what he'd done.

She had her own stuff to handle and she was way too busy to do this for him, even if she'd wanted to. And she didn't. If Vaughan really wanted her back, he had to work for it. She could only let the hope remain that he'd actually open up and own what he did.

And, if he really wanted to be a more involved dad, she'd take him at his word. "Kensey needs to be up at seven. I'll handle Maddie tonight. I'm going to sleep in her room."

"Are you worried?" He shifted closer, concern on his face.

"No. But I'm her mom." She shrugged. "I just want to be close if she needs me. As for Kensey, I suggest you get up at least half an hour before she does. You'll need the time to wake up, get dressed and have coffee." Their youngest was an absolute horror to get out of bed in the morning. "You need to be out the front door by five after eight or you'll have to run."

She stood and went to the door, opening it up. "Good night, Vaughan."

"Wait, you're kicking me out? I thought we were going to talk."

"So did I. You can try again in the future. When you're ready to really open up and talk." She put the bottle of wine and her now-empty glass in his hands and pushed him into the hallway. "See you tomorrow."

She closed the door, leaning against it to keep herself from opening it and inviting him back inside. A little roll between the sheets could work out a lot of energy. But it would be a supreme mistake.

She headed for the shower instead. A detachable showerhead was a girl's best friend.

VAUGHAN LAY IN his bed, a yellow, lined legal pad at his right hand as he scribbled things here and there. The lyrical beginnings of a new song.

He found, even though he'd hoped she'd let him back into her life that night, that he wasn't down that she'd kicked him out of her room.

That she'd snapped at him and kicked him out of her room had only underlined to him that she did care. She hadn't tolerated him, or been barely interested in him. Not at all.

No longer remote, this Kelly was going to demand that he work for his redemption.

He could have said the words. But they taunted him. Just out of reach. Like if he said them, if he came out and said he'd betrayed her and violated her trust and his sense of honor and he'd ruined everything because he'd been a selfish asshole that she'd say, *you're right, get out*.

And it would be over and done.

He had done those things. And yes, she'd made mistakes, too. But she'd come here to this suburban wonderland to build a life for their children. She'd given up nearly all modeling and put her focus on them.

And what she'd built was amazing. Their girls were lucky for it.

He rolled to his belly and began to write again.

## CHAPTER SEVEN

KELLY FLIPPED THE sign on the door and unlocked it to admit Stacey.

"I brought you a smoothie. It's got that powder you like." Stacey's lip curled. "I have to be in court soon, but you're on my way and I really need to get all the details about yesterday."

"I don't even know where to start." Kelly took the smoothie with her thanks.

"Biggest news, then. Go with that."

They hadn't been able to really have enough time the day before to get the whole story out. All Kelly had been able to say was the engagement had been broken so she took a moment to get her friend up to speed.

Stacey's mouth dropped open. "I get that he'd be a little jealous. Vaughan is one of those people everyone likes to be around. But this?"

"Right? I know they don't like one another. That's *normal*, for God's sake. He sounded like a stranger yesterday. The words he used made me believe he meant them. I just feel nothing for him now. He killed it all. I don't hate him. My overwhelming reaction is relief I'm not marrying him."

"Well, jeez. You know my opinion of the engagement, but I'm sorry it was painful for you both. And yes, you can't respect a person who'd do that to those girls."

"How could he have trusted *me* if I'd have gone along with it? He's got kids, too. How could he have wanted me to do that to my children?"

"Because he wouldn't have asked his ex to do such a thing."

"And I wouldn't have asked. The world is full of parents who walk away. Vaughan didn't walk away from them when he left me." Kelly rubbed her hands up and down her arms a moment.

"What did Vaughan say when you told him?"

"I didn't tell him any details, really. He asked if he was the reason. I said Ross and I were the reason. That we'd had a disagreement about something important and weren't going to get married after all."

"Did he believe that weak-ass response?"

"It's true! Even if Vaughan…"

"Even if you weren't still in love with him, you mean?"

"I'm not an idiot. I can't help loving him, but I know what he is. Or maybe what he was. But I can have feelings for him and still not fall for his crap. Anyway, the last thing I want is for Vaughan to think I did it for him."

"And why is that?"

"He told me he still loved me and wanted another chance. And I need to have it be apart from the Ross situation. I can't run from one man to another. It's a bad lesson for my kids and it's stupid."

"You're not running anywhere. He said all those things and you said what back?"

"He said lots of things." Kelly shrugged. "None of them was enough. He's dancing around what happened. I get it. He doesn't want to admit it out loud. But there's no way I could even consider letting him close enough to maybe work things out unless he does.

"Anyway, I'm too busy. Maybe I should give up on the idea of settling down with anyone. I can buy one of those boyfriend pillows instead. I have a vibrator. It's not like I don't know how to take care of business when there're no penises around."

Stacey nearly choked on her coffee.

"I think it's fair to make him come clean. That way you both go forward with a clean slate. Why don't you see where this goes before swearing off men in favor of silicone and pillows first?"

Kelly wiped a fingerprint off the display case that surrounded a nifty point-of-sale hub that was all discreetly out of the line of customer sight.

"He says he wants to be a daily help with the girls. I have to admit, I sort of expected him to mess up today. I slept in Maddie's room last night. Got up early to exercise and by the time I'd finished, showered and dressed, he was up, coffee was brewing. He got Kensey up at seven, though I thought I'd lose him a time or two." Kelly laughed.

"That child is an absolute bear in the morning. She's slept over at his house many times over. How is he just figuring this out?" Stacey asked.

"He's been vacation dad. You know? At Daddy's house they get up when they want. They go to bed when they want. He lets them eat too much crap and he hates to say no."

"That's going to be a cold hard slap in the face." Stacey grinned as she said it. "Man, that puts a spring in my step."

Kelly couldn't stop herself from laughing. "He has it so easy. Shurley does everything for him."

"You said I wasn't fair because I called him a man-boy who lived with his mom!"

"He has his own house!" Kelly protested.

"Which can be seen by standing on the front porch of his mom's house."

"You're going to make me pee my pants if I can't stop laughing." Michael and Sharon's house sat at the highest point of the ranch, on a rise. They could probably see lots of houses from there.

Kelly continued, "Back to my point. He's never had to manage their schedule. Never had to wake them up for school and get them there on time. This is going to be a challenge for him."

And for her. Because she wasn't going to believe anything he said until she saw him living his words.

"He's good with them. They like being around him. That's a big step right there. We'll just see what happens next." She'd left a detailed list for Vaughan to refer to during the day. What time Maddie needed medication, how much to give her. What she could eat and drink and where it could be found. Numbers for everyone important.

She planned to leave at her usual time to be home for the school bus arrival. Hopefully Vaughan would be okay in the time between now and then.

"I have to run now to make court, but I want you to keep me updated on what's happening with you. I told

Maddie I'd stop by later on. I was planning on bringing lunch, though hers was going to be pudding. I'll work that out with Vaughan, though, so don't worry."

Kelly tried not to but it was hard.

Stacey sighed. "You look like you have to poop. Stop. Maddie is old enough and recovered enough that she won't need a lot from him. As long as he watches movies with her and lets her tell him all the facts in the world about Pokémon he'll be fine."

"I know. He's had them on his own lots of times." Stacey knew this, but it felt better for Kelly to repeat the words. To remind herself.

Stacey hugged her on the way out and then the first customer came in, and the day got started and kept her so busy she didn't have much of a chance to worry until her afternoon employee showed up to take over.

It had been a way to be present at the store and still home to pick the girls up from school several years ago and she had kept it up ever since. She knew how lucky she was to have the luxury to do it. Kami, her business partner, had a two-year-old and they'd both wanted to keep their business as family friendly as possible.

She came into the house and stopped to watch Vaughan and Maddie tucked up on the couch, watching a movie. They looked so much alike it always punched her in the gut.

His hair was messy and he smiled sleepily Kelly's way and a deep, craven greed to touch him bloomed. "Hey."

"Afternoon." Kelly put her things down and moved

to check Maddie, kissing her forehead and then testing it for fever. "How're you feeling, bug?"

"I had pudding and it was very good."

"Pudding makes every day a great day. I totally agree."

Maddie laughed.

"You can have some soup tonight for dinner. And some toast."

"Party!" Vaughan joked before he got off the couch and stretched. The hem of his worn T-shirt rose, exposing hard, muscled abs, defined at his hip bones. She had stretch marks and he had an eight-pack. Figured.

"Why don't I go pick Kensey up from the bus stop and you can stay here with Maddie?" Vaughan offered and it took Kelly a second to hear it all because of the roar of white noise at the sight of that damned belly of his.

"That works. You need to change, though."

"Huh? Why?"

"Because you show up to the bus stop looking like that and the other mothers are going to eat you up. We'll never see you again."

He paused, a smirk on his lips for a brief moment. "Too bad I already have all the women I want or need."

*Have?* Puhleeze. If he wanted to have her, he had a lot of work to do to make that happen.

Vaughan jogged off to change.

"I'll be right back, bug." She had work clothes on, which were gorgeous and expensive, and what she wanted was something casual, loose and not a disaster if it got ripped, stained or otherwise ruined.

The hallway near her bedroom smelled like him. The guest room was down at her end of the house. It had taken her a long time to get over her sheets not smelling like him anymore and this felt very similar.

By the time she'd returned downstairs she realized her house had started to change. Just a little bit. A guitar case was casually leaned against the back of the couch, in a corner. His ebook reader was on the side table near the couch.

This was disquieting. Because she liked it so much and she shouldn't. Not until he'd done a lot more work.

Vaughan headed out and Kelly tucked onto the couch next to Maddie. "I missed you today. How are you feeling?"

"Auntie Stacey came over with pudding. She brought Daddy a sandwich and some chips, too. That was very nice. I like it that he's here. He watched *Brave* with me. Twice. Isn't that nice?"

Their daughter sounded as if she were making a pitch for a puppy. Only Vaughan was way more trouble and there was no doubt Kelly would have to do all the care and cleaning.

"It *is* nice." It was also what parents were supposed to do so she wasn't that inclined to give him a gold star for it.

Vaughan came back shortly, an excited Kensey chattering endlessly about her day. He had a slightly dazed look on his face that Kelly could totally identify with. Their youngest only stopped talking long enough to eat, drink and sleep.

She gave Kelly and Maddie kisses and told them

about her day as she handed over a packet of homework for Maddie to do that week.

"Your teacher left this for you in the attendance office and I got called in! Over the loudspeaker and everything."

"Uh-oh. Did you think you were in trouble?" Vaughan asked.

Kensey's eyes went big as saucers as she nodded excitedly. "But I didn't do anything so I was worried someone told a lie on me. But it was just all this homework for Maddie."

"Did you make up a good story about why you got called in to the office?"

"No. I said it was for my sister who got her appendix out. Making up stories when it's not for a book is bad, Daddy."

Vaughan tried not to smile so Kelly tried not to sigh wistfully. There were few things sexier than a man being a good dad.

"You're totally right." Vaughan kissed the top of her head as he made his way to the couch. "What are our plans for the evening, ladies?" Vaughan asked, tucking in on Kelly's other side without even a by-your-leave.

"Kensey has reading to do." Kelly looked through the stuff for Maddie. "You can do all this homework in your sleep, bug. If you do one piece every day, you can enjoy the weekend and still be ready for school Monday."

"I think if you have to get cut open you should get a pass for all homework while you're out sick," Maddie declared.

"Thinking is good for you." Kelly smiled when Kensey wormed her way between Kelly and Vaughan.

"I have to do homework. You should, too. Aaron Bertis asked about you today," Kensey explained to her sister, eyes wide. "He said to tell you he said hi."

"Who's Aaron Bertis?" Vaughan asked.

"He's Maddie's boyfriend."

Maddie squealed, "No, he is not! He's a boy in my class. He's nice and his hair is perfect." She looked to her dad. "Like, as nice as yours. But he's *not* my boyfriend."

"Boyfriend? No way." Vaughan's features hardened and Kelly snorted a laugh.

"He does have great hair genes, but she knows the rules. She's only in fifth grade." Kelly winked at Maddie, who blushed so hard. "If he still has perfect hair and an interest when she's fifteen, we'll talk."

"Fifteen?" Vaughan's voice cracked. "That's too early!"

"When did *you* have your first girlfriend, Vaughan?" Kelly asked, pretending to be innocent.

He blushed. "That was different."

"Why, Daddy?" Maddie asked.

Kelly nodded. "Yes, why is that?"

He frowned at her and she still didn't laugh, though she wanted to.

"I think seventeen is better."

Both girls started to argue and Kelly got up, leaving them to it. His reason was that he was a boy and their daughters weren't. He deserved to be pecked by two little girls over that logic.

Her phone rang and when she saw who it was she

sighed. "Vaughan? I need to take this. I'll be back in a few."

Concern lit his eyes but he nodded.

SHE STEELED HERSELF and answered, heading down the hall and outside. She did her best to shield the girls from their maternal grandmother.

"It's been weeks since you've called me last." Rebecca complained without bothering to say hello.

"Been a little busy. What's up?"

"You need to let your employees know I'm your mother and deserve a discount at your Manhattan store."

"We've talked about this before. Is this what you called about?" Rebecca believed Kelly owed her a piece of everything she had. And to keep her satisfied—and on the other side of the country—Kelly kept her mother's bank account full and sent clothes to the house in the Hamptons she'd bought her mother before she'd even turned eighteen.

"I was in the neighborhood!"

"I've told you before, you're not allowed inside the store. You won't get a discount. You won't get anything. I send you all the stuff you'd like and that will fit you. Leave my employees alone."

Kami must not have been at work when Rebecca stopped by. Her business partner and friend loathed Kelly's mother and had zero issue with saying so straight to Rebecca's face.

"Just for once you could take my side. But you tossed all my advice when you moved to Oregon and started popping out babies instead of making all your money while you were still young and beautiful. Now look at you. Over thirty, twenty pounds fatter than you were. Couldn't keep your cash ticket and divorced him. You don't know what it takes to survive."

It did no good to engage and yet, Kelly found herself at the end of her rope and the words came anyway. "Yes, look at me. Gosh, it must have sucked for you when your cash cow decided to be an actual parent. However do you survive me supporting you since I was fourteen? Your bills are paid, stop crying about it."

"I can't believe the way you talk to me."

If only it drove her away. "I'm hanging up now. Stay away from the store or I'll let Kami get a restraining order."

Her mother didn't comment on that, but she wasn't done. "Your employee told me your daughter was sick. I said I had no idea as you didn't bother to inform me."

"I don't know why I would bother to tell you. Also, nice that you bitched at me for ten minutes and didn't ask after her until now. Even when you comment it's about you and your feelings. Why are you *really* calling me?"

"I hope your daughters are more grateful than mine."

Kelly sure hoped so as she was working to be a better mother than she had. "Have a nice night, Rebecca. I have things to do."

Kelly hung up and turned her phone off. There would be at least a call back or a text and she didn't want to deal with either just then. Or ever.

# CHAPTER EIGHT

VAUGHAN TUCKED MADDIE IN, kissing her forehead. "Night, baby."

"Night, Daddy. I love you."

That his daughters loved him was the finest thing he had.

"I love you, too. Sweet dreams."

Kelly was leaving Kensey's room as he went in. They'd never had this unified parenting. It seemed to fill him up and yet he craved more and more.

The whole day had been a lesson.

He said his good-night, his love yous and gave several kisses and hugs. When he ended up out in the hall again, he wore a goofy smile.

Vaughan could have gone to his room. But he wasn't sleepy. Tired, yes, sleepy, not at all.

Following the sound, he headed down to the kitchen where Kelly had just been checking the door to the garage.

"Just my nightly lockup." She smiled and he wanted to kiss her so badly he licked his lips, trying to remember her taste.

"Are you going to bed right now? Want to hang out with me awhile?"

She watched him with careful eyes but everything

was all right when she nodded. "Sure. I've got beer if you want. I'm having a glass of wine, but if I remember correctly, you like beer better."

She grabbed a bottle of white wine she'd had chilling and a glass.

He followed her back upstairs, a beer between his fingertips. "You offered me wine last night."

"I did. I wasn't inclined to give you any other options then. I'm feeling nicer now." She opened her bedroom door, looking back over her shoulder, saying softly, "Don't ruin it."

He'd ruined it eight years before. That hung between them. And, he supposed, it should have until he dealt with it. Being an adult sucked sometimes.

Then again. The scent of her hit him as they settled. This was her space. Soft bedding in blues and grays. The chairs they sat on in her room were a silvery purple. Framed pictures of the girls, some nature shots, a few of Kelly with friends dotted the walls and shelves.

The rugs on the floor were lush. Feminine. Not even a trace of Ross here.

Instead of starting slow, Vaughan found himself blurting out, "Did you really want to marry him?"

Kelly shrugged, tucking her feet beneath her. "Doesn't matter now. It's over."

"You don't even have his picture in here."

"I had one of the two of us together on my dresser over there. I put it away when I gathered all his things to return to him. Why do you care so much?" Even with her gaze narrowed, the pretty sky blue of her eyes still made his heart beat faster.

"You know why."

She flipped him off.

"What's that for?"

"You come into my house with all this talk about how you want this or that. How you're sorry for *a lot*. But you can't even come out and say what you want so why should I give it to you? I don't really care if you don't like getting flipped off. Be honest or get the fuck out of my bedroom."

This Kelly wasn't one he knew how to get around. And…it made him want her even more. This Kelly was pissed off and wanted some groveling. Maybe a lot, given the gleam in her eye.

She deserved all she was asking for and more.

"I care because it makes me jealous. I don't want you to love anyone else. Or marry anyone else. I don't want my daughters to be raised by another man they call Dad."

She lifted her glass and took a sip. "See? How hard was that?"

He frowned. "Hard! It's not easy admitting stuff like that."

One of her brows rose slowly. "Really? Gosh, I have no idea about such things."

He sighed. "All I can say for totally sure is that I fucked up. Okay? I did and I know it and now I'm old enough to really see it. You never had any reason to doubt my commitment."

"I'm about two seconds from throwing this wine in your face. So adjust your speech accordingly."

*Wow.* He shifted, uncomfortable but also half-hard. "I never loved anyone else." Even to that moment, it had only been Kelly.

"And yet, it didn't stop you from letting a stranger give you a hand job after a show when you had me."

And there it was.

But she wasn't done. "You. Had. Me. I was there, Vaughan. Pregnant, exhausted but there because you asked me to be. And I wasn't enough. Do you have any idea what that feels like? Madeline wasn't enough. Kensey wasn't enough. None of us was enough and I could see in your eyes that you wanted me to know it."

Each word she gave him sliced deep. He wanted to turn away, wanted to deny and protest that she misunderstood. But she laid herself bare for him and it seemed like more betrayal to disrespect that with lies.

He'd begged Kelly to visit him on tour. Maddie was still a baby and Kensey was on the way. Restlessness had gripped him during that tour. Each day without her he'd begun to itch, feel weighted down by his family. The spiral of his behavior spun in wider and more erratic circles, more and more destructive until the moment his wife had walked around the corner and caught some random groupie with her hand down the front of his pants and her mouth on his neck.

And then he'd asked Kelly to join them. He'd never forget the look on her face.

He breathed out, trying to ignore the pain in his chest. "I did have you. Damn it, Kel, I miss you. I miss your being mine. I'm sorry I had no self-control. I'm sorry I was careless with what we had. I'm sorry I couldn't see what I had until it was too late and then I was too stupid for years to realize how special it had been. I'm sorry I threw us away. Sorry I hurt you. God, so fucking sorry."

Tears glistened against her lashes.

"You and the girls are the most important things I've ever had and I didn't act like it. I didn't and I'm standing here telling you I'm sorry."

She cleared her throat. "And then what?"

"I meant it when I said I wanted another chance. I want us to be together. I want to be a real family. You, me, our daughters. I want you to be mine again."

"Just like that? No harm no foul, we're okay again?"

Defensive words rose to his lips but the pain in her tone stopped them. "I know it's not going to be that easy."

"What exactly are you proposing? We tried marriage. It didn't work. It took me years to get over you, Vaughan. I can't do that again."

Why he was so surprised by the depth of her pain he wasn't sure. Shame that he hadn't really examined it more rode him.

"I was an asshole. I swear to you on my life that I didn't… Nothing happened more than what you saw." He scrubbed hands over his face. "I know it was wrong. But I didn't cheat on you."

"Before that moment, you mean? Because if you think you can sit there and tell me another woman's hand on your dick isn't cheating you better wear a cup every day for the rest of your miserable, lying life. If I recall, you punched someone once for telling me I looked pretty. That's some double standard you have. How'd that work out for you? You're going to sit there and say with a straight face that it's cool to get jerked by a rando you tossed aside after you blew all over her hand?"

"I didn't! I didn't come. I stopped everything."

"You want a gold star?"

"I said I was sorry."

"Oh, did you?" That she'd nearly yelled it startled them both. She clapped a hand over her mouth, tears in her eyes. "I'm sorry. Just go, please."

"I don't want to go. I'll tell you I'm sorry every five minutes forever if you just give me another chance."

"You think I want that? Some sort of man-child I have to monitor and parent? I have two kids already. I don't want to be your conscience. I wanted you to use your own."

IN THE YEARS since that night, Kelly had thought about that moment, over and over. When she'd looked at him and seen just a glimmer in his gaze. As if he'd wanted her to see it and push her away.

It had made her deeply sad. Filled her with regret and sorrow. That glimpse was it. The final, last thing. She could not be with someone who'd treat her like that.

She'd never raged at him. Not like this. Oh, they used to have their stupid fights. They both had artistic temperaments and were independent. Shallow, passionate, stupid arguments that ended with ridiculously amazing sex and lots of laughter.

No one could make her laugh like he had.

Which just made her angrier.

"I was young and stupid and selfish. Destructive. I made mistakes. I hurt you. Broke things. We can't have back what we were, and maybe that's for the best. You've grown up, way before I did. Let me prove to you I've changed. Grown. I can be the man you need me to be. Take me back, Kelly. Be mine. This time as equals. I love you."

For a long time, she'd wanted those words. If he'd said them even two years before she'd have already been naked with him.

But he was right about one thing. She'd grown up. Enough to know that despite the fact that she'd never gotten over him, she couldn't let him close enough to break her apart. Not until he'd done some major showing and not telling about this whole apology-and-wanting-another-chance business.

"What's different for you now? You're asking not just me to take a risk on you. The girls are old enough to understand it when you leave. I have them to think about, too." They adored Vaughan. If he disappointed them like that, it would hurt their relationship with him for the rest of their lives.

He took her hands. "Another reason I love you. I'm thinking of them, too. Hell, this is about them, as well anyway. They visit my house. This is their home. I've missed out on a lot. Enough to know how happy I've been to do something as mundane as walking Kensey to the bus, or to see the way she looked when I picked her up. I want that. Every day. I want it with you."

She shook her head, dubious. "How do you know you want it, though? It's been a few days. The truth is, you've never been a family with me. Even when we were married and had Maddie you weren't around much."

"Being here, with you three, has made me happy in ways I can't explain. I've known for some time I needed to find a way back to you. I'm asking you for a chance to show you I'm ready to be your husband again. Ready to be part of this family with you and our daughters."

She swallowed and then licked her lips, nervous. She wanted this. Wanted it so much the depth of it scared her.

"It's harder than you think. Being in a family. Being stable. Being reliable. You have to make decisions based on what they need. And a lot of the time it's not the most fun choice. You need to put your family first."

"Then let me in. Let me show you."

Kelly had been thinking of little else. Wondering if she was a fool for even considering giving him another chance. Loving him so damned much the hope of it, of having him back in their life, edged out the fear. Just barely.

She blew out a breath. "If we go down this road I have rules. Conditions."

"What are they?"

"They're what you need to agree to if you want to pursue this."

"Whatever you want."

She chewed her lip a moment. "I'm not convinced you know what it really is you're saying you want. Love is necessary. And I can admit I never stopped loving you. But it's not enough. What you're asking for, the only thing I can see working, is to make yourself a space in the family the girls and I have. You say you want me back and you want to be the man I deserve and that comes with you being a present, engaged father. A co-parent."

He nodded.

"You need to be here. Every day. Up early to get the girls ready and out the door for school. Then in the afternoons to pick them up, help with homework, dinner, bedtime. I want you to deal with tantrums and slammed doors. I want *you* to know they're going to be mad at you for saying no but you say it anyway because that's your job.

"What we had before? It's nothing like my life now. I'm not…that girl." She had stretch marks and cellulite, dark circles under her eyes and two kids.

A smile touched his mouth. "Neither of us is. I want to know you. The Kelly of now. I want waking up early and tantrums."

She laughed, unable to help herself. "You're so full of shit, Vaughan. You have no idea."

"Okay, so I probably don't. I want to learn. What are the other rules?"

"Why are you being so amenable?"

He frowned. "I'm being too nice?"

Kelly crossed her arms across her chest. "It's been eight years. You tell me why I *shouldn't* be suspicious."

He put his hands up. "I told you, I know this isn't going to be easy."

"My rules are as follows. Total honesty. Lies are bad for a marriage. Not the small ones like who ate the last piece of pizza, but did strange women touch your junk. I need to know that when I ask you a question, or when we're talking that you're being totally truthful. If I find out you're lying, it's over. I can maybe get past something hurtful you think or have done, but lying about it is an automatic ticket to your stuff on the lawn."

"Honesty and being here for real for you and the girls. I agree. What else?"

"You will stand between me and your mother. I'm done paying for your sins with that woman. If you're here, and that's another one of my rules, this experiment takes place here, not at the ranch. I will not live there."

There'd been a time when she'd wanted Sharon Hurley to welcome her into the family. To be the kind of mother figure Kelly'd never had. Vaughan's mother had hated her from the start. During the divorce there'd been some intense and harsh words between them.

That's when it had become clear to Kelly that Vaughan hadn't told his mother the whole story about why they'd split.

"I know she's been less than pleasant at times. I thought it was getting better. She's…"

Kelly held up a hand. She didn't want to hear any excuses. "I don't care what she is, or isn't. Back when we broke up I was different. I'm not that woman. I will not tolerate any of that bullshit from her again."

He nodded quickly. "I understand. I agree that here is best for a host of reasons. This is where Kensey and Maddie need to be. Their school and Kensey's dance classes are here. And it's got some distance between you and my mom. I need to talk to her, to come clean and own what I did. I'm sorry I didn't protect you before. I should have."

Kelly wasn't holding her breath but she was done letting Sharon Hurley hurt her, and if he wasn't willing to shield her, it was best to know early on, before she allowed herself to get too close. She had no desire to be with a man and his mother. Sharon needed to back the hell off and learn her place. Which was not in the middle of Kelly's family.

"Essentially, if you want us back, you need to put us first and protect us. That's really the bottom line."

He nodded. "Okay. That's fair." Vaughan's lopsided smile did her in. There was nothing else but to smile back. "So, we're good? I mean, on the way to good?"

"There's one more thing." She blew out a breath. "I need you to give me some time and space with the um, sexytimes stuff."

He guffawed and then quieted down. "Sexytimes?"

"Look here, buster. What's between us, what's always been there between us, that's so good that it sometimes makes me forget the other stuff because all I want to think about is the sex. Or be doing it, or figuring out how to do it. I want us to have some, oh, I don't know what to call it."

"Wooing? Courting?"

"Yes, but those seem sort of innocent words for what you do to my wits when sex is in the mix."

"Damn, you're really going to get some fantastic presents for your birthday for this."

She liked that he teased her. That he was also clearly

listening and willing to work things through pleased her even more.

"I wasn't stupid enough to think we'd end up in bed tonight—though I do live in hope. We have some getting-to-know-you catch-up stuff to do. I agree it's good to wait. Like a few days, right? Not a year or anything?"

He looked so adorably panicked all she could do was laugh. "Not a year or anything."

"Okay. I'll try to keep the smolder down to a reasonable level. A tough job, you know."

She snorted. "Okay, then. I'll do my best to resist. So, we have an understanding. That's a step on the way to good," Kelly said.

"Cool. And just to be extra clear, I'm very glad you broke the engagement with Ross. But I should be thankful that he proposed. It was like a stone in my shoe that finally made me act. I kinda feel bad for him."

"Why?"

"He had you for a brief period of time and now he doesn't. I've been there. It sucks. He seems okay and I came in here wanting you back. He handled himself pretty well. I probably would have in his place."

There was no reason to tell Vaughan the things Ross had said in the heat of an argument. It didn't matter anyway so there was no use in spreading negativity.

"So, would it be okay with you if I changed into sleep pants while we talked more? I wanted to chat with you about your business."

If she meant to really give this a chance, she had

to truly be open to it. That, and she wanted to spend some time with him.

"Sure. I'm going to change, too."

He grinned and she enjoyed the view as he left the room.

## CHAPTER NINE

KELLY MET STACEY at her office for an early lunch.

The boutique firm Stacey started with three friends three years before lay between Kelly's store, Chameleon, and her home in the nearby suburb of Gresham, so if Stacey wasn't in court, they had lunch like this at least once a week.

It had been several days since she and Vaughan had the talk about him wanting a second chance and moving in for a while. She'd only been able to have brief text exchanges about it with her friend, and Kelly had so much she wanted to share.

They settled in at the table in the comfortable kitchen area.

"How's Miss Madness?" Stacey asked as she unwrapped her sandwich.

"You know we had a doctor's appointment on Wednesday and she's doing great. Healing well. Enough to be more and more impatient with not being at school. Thank goodness she heads back on Monday."

"I've been here at work until ten at night pretty much all week long. I'm sorry I haven't been over to see her in a few days."

Stacey and Kelly's girls had loved one another from

the start. It had been lovely to have that sort of support for her kids, and from a friend, that love meant even more.

Kelly waved a hand, purposely not allowing herself to think about how many calories and carbs she was putting into her body. She'd allowed herself to think about calories only when she was making a choice on what to eat and even then, only for five minutes or less.

"They know you're busy."

"Still. I have to go out of town to deal with my grandmother but I'll be back late Monday. Then I'll come over so we can have a girls' day. But right now you need to tell me about Vaughan. I'm dying to know what's been going on."

"Well, I told you about his promise to work to get us back. He gets up early and wakes Kensey. She's so, so happy to have him in the house. I'm watching him so closely, though. I'm…I don't know, nervous maybe? Like he thinks this full-time parenting and family thing is great but it's hard. He's capable of hard work. He lives on a ranch as well as being in a supersuccessful band. His problem isn't laziness. Not really. But I keep wondering if he's going to realize how hard it is and panic."

"Has he shown any signs of that?"

"No."

"Exactly. He's been their dad all this time. Even when they aren't in school, when they're with him, he makes sure they're fed and sleep and are told they're loved. I know what you're afraid of. But he's not your fucked-up mother."

"Every night he and I hang out for a few hours in my room, just chilling with a glass of wine or a beer. We talk. Nothing important. Just normal stuff." Which was why it was integral because they were re-building trust.

"Have you nailed him yet?"

"I'd tell you if I had! Jeez. Not yet. I told him I needed some space and time and he's been giving it to me. But holy hell, the man can flirt me right out of my panties. I'm weak against his powers. And let me assure you, his powers are mighty. It's just a matter of time. Unless he does something stupid first."

"Any visits from Hurleys?"

"They've called to talk with Maddie and Kensey but none have shown up. I think he's asked them to give us space. I hope he has anyway. I like some of his family well enough, but I don't trust them all when it comes to my relationship with Vaughan. Not yet."

"Fair enough. Paddy was a dick after the divorce for a while if I recall."

"Ezra has always been friendly. Good to the girls. He knew what Vaughan was up to. I think Paddy does but maybe didn't for a while. There's weird money stuff, you know that."

"I do know it, but I also think it's total shit. Utterly stupid."

"The issue is that they never took the time to know me. They saw a young, pretty woman who they didn't even meet until after she'd not only married their son but also did it pregnant. Sharon always thought I was fluffy and weak just because I didn't strap a baby to my back to rub sticks together to make fire. And then when we divorced and he gave me our apartment in New York and insisted on paying for my tuition when I finished my degree so I could be home with the girls. I have my own money! I don't need his. He's the one who put it in the settlement. I didn't ask for any of that. You know I didn't."

"It's none of their business if you did. You had a house. You had a successful career. In Manhattan. And you left that behind to live in Gresham for Vaughan. So he could see his kids more often. What anyone but you and Vaughan think about it isn't relevant."

"I just get wary about them. He's so close to them. I don't want to take him away from that. It's good for my kids to have his entire family so nearby."

"It's all right, you know, not to want his whole family in your business. Or to at the very least be suspicious of their motives until you know them better. You've changed. Vaughan has changed. I'm going to hope they've all changed, too."

"We were very young."

"All of us." Stacey winked.

They hung out for another half an hour before both women had to be on their way, Kelly to pick Kensey up and Stacey off to court.

VAUGHAN REALIZED, AS the four of them ate dinner, passing around platters and bowls, laughing and sharing their day, he'd been missing so much wonderful, normal stuff with his family.

Guilt hung around his neck like a stone, equally useless. He needed to talk to Ezra or his dad. Someone he could trust to give him good advice. They'd just spent a really nice weekend at home with a movie-and-board-game marathon. He'd been all over the world, seen and done a lot of things, but the days had been the most fun he'd had in recent memory.

All of this in a period of a week.

Maddie was headed back to school the following day and he planned to drive to the ranch, pack more appropriately to live with Kelly and his girls long-term. Kelly had offered him the office space above the garage for a music/work space. He'd bring over some of his equipment from his studio at home. Hopefully he'd be able to connect with Ez when he stopped over.

"Are you excited to go back to school tomorrow, bug?" Kelly asked Maddie.

"I'm not excited for homework, but I want to see my friends."

"I'm excited!" Kensey grinned. "I don't have to sit next to anyone yucky on the bus when you're there."

Kelly laughed.

"I know you've already been here a week and you probably have to work, but would you stay through next weekend, too, Daddy?" Maddie's eyes went wide and round and it tore at his heart. "We can see a movie at the theater now that I'm better!"

They hadn't really discussed too much with their daughters. He got the feeling Kelly didn't want to get their hopes up. But each day he'd been there he'd fit a little more. Got more confident at the basics. He already knew how to take out the trash and get the mail. He'd really dug walking with Kensey to the bus stop each day. One of the moms had been a little too friendly, but his daughter had gotten right between them as he'd stepped back and made it clear he didn't want the attention.

She'd backed off and it had seemed to Vaughan as if he'd passed some sort of test for Kensey, who'd thrown herself at him happily each morning when he woke her up.

He liked it a whole lot that she'd stopped being surprised. Kensey knew he'd wake her up. Knew he'd be there to be hugged and kissed.

It had brought something to life, a deeper need to protect what he had because he was fast getting used to the love and connection he felt every night as he ate at the dinner table with them.

He looked to Kelly, letting her make the choice about how much to tell them.

"Your dad is going to be living with us for a while. Cool with you two?" Kelly asked.

They turned their attention to him, so pretty, faces so open, expressions trusting and full of hope. Resolve strengthened him. He needed to make this happen.

"I sure like being here to take care of you two. Your mom is nice enough to share the family you three have made with me. Do you think you could teach me all the stuff I need to do to be a better dad? I need your help."

Both his daughters flung themselves at him, covering his face with kisses.

"I'm going to assume that's a yes." Kelly smiled at him briefly. An unguarded moment, maybe the first one since they'd laid things on the table a few nights before.

"I'm glad you two think it's a good idea." He wanted

to tell them he was there for good, back with them where he should have been all along. But he knew better.

Not that he planned to fail; he didn't. But he wanted to show them, not tell them.

"I bet Sierra's mom will be happy, too. She likes to look at Daddy." Kensey made a face at Kelly.

Vaughan didn't want to hold his breath, or make it weird, but he was relieved when Kelly rolled her eyes, but didn't seem overly bothered.

"He *is* nice to look at."

Kensey shifted her attention back to Vaughan, who made a face and she laughed. "Yeah. He has a handsome face and nice eyes."

"*We* have his eyes, too," Maddie informed her little sister. "Everyone looks at Daddy. Sometimes it makes everything go faster, because they want to make him smile at them."

Kelly smirked.

"Mostly, though, it makes everything take longer because, as Nana says, they lose their wits because he's so pretty," Kensey said.

Kelly's surprised laughter made Vaughan relax.

"Your grandmother does have a point. Though she's quite susceptible to your dad's charms, too."

*Danger!* He changed the subject. "Hush now." Vaughan gestured at Kelly as he spoke to the girls. "Look at your mother. Talk about pretty."

"The principal ran straight into the flagpole because he was staring at Mom. He had a big bump on his forehead all day." Maddie wrinkled her nose.

Clearly Vaughan needed to accompany Kelly the next time she went to school.

"Your mother is impossible not to look at." The first time he'd seen her had been at some ridiculous Manhattan shindig. Rock stars and models milling around, drinks in hand, and there she'd been, in this dress—a shining, shimmering gold thing—skimming her body, the material catching the light as she moved. That night she'd looked like an avenging angel; her hair had been slicked back, away from her face. No jewelry, just all that skin, that body and the golden dress.

"I saw your mom across the room at a party. I wanted to know who she was but didn't get the chance to meet her that night. And then I saw her in a magazine on the airplane coming home from the East Coast. She was in this dress that looked like a flower." He could still remember that shot. "I arranged through a mutual friend to get an okay to call her and introduce myself."

Kensey and Maddie's attention had locked on, not often getting those details. Neither of them were old enough to remember their parents being together. Another mistake he needed to make up for.

"Where did you go on your first date?" Kensey asked.

"He bought me street meat and we went to a movie afterward," Kelly answered, a smile in her tone.

"I'm still not entirely sure what *Lost in Translation* was about," Vaughan admitted.

"Daddy, you bought your date a hot dog?" Maddie shook her head.

Vaughan thought back to that night. "I know! But luckily, she forgave that error. It was late. Your uncles and I were in New York making a music video."

"I was flying to London that following morning for fashion week."

He'd followed her, but that part of the story wasn't necessarily something he'd share with the girls. Not without some heavy editing.

"I called her and she came down to where we'd been filming. I offered her something way better than meat stewing in water in a cart all day." She'd shown up from a shoot of her own. Effortlessly beautiful and glamorous. At home in New York on her own in ways he still hadn't managed when staying in Manhattan.

He'd expected her to be fussy but found her to be incredibly down-to-earth, even as she managed to dominate the world she worked in. Intense and ambitious even as she could be obsessive and melancholy about her place in the world apart from what she looked like.

"Don't impugn street meat that way." Kelly laughed. "There are days when I'd like nothing more than to get a dog on the way home from work. Don't worry, girls, he took me to nice places, too."

They'd gone to a movie because he hadn't wanted her to think all he wanted was to get her naked. When, in truth, there was little else he could think about as they sat, side by side in a movie theater at nearly midnight.

He'd started to kiss her in the cab, on the way to her apartment and then there'd been little else but his hands and mouth on her, being inside her, over her, under her, laughing and coming harder than he ever had or had with anyone since.

"She got on a plane that next morning and I managed to make it a whole day before I was also on a plane to London."

Maddie's attention hadn't wandered at all. "You chased her?"

"Your mom was a star when we met. She traveled more than I did. But I liked being around her a lot. Way more than not being around her so yes, I showed up at Heathrow, called her and found myself surrounded by the insanity of fashion week."

They'd conceived Maddie in Paris and married a month later in a private ceremony at Kelly's Manhattan town house.

"We seen pitchers of you two from back then. Uncle Paddy has lots and lots of pitchers at his house." Kensey wiped her mouth on her napkin as she finished her dinner.

"Ugh, Kensey! We saw *pictures*. You drink from pitchers. You look at pictures," Maddie said with a very big-sister attitude.

Kensey's face was a near perfect imitation of one Kelly had used on Vaughan several times over the past week. Annoyed. Incredulous.

Kelly clapped her hands and the brewing spat dissipated as they turned to their mother. "Enough walking down memory lane for now." Kelly stood and began to clear the plates. The girls jumped up to help.

"Tell us more," Maddie begged as they began to put away leftovers.

"Like what?" Kelly asked. "When he called me the first time I thought he was actually your uncle Damien. I said no, but I was sad because I thought his brother was actually pretty cute."

Kensey giggled behind her hands.

"I realized she thought I was the wrong brother right as I was hanging up. I clarified which brother I was and then she said I could call her the next time I was in New York."

"Tough luck for Uncle Damien, I guess."

Vaughan agreed. He kissed Maddie's head as he brought the last of the dishes over from the table. "I'm going to take the trash out when you're done in here."

Kelly looked up from where she stood at the sink. "Okay, thanks. Can you move the clothes from the washing machine to the dryer, please?"

He realized he was actually excited to be asked. "You got it."


BY THE TIME he came back downstairs, the girls met him as they came up.

"Don't forget to brush your teeth before your showers," Kelly called out.

"Thank you," he said, pulling Kelly into a hug he hadn't planned but didn't stop.

She didn't pull away, instead hugging him back, which felt amazing on a whole new level.

"Why are you thanking me? Did I buy your favorite laundry soap?" She smiled at him, nearly shy as she pulled away and went back to what she'd been doing.

"For letting me be part of this." He motioned between them and then at the house. He wasn't sure how to explain how it felt to be involved in their family. Being a dad whose kids visited wasn't the same. And now he understood that in a new, more painful way.

Kelly turned from the dishwasher, drying her hands. Her smile went tender. He hadn't seen that smile directed at him in a decade. He grabbed the counter as it hit him.

"Oh," she whispered, stepping close enough to briefly cup his cheek. "Guilt does you no good. Not right at this moment."

"You looked at me just now." Vaughan cleared his throat. "It's been a long, long time. I missed it. Like I missed eating dinner with you and making lunches and going to the doctor." He shrugged, the weight of it stealing his words.

He'd grasped how much he'd missed, but the reality of it being his own fault, the real loss because he'd never get it back, really hit him. Those years as his daughters had grown up, it had been Kelly and the girls struggling and triumphing and he'd visited and thought it was enough.

But it wasn't. It hadn't been. And he hadn't even known it.

She paused, clearly thinking and then swallowed hard. "I'm glad you're here. I'm glad it makes the girls happy. I'm glad it's making you happy. It makes me happy, too."

Otis Redding came on and he grinned. "'I've Been Loving You.'" He held out a hand. "This calls for a dance. It's meant to be. You can't fight fate, Kel."

She took his hand, letting him pull her close, snug against his body, his arm around her waist as they began to sway.

KELLY TEETERED ON the edge and once he'd thanked her she'd let go. Let herself fall into that place that had always fit with Vaughan.

She'd ached for this. For years and years after she lost it. At times Kelly had wondered if that ability had died along with her marriage. And it was right here, all along.

Tipping her face up, she let herself be kissed.

She'd expected something slow and gentle. But what she got seared her. Stunned her as the raw, sexual heat of his mouth, his tongue and teeth destroyed every last bit of her remaining defenses against him.

This was how he'd kissed her that first date that had spanned two days. The need of it flowed through her, barreled straight to her nipples.

Kelly gave in and slid her fingers up and into his hair, tugging to keep him close.

He growled into her mouth, pressing himself closer.

He didn't apologize for his hard-on and she didn't apologize for how much she wanted him to take her right then and there, in her kitchen.

The song ended as he spun her, backing her into the pantry, closing them both inside.

And then his hands were inside her shirt, his bare skin against hers. Need raced along the wake of his fingertips. She hissed at the wave of sensation. He bit her lip, tugging. She tried to keep her groan as quiet as possible, in the back of her mind, listening for the water upstairs to turn off.

Not so much she wasn't able to copy his movements, her palms sliding all over his back underneath his T-shirt.

"Jesus," he gasped into her mouth.

"Yeah." She moved closer, taking his mouth again briefly until she kissed down his neck. He grabbed two handfuls of her ass and held her close, grinding into her until she started to see little white stars against her closed eyelids.

Holy cow, was it even possible to come from a clumsy, furtive dry hump like she was back in high school?

The water turned off upstairs and she groaned. "Wait," Kelly managed to say, her hand on his chest to hold him back when he went in for another round. "The girls." The other shower turned off. "Both are out of the shower. I need to be out there where I can hear if someone slips. They'll come down here anyway. You promised to sing to them."

He leaned his forehead to hers, breathing hard. "Give me a minute or two." He took her hand and put it against his cock, through his jeans.

Kelly squeezed a few times. "You're going to need a lot more than a minute so don't get cocky."

"Are you trying to kill me?"

"No. I plan to ride you until you sweat," she whispered before she nipped his earlobe.

He grabbed her close again. "You'll pay for that."

"Can't wait." Still laughing, they spilled from the pantry.

He headed off, the garbage bag and recycling in his arms. "I'll be back, uh, as soon as this is less noticeable."

As long as it came back when she needed it later, she was just fine with that.

## CHAPTER TEN

HE SHOWERED AND waited for the girls to fall asleep. Stupid, as he'd been going to Kelly's room for a nightly chat and glass of wine for a few days and he hadn't hid it.

He planned a lot more than a chat and some booze and he had zero intention of walking back to his room and jerking off at one in the morning, either.

She opened to his knock, wearing sleep shorts and a tank top. Without a word, he went inside, smiling when he heard the click of her door being locked.

"I've never snuck into a bedroom to keep my kids from hearing me sex up their mom before," he murmured when she got close enough to touch.

"Sex? I thought we were going to play a rousing game of Uno."

He barked a laugh. "I played Uno last night after I left your room. There's only so much Uno a man wants to play."

Her reply was a slow raise of her right eyebrow and a smile that sent his system into overdrive.

"Damn it, you're so beautiful." He fisted his hands a few times to conquer the shakes. "You give me butterflies."

She took his hand, tipping it, bending to brush a

kiss over his palm. "That makes two of us. But I think between the two of us we could work something out. We've done it a time or two. It's like riding a bike."

One-handed, he pulled his shirt up and over his head. Her eyes went wide and then settled half-mast as she took him in. "Damn, I like whatever it looks like you're thinking."

"I saw the nipple ring in a video a few years back." She stepped close enough to run covetous hands all over his arms and chest. "New ink, too."

He looked down at the chest piece she meant. A heart with wings. Maddie's and Kensey's names had been interwoven.

"I knew about it. The media loves to talk about you." Kelly traced over their daughters' names. "But obviously I had no real reason to get this close until now. This is gorgeous work."

"Thanks. You should take your shirt off, too. That's only fair."

She whipped her tank top off, tossing it behind her somewhere.

"You have ink, too."

"Mine is on television a lot less," she said, not keeping the smile from her tone. "Crocus. A reminder that even in the dead of winter there's beauty just around the corner."

He licked over the purple and white blooms inked just to the left of a spectacular breast.

"It tastes as good as it looks."

He sighted one more as he began to circle her. At her shoulder blade, near her spine, a small, curled up lizard. "I don't remember anything about you loving reptiles."

"It's a chameleon."

"Ah." The name of her boutiques.

He came to face her again.

"A chameleon can hide in plain sight, all while still remaining essentially what it is. I guess I take some meaning from that."

He wouldn't have understood it as well if she'd told him when they were together before. Then again, she hadn't had any ink when they'd been together.

"Some things have changed. I'm looking forward to seeing everything old and new."

She looked down a moment. "Everything's not, you know, where it was. Before having kids, I mean."

Vaughan stepped back and took her in, shaking his head. He hadn't seen her topless in eight years. It still rendered him speechless. At her striking five feet nine inches, she stood head and shoulders above most women. A tumble of honeyed gold framed her face and shoulders.

Long-as-sin legs led to strong thighs and the hips he'd held on to more than once as he thrust into her body. The flare at her hips was softer now than it had been when he'd met her, sure. She'd been twenty-two years old then! These days she was no less stunning. In fact, he found her even more beautiful. It could be the bare tits in front of him, but she dazzled him. Always had.

The problem was Kelly's mom had done a number on her head. That stupid, horrible cow had beat it into Kelly that her entire life was how she looked. Rebecca had weighed her daily and if Kelly had gained even one pound her mother would put her on an even more restrictive diet than her normal one.

He was sorry she still had remnants of it. But he sure as hell wasn't going to let that pass without a reply.

"Without a doubt, you are the most beautiful woman I've ever seen." He shrugged. "Right here, right now. There's not a single woman on the planet who could hold a candle to you."

He cupped her breasts, taking them into his hands with a happy sigh before brushing his lips over hers.

Her eyes, deep blue, so big, held less wariness and a lot more willingness.

"I want to see the rest," Vaughan urged.

She shoved her shorts and panties down and sent him a look of challenge. Relieved all her wariness was gone, he got naked, too.

She took his cock, squeezing at the base, and he nearly choked as he sucked in air.

"Still works, I see."

"Oh, is that how it is? You're all saucy now?" He stalked her backward through the room until she landed on her bed.

"I'm always saucy. It's one of my finest qualities."

He paused, his knee on the bed between hers. "I've missed this. You all spread out below me just waiting for me to get close. Your attention all on me."

KELLY LOOKED UP into that face. This was one of her favorite ways to look at him. Right before he put his hands and mouth on her. The green of his eyes deepened, his lips swollen from kisses, framed by the beard he'd grown a few years back. She liked it.

His hair was a little too long. He'd just come off tour so he was a little shaggy all around. But it only made him hot lumberjack instead of scary hobo.

He'd grown into his handsomeness. He'd be more like his oldest brother, Ezra, and their father. That sort of handsome that deepened as the man aged.

The heat of the beard burn he'd left on her neck seemed to flow into the flush of desire. She was so wet she should have been embarrassed. Instead she wanted to toss him on his back and climb on top.

"Tell me what you're thinking," he said, lying next to her, his leg over hers as he kissed her shoulder and up her neck. He'd *always* made her feel this way. The center of everything. It had been amazing until she realized he showed it too rarely.

But now? She took it for what it was. And hoped it was more. But she didn't count on it, because he hadn't earned it yet.

But she wanted him to.

She could have said all that, but she didn't want to talk. She wanted him in her. More than she'd wanted sex in a very long time. It didn't matter that she'd been engaged to marry someone else just a week before.

She'd wanted *this* with Vaughan for so long. Guilt over messing up with Ross would return later.

"Fuck me. That's pretty much it. Over and over."

He laughed. "Oh, I will. I promise."

"Less promising, more doing. I'm all about action, Vaughan."

He kissed her long and slow. Tasting, taking his

time. "You've always been bossy. In bed it's a fantastic quality." He paused the kissing to look her in the eye. "I haven't seen you naked in a really long time. It's as fine an experience as I remember. Don't rush me."

"I can tell you've never had sex in a house with two small children in it." She scrambled atop his body like she'd wanted to and when she ground herself, hot, wet and ready, over his cock they both groaned.

"When they're gone is the time for long, slow fucking."

"I'll keep that in mind for future reference." He tried to keep his tone cocky, but she knew he was as hot for it as she was.

He slid a hand up her arm, caressing her shoulder. She shivered at the contact, at the reawakening of all that feeling she'd buried when they fell apart.

It rushed through her. Bittersweet. There was still so much between them. He seemed to fit her in a way she never found with anyone else. Like this, skin to skin, she trusted him. Their bodies remembered what they had before.

He knew just how hard to graze his teeth over her collarbone, rendering her shivering, a muted moan of pleasure sliding from her lips.

She dragged her fingernails down his chest, over nipples she knew were sensitive. Beneath her, his body shifted, muscles of flexing against her inner thighs. That sensual caress turned her inside out.

So much. He made her feel so much.

And then she'd never had it again. No matter how many hands touched her, even in the same way he did then. Only this man seemed to render her bare, every nerve on fire, supersensitive. He played her body, and her heart followed.

Even the way he fucked was like music. One of those slow, ragged rock-and-roll songs about desire and longing.

All that intensity he exposed left her utterly defenseless, not just to how he made her feel physically, but the deep and until last week, hopeless love she'd carried all these years.

"Come back to me," Vaughan said as he tipped his body, reversing their positions as he knelt between her thighs.

And there she was, physically open to him, as well.

"There hasn't been a single moment since you left that I haven't wanted this." His teasing sensuality had gone very primal. Regret was in his gaze, but so was resolve.

"That's the same." He petted down her body. His gaze following her hands. "I could never get enough of you." His thumbs spread her wider and then together, squeezing her clit that way.

An intense ripple of pleasure hit and she gasped.

"That, too." One corner of his mouth hitched up. "I'm going to be here tomorrow. And the next day. I'm here. That's changed. I'm aware of how much I've lost. That I'll never, ever get back."

He continued to speak while he squeezed her clit over and over. It got hard to listen, but she fought against climax and kept her focus on him.

He'd told her what she wanted to hear. What she'd needed to hear. And she wasn't the only one laid bare.

He was trusting her, too. She needed to let go of

the past she'd been using as a shield against him. She already loved him. If he left she'd be hurt either way.

She nodded. "You're here now."

He bent to kiss her stupid and she wrapped her legs around him, urging him closer.

"I'm not done." Vaughan kissed her again before moving down her neck, across her collarbone. Down her sides, against her ribs, feathering against her hip bones and then back up to her nipples.

That was certainly worth waiting for. Kelly arched into his mouth, her fingers digging into his biceps and finding a lot more muscle than before. Mmm.

HER SKIN WAS still so soft and tasty. The warmth of her scent when he'd breathed her in at that place her neck met her shoulder incited him. He wanted more.

He liked sex, yeah. A lot. But with her it had been far more intense than it had ever been with anyone else.

*This* was what it was to love the person you had sex with. In the to-my-very-bones-love sense. He'd been lying to himself that it was just amazing sexual chemistry.

It was love.

And a lot of sexual chemistry, no fucking lie.

She writhed beneath him as he tugged a nipple between his teeth.

"Good to know that still works," he said before licking against the sting of the bite.

"Yep," she squeaked out and it filled him with even more joy when he'd been pretty sure he was so happy it wasn't possible to feel even more.

"I'm going to need to conduct a few tests." He kissed his way down her belly, taking a long, slow lick once he reached her pussy.

So. So. Good.

It was the gentlemanly thing to do, to go down on your partner. Especially when you expected your partner to do the same. He didn't resent it. He dug making his partner feel good. But this—with Kelly—it was so much more devastating. Intimate. The taste of her sang through him, settling in as if it had never been gone.

He didn't stop until she trembled against him, her fingers knotted in his hair, her back arched, a hoarse whisper of his name on her lips as she came.

He kissed his way back up her body, resting some of his weight over her.

"That still works, too. Just in case that wasn't clear." Her voice had gone whiskey-rough.

"I'd forgotten you sounded like a torch singer every time you came." He kissed her.

"Only with you." Her smile was a little shy, a little surprised. He couldn't tear his attention from her neck as she reached back, under her pillow, and held a condom aloft. "Show me if you still make that growling grunt right before you climax."

He managed to tear the packet open and get the condom rolled down his cock and was back, teasing them both, pressing in just slightly and retreating. Getting deeper with each thrust but making it last.

Kids in the house or not, the door was locked and he meant to make this something special.

Even if he wanted to rut. To mark her as his so everyone could see it. But he had to earn that.

KELLY KEPT HER eyes closed as he thrust deep and slow. Over and over until he'd lodged himself to the root.

He kissed her closed lids and then over her cheeks. Touching her with so much tenderness she was crying before she could stop it.

He paused as she wiped her face on the back of a hand. "Am I hurting you?"

She took his face between her hands. "Not anymore."

Wrapping her legs around his waist, she held on as he continued to keep his pace. Slow torture but it was the best kind.

And when he finally came—after making her come another time, too—he left her boneless as he went to deal with the condom and then came back to her, sliding in behind her body, tucking her close.

"Why did you cry?"

She turned in his arms. "Because you touched me tonight and made me feel something I wasn't sure I even could again."

He smiled, his worry past.

"Oh. I like that. I feel the same. It was right there. The way I am only with you. I just reached for it and it was ready."

She knew exactly what he meant.

"I'm going to the ranch tomorrow morning after the girls get on the bus. I need to pack some more stuff. I'll be back in time to have dinner with everyone. I figured I'd bring back some takeout."

She nodded and tried not to think about him not coming back. About him getting to the ranch and his mother talking him out of getting back together with her.

"Have you told them yet? Your family?"

"Ezra knows. I talked to my dad the day you broke the engagement with Ross. I'm going to talk to my parents tomorrow. Do you want to come along? I don't want to exclude you. Especially after the way things have been."

"That would be negatory. Maybe one day I'll feel as comfortable around her as the new crop of Hurley women, but for now, I think it could be really bad."

He sighed. "I'm sorry. I didn't think… I was about to say I didn't think it was that bad, but I guess it's more like I didn't think. I made the mess, though. She's just reacting to what she thinks."

Kelly rolled her eyes. "Your mother is not stupid. Or naive. Not even when her precious sons are concerned. She knows you and your tricks. She didn't want to confront it. And I get that, too. But I'm not ready for that. Not yet." Maybe not ever.

"All right. But I *am* coming back. We have dinner plans."

"Okay. Oh, and I need Tuesday's phone number so if you see Ezra tomorrow can you get it for me? I want to talk to her about the jewelry she makes."

"You two seemed to get along pretty well when she was over here last weekend."

"I liked her a lot." Kelly really did click with Ezra's new girlfriend. The other woman seemed to love clothes in the same way Kelly did. She had a fantastic sense of style and if her work was half as stylish as the rest of her, Kelly wanted to feature Tuesday's designs in her boutiques.

"Do I have to go back to my lonely bed or can I sleep in here with you?" Vaughan asked.

"I want to be careful. This thing between you and me is complicated. But we're adults. It's *their* happiness I worry about. I have to trust you to keep your word. It's not just my heart you'd be breaking, but theirs, too." Being a grown-up sucked sometimes. But she wasn't going to be like Rebecca.

If the girls saw him in here they'd assume things Kelly wasn't ready to fully admit yet.

"I think for the time being we should sleep in our own rooms. Sometimes they come get in bed with me in the middle of the night. They'd be so ridiculously excited to find you here, no kidding. But I think taking it slow is good when it comes to them. But you certainly don't have to go just yet." She smiled.

He pulled her more tightly against him. "Sounds very good. Now. I think we should investigate round two."

He pulled the blanket above them both and when his hands were everywhere at once, she readily agreed about round two.

## CHAPTER ELEVEN

CONFUSED, VAUGHAN LOOKED over at Kensey, who'd just dissolved into a mass of tears on the floor next to where he stood.

He cast his glance Kelly's way. She sat at the table, a bunch of spreadsheets in front of her. And she smirked behind her coffee cup, not moving to intervene.

"What's the problem, Miss Kensey?" Vaughan asked.

She answered in a rush of gasping sobs and hiccups so of course he had no idea what she'd said.

"She says, what if the girls in her class say corduroy is dumb?" Maddie explained. "And she doesn't like mustard on both pieces of bread."

He had zero idea how to deal with the pants issue, though he got out another piece of bread, this time with no mustard on it. The week before she'd had school lunches so he hadn't made her a lunch yet.

But Kelly spoke, interrupting the process. "Kensey, get up off the floor immediately. Go upstairs and clean your face. You *will* have mustard on both slices of bread today. You *will* come down, apologize to your father for this behavior and get it together."

Kelly's tone caught his attention as quickly as it

got Kensey's. Not angry, but full of command and not an inch to be given.

Kensey sniffled, hauled herself up and ran out of the room.

Vaughan, undeniably impressed, finished up with sandwiches for both girls' lunches. Maddie patted his arm once he handed her a lunch bag.

"She's a handful, Dad. You gotta be tough with her."

Kelly had to cough to hide the laughter Vaughan also fought against.

"You're an artist. You know how you guys are. Temperamental. But she's like a kitten." Maddie turned to Kelly. "Right, Mom?"

Kelly blushed, shaking her head and giving in to her laughter. "Kensey likes shiny things. Sometimes you just kind of shake something pretty and it breaks the spell and she gets back on track."

"Oh, and artists need to be handled that way?" he teased Maddie.

Maddie gave him a serious nod. "Yes. We're all quite individualistic. We're snowflakes, Mom says, but not special snowflakes because special snowflakes think the rules don't apply."

"Your mom is very wise." And way better at this parent thing than he was.

Kensey came back down and her attitude had shifted. She hugged Vaughan and apologized. He would have told Kensey it wasn't necessary to apologize, would have if they'd been at his house. But he didn't countermand Kelly, knowing that would be a disastrous thing.

"Will you both walk us to the bus stop? It's my first

day back." Maddie gave those eyes Vaughan had no idea how to refuse.

"I was thinking of driving you both. You'd rather go on the bus?" Kelly had gotten up to pin Kensey's hair back from her face.

Maddie nodded. "My friends are on the bus. I won't roughhouse or anything. I promise."

The doctor had told them at the appointment just a few days before that Maddie would be fine to return to school by week's end, and here they were. But she seemed so small. So fragile. Maybe she should be driven. What if she got jostled and hurt?

Everything seemed to scare the hell out of Vaughan, but Kelly had seemed to handle it perfectly so he'd leaned on her.

"We can all walk together, if that's cool with your dad." Kelly kissed Kensey's head.

"Yeah, I'd like that." He looked at the clock over the stove. "Okay, ladies. Bathroom break and then we'll go."

The girls headed off and he moved in close to Kelly. "Hi."

She smiled. "Hi."

"I'm impressed with how you mother them. I feel like a total amateur."

"You love them. That's the biggest thing. You just have to be tougher sometimes. You'll learn. They'll still love you. It's going to be okay."

"I've made so many mistakes already." Sometimes that shook him. Made him wonder if he had it in him to do this. But then he looked at his ladies and he knew it was worth the effort.

"Everyone makes mistakes. I sure do."

He kissed her quickly but stepped back when he heard thundering feet coming back downstairs.

IT WAS THAT FEELING, that sense of fitting in a place that was distinctly unique. Not Hurley, but something more.

"I'm heading out," he told Kelly as they returned home. "You sure you don't want to come along?"

"Uh, yeah. Totally sure. I'll handle picking the girls up so if you want to spend more time with your brothers, you can."

He took her hands. "I'll be back. I swear to you."

She took a breath and then shrugged. "I can't do anything but trust your word."

He kissed her. Right there in the driveway. He pulled her close and showed her how much he'd missed her. Of course when he broke the kiss, he, too, was nearly panting and totally not wanting to go anywhere but upstairs back to her bed.

"That's a down payment. Tonight we fuck in my room. I have plans. And because it's even farther from the girls, I'll happily make that growling grunt you seem to like so much."

She shivered, blowing out a breath. Her eyes were clear when she smiled. "All right, then. I have very high standards so I'll hold you to that."

The last thing he wanted to do was get in his car and head away. But she had work and he had to get moving so he could return in plenty of time for dinner.

VAUGHAN HAD DRIVEN the same route to and from Hood River from Kelly's house dozens upon dozens of times. Usually, he came up the hill, the road curving ever so slowly and then *bam* he was home. The big iron gates with the Sweet Hollow Ranch logo on them welcomed him as he drove through.

Even as he knew every bump in the road, he thought about how to make the office above the garage a more useful work space. Because he'd begun to think of that house in Gresham as home, as well.

He parked at his place, noted the mail Ezra had left on the counter in the kitchen. The dog had long since given him up for the far more lavish surroundings his mother provided so he didn't have to worry about feeding anyone but his daughters.

Ezra had left a note saying he'd put Vaughan's sprinklers on a timer so his landscaping didn't die in his absence. *It's May already, dumb ass* was implied. Vaughan snorted as he pulled his phone out to text Ezra.

If his brother was on horseback or on an ATV he wouldn't even hear or feel his phone so it could have been anywhere from a minute to hours before Ezra replied.

Vaughan had two of his guitars with him in Gresham already, but he grabbed his mandolin and slide guitar along with some equipment. Before he'd left Kelly's he'd pulled the seats out of the back of his SUV so he had enough space to pack enough to get set up to work.

He'd already loaded his equipment and was in his room filling suitcases with his things when Ezra came over.

"Look what the cat dragged in." The brothers hugged.

"I put some soda in the fridge when I got here. You want something to drink?" Vaughan asked.

"Yeah, that'd be good."

Once they'd retrieved their drinks, Vaughan began to pack some things from the kitchen and family room into a box.

"Well." Ezra gave him a look. "That looks like more than just what you'd need to hang out until your daughter goes back to school."

"Which is today. I walked her to the bus this morning before I came out here. Damn, Ez. That kid is strong. She was operated on just a little over a week ago and she's ready to go back to school. It's not just staying there until Maddie gets better. It's more. I'm moving in. In my own bedroom still. Which sucks. But I can deal." He paused after tucking a few of his favorite books into the box.

"I want you to know I'm still going to be here to do my part." It was coming up on the alfalfa harvest and then a whole lot of busy months as summer came and that melted into fall. Harvesting pears would take up much of August into October. The pears were picked and then sent to cold storage to continue the ripening process. Each step of the process had its own set of challenges.

Ezra did a lot. Far more than anyone else. When the brothers were off the road they made it a point to pitch in and be as much help as Ezra would allow. It was, in a very real way, their big brother's ranch now. He had staff to handle all things that needed doing. But he was there when the band wasn't. He kept their roots deep and something their parents had built chugging along.

And he had his own way of doing things. So the rest of the brothers just pitched in and if Ezra didn't want them doing something he aimed them elsewhere and that worked, too.

"You're dealing with something way more important right now. Focus on that."

Vaughan wanted to tell his brother that he'd slept with Kelly at long last but something made him keep it to himself. Ezra had enough on his plate just then anyway.

"You work too hard. You need to let people help."

Ezra rolled his eyes. "I have employees, Vaughan. I keep telling you guys that. Has the ex shown up yet?"

"He drove by when I was out in the front yard last week. When he saw me he left in a hurry." Vaughan had wanted to punch the guy, but then he'd thought about it and felt sorry for him.

"He in stalker mode?"

He liked that his brother had worried for Kelly.

"I don't think so. It struck me more like regret that she'd gotten away than him having a secret shrine to her in his basement. She took some stuff over there last week, but Stacey was with her. I'm scared of Stacey. I imagine she inspires that same fear in Ross."

"Stacey is the lawyer? Killer legs? Redhead?"

"Your memory for women rivals Paddy. Damn."

"Some gifts you never lose." Ezra grinned and then got serious again. "You happy?"

Vaughan leaned back against the counter. "I am.

It's hard. I make mistakes. The girls know I'm a rookie so they try to work it to their advantage."

Ezra found that hilarious. "They're Hurleys, all right."

"Kelly deals with discipline better than I do. She's calmer about it. Firmer. I'm just watching and learning."

"You've always been a pushover when it came to women anyway. She is a good mother. I misjudged her at first. But your daughters are amazing and she's definitely part of that. Speaking of Kelly... How are things between you two?"

He smiled as a flash of memory hit. Kelly arched, flushed from climax, and his brother's face told Vaughan Ezra knew they'd had sex. Just from one look. He was going to be such a great father someday with that kind of radar.

"Slow. She wanted to take it slow and while parts of me thought it was a bad idea, I have to admit she was probably right to keep it careful and be cautious," Vaughan said.

Because sex between them had been perfect. Messy and sticky, too, but it had always been a part of their relationship that had worked.

But it was so good, and made them so close that it was easy to forget all the work. Easy to coast on the fucking and forget the rest. Which was why she'd wanted to wait, of course. But damn, he was glad she was as powerless against their sexual chemistry as he was.

"It's good. All of it. Uncomfortable sometimes. I did some damage, you know?"

Ezra snorted. "Yeah, I think I can imagine what that might feel like."

His big brother had fallen down the deep pit of addiction. Driven himself right off the road of life, had to go to rehab and rebuild everything, including all his relationships. Which he had.

Ezra, being who he was, though, carried it around, all that guilt, as if he hadn't made up for his mistakes a thousand times by then.

"I say this with love, Vaughan."

Vaughan cringed at whatever his brother was about to say.

Ezra laughed. "Calm down. You've been given a pass. Most of your life. Now you have to face some shit you pulled. Bad enough to have derailed your own damned life. Own your shit and then move forward with these women who adore you. Don't look back, Vaughan. Once you've dealt with the hurts of the past, it's time to look to the future."

"I'm trying."

"You're out of your element, too. Not here, but at Kelly's house. How's that feel?" Ezra asked.

"She's got reasons for that," Vaughan said, defensiveness in his tone.

"I imagine she does. We're all responsible for that. In protecting you, we were less than kind to her."

How could Ezra be so spot-on about everyone else, but never cut himself a break?

"And now she doesn't trust you all," Vaughan said. Which he really hated. This was his family; he loved them. They were an incredibly important part of his life and he wanted her to feel that, too. Though his family had opened their hearts up to his sister-in-law Mary, Natalie, his brother Paddy's girlfriend, and even to Tuesday, the woman Ezra was just starting up with, they hadn't with Kelly.

"Fair enough. You have to get her trust back first. And then you have to lay out the whole truth. Mom will do the right thing once she knows."

Vaughan blew out a breath. "Maybe. She seems pretty invested in not liking Kelly."

"Sure she did. You're her son. She'd cut someone to protect any of us." Ezra shrugged. "Back then the whole family was different. You brought this woman around and she was pregnant and your wife before they even met her?"

"Mom took one look, got how pretty Kelly was and then wrote her off. You can't pretend that wasn't part of it."

Ezra nodded. "Yeah, most likely. We never got to know her very well."

Vaughan just hoped he got the chance to get his family to open up in ways they hadn't before. If they gave Kelly the time, they'd see she was so much more than a pretty woman who'd had his kids.

"Step one is to get her back. Then I guess the rest of it will follow," Vaughan said.

"Only if you work your ass off for it."

"That so? How are things with Tuesday, then?"

His messed-up brother had found a woman with her own set of vulnerabilities. The two fit in ways Vaughan could see made his brother uncertain. But that he kept at it and continued a relationship with her was a good thing.

Ezra smirked. "I'm keeping it close for the time being. We like each other."

"Fair enough. Help me load this stuff into my car."

As they did, his father approached with a wave, a few dogs and a pig in his wake. "Ezra, your animals came to see me this morning. Your mom loves the visits but your pig roots in her flower beds and then I have to listen to her rant about it. You know how she is about those beds. It was your goats last time now it's the pig again. Don't do that to me, boy."

Ezra was a burly man. Broad-shouldered. He didn't speak unless it was necessary most of the time. Taciturn. Gruff. But that was all for show. He was a giant marshmallow when it came to his animals and his family. He had a sweet but not exceptionally bright Lab named Loopy and a pig named Violet who seemed to think she was a dog and Ez let her.

Currently though, Violet knew she was in trouble for digging and she made a cute little squeaky grunt. Ezra rolled his eyes, went to his haunches to dust the dirt from her snout.

"I thought we had a deal?" Loopy licked the side of Ezra's face. "And you? You're supposed to keep her away from those flower beds."

As Ezra pretended to scold his pig who thought it was a dog, Vaughan hugged his dad quickly.

"Hey there, stranger. How's my granddaughter today?"

"First day back to school. I made Kelly promise to text if there was a problem, but she was strong and happy when she left this morning."

"Good. Bring them over to see us soon, all right?

She brought them out here, you know. While you were on tour," his dad said quietly. "For your mom's birthday. We had them for the weekend."

"I didn't know." Though he wasn't surprised. Despite her feelings about Sharon, Kelly had gone out of her way to be sure the girls saw his family.

"She gave up her career to move here. She didn't have to. She could be making a huge amount of money if she was modeling regularly."

"She sure did." His father clapped his shoulder.

"He's sneaky with the lessons," Ezra said as he stood, brushing his hands down the front of his jeans.

"Vaughan knows a dad has to get his lessons in whenever he can. You'll know this one day, too."

"I have a long way to go to be half as good at this as you are," Vaughan told his father.

"I've been doing it longer. Parenting is a lot like a marriage. You have to consistently work at it or things turn to shit. Hopefully you'll all have children who are easier on your hearts than mine. Though I'll laugh my ass off when one of you has to go to the school to deal with some stupid bullshit one of your kids pulls."

He took Vaughan by the upper arms for a moment. "You can do this." And that moment passed.

But it was what he needed. Enough to spur him on. To remind him of what was important.

He could do this. He would do this.

## CHAPTER TWELVE

KELLY LOVED CLOTHES. That one part of being a model she'd loved. She'd never have been exposed to the depth and breadth of design, fabric and style otherwise. As she grew more successful in the modeling world clothes began to come with the gigs.

When she left modeling full-time she hadn't relinquished her love of clothes. She'd kept a huge closetful in her condo in Manhattan and the one she currently stood in was similarly full.

Her closet was a place she often escaped to after a frustrating day. Organizing, shifting things around that she hadn't worn in a while. She liked to do a cull each season and those things were either donated or traded with her friends.

Some of her pieces were like art. Kelly didn't attend as many parties as she once did, though she still did modeling campaigns for two design houses, but she built her time in New York around the girls' school schedule and kept a place there.

The money was good. It kept her working and relevant in that world, which was helpful to her boutiques, and she couldn't deny she was proud of what she'd built.

It was fitting that she'd been able to take her love

of clothes and fashion and make it into a way to continue to support herself and her girls. More than that, she'd begun to construct what Stacey liked to call Kelly Hurley, Inc.

She didn't much want to act or sing or do any of those things. But there were things she was good at. Things she was proud to add to her résumé. It was more than throwing money at a storefront. She was involved with the direction of her business. She and her partner liked to innovate.

Which was why she'd just pulled on one of her favorite outfits and was heading to Hood River to have lunch and a chat with Tuesday Eastwood about her jewelry.

There was a tap on the door just as she'd slid a blue Lucite bangle bracelet into place.

Vaughan stood there with a smile. "Wow, I'm impressed. This is huge."

She looked around the room, proud. "Yeah. This was supposed to be another bedroom with an en suite bath but I made it into my closet instead." And a dressing room—a place she put on her makeup and did her hair, as well.

"You're off to have lunch with Tuesday now?" He'd retrieved Tuesday's number from Ezra just a few hours before so he knew where she was headed.

"Yes. I'll be back in time for the bus, though."

"No big deal if you aren't. I'm here. I'm working in the office, setting it all up in there, but I have my phone and the house phone up there so I'll be available if there's a problem. Tell her I said hello."

"You really want me to like her, don't you?"

He brushed the pad of his thumb over her bottom lip. "Well, sure. She's my brother's girlfriend so it would be nice if you were friends with her. And she's close with Natalie, and that's my other brother's girlfriend so that's a good thing, too. I want you to like my family."

"I like the way your family treats my children." She smiled brightly, pleased she'd found something positive to say that was actually believable. "That's a lot to me. As for the rest, it's a conversation we need to have, but not right now." She stepped back, breaking contact or they'd end up in bed and she'd never leave the house at that rate.

Avoiding any more discussion of his family, she grabbed her bag, slid into her shoes and headed out.

"You tell me to share but then when I do you're too busy for it?" he called out from the doorway to her bedroom.

The words to agree with him rose to her lips and then she stopped, frowning. Her normal instinct was to defer, even when her feelings were being ignored. If he meant to be around she couldn't let their daughters see her be anything but strong, them anything less than united and always respectful of one another.

It seemed that now she was confident—and wary—enough to demand respect. And not all anger was destructive and ugly.

Which was good because he could make her angry in ways no one else on earth did. But instead of running from it, deferring to him to keep the peace or shying from conflict, she let it come.

They promised one another honesty so she gave it to him.

"Oh, I see. So when *you* decide you're ready to talk about something you've been avoiding for eight years I'm supposed to drop everything. Do I have that right?"

"We can't work things out if when I finally talk about them you run off." Vaughan threw his hands up.

"It's really a good thing you're going to continue to be hot when you get old."

His eyebrows rose. "That sounds like an insult."

"Smart. Also, self-centered. I'm meeting with a potential new business associate and you really expect me to toss that? Eight years *you* said nothing. Two weeks of being back in my life doesn't give you the right to stand there and be hurt or mad or anything but accepting of my saying, *yes we need to talk but not right this moment*."

He froze as the point hit home.

"I'll see you later. Make sure everyone has a backpack when they get off the bus." She walked downstairs, snatching her keys from the hook near the garage door and scooting out.

She'd had the last word and he needed to chew on that for a while.

THOUGH HER TRIPS to Hood River were usually far less pleasant than the one she undertook that day, the skies above were brilliantly blue. The weather was gorgeous and she was hungry and going to have lunch with a new friend and hopefully a new business contact.

It wasn't a city, not even a small city. But Tuesday's

custom frame shop was located in a cute, well-traveled part of town in a busy retail-dense several blocks.

But when she went inside, Kelly realized this was far more than a place people got art framed. This little shop had the bones and heart of a gallery.

Tuesday was up front, dealing with a customer, so Kelly strolled through the space, pausing to look here and there.

Once the customer had left and it was just the two of them, Tuesday smiled and welcomed Kelly with a hug. "Thanks for waiting."

"No problem. I run a shop, too. I know what that's like." Kelly indicated a glass case. "Is that yours?"

Tuesday nodded, pulling some trays out.

Like Tuesday herself, the jewelry was vivid. Bold and beautiful. She liked to work with a variety of stones and findings but everything was crafted incredibly and priced fairly. In fact, Kelly would sell these things in her store for at least twice as much and they'd still be a bargain.

"Let's go to lunch so we can talk about what I've got in mind."

Kelly didn't have many close friends but when she liked someone she tended to just like them intensely enough to be real friends with them, or they became acquaintances.

Tuesday was one of those souls Kelly had liked the moment she'd come into Kelly's house with Ezra at her side. They had lunch, talked about the kids and how they were feeling and the discussion landed on how Kelly felt about Vaughan living with her.

Kelly hesitated because she had a million different feelings about it.

Finally, she managed, "It's complicated."

Tuesday laughed, patting Kelly's hand. "Girl, I bet. I'm around if you want to talk about it. You don't know me very well, but sometimes that's a good thing."

Maybe it was.

"I'm so confused right now. To be honest, I couldn't answer you because I don't know. Well, no, that's a lie. I like Vaughan. I mean as a person separate from my ex-husband or as the father of my kids. I've always liked him, since the start. And it hasn't served me well in every circumstance. I have a lot to figure out. Right now I'm just trying to figure out what it is I want."

She wanted what it was between them when they were having sex. It wasn't awkward or uncertain then. Her body trusted his. In the four days since they'd slept together, they'd been together every single night after the girls had gone to sleep.

She'd gone back to her room, or him to his own, but he chafed at that, she knew. He wanted the girls to understand he was there to get all of them back.

The truth was, sleeping with him had been a stupid, impulsive mistake. Kelly had wanted to wait, take it slow. But she'd given in and at this point, since the condom was out of the wrapper, she didn't regret it because it felt so good.

She never wanted her children to feel what she did when their father lost interest. And though she'd forgiven him and believed his apology was genuine, there was no forgetting.

And that still loomed between them whether she wanted it to or not.

Illicit sex was one thing. Mom and Dad sleeping in the same room was something a lot more than, "Dad's staying with us awhile."

They paid for their lunch and began to make their way back the few blocks to Tuesday's shop. Her new friend was equally skittish it seemed about the Hurley she was with.

Neither of them seemed to want to talk about it in too much detail but Kelly felt a little better anyway that someone else was trying to work out a complicated-type romantic thing at the same time.

"Vaughan isn't a bad man." Kelly began to speak as she arranged the jewelry she'd asked Tuesday to pull out of the locked cases, taking pictures and sending them to her business partner. "He just didn't want a life with me and the girls. It took me a really long time to get over that."

When Kelly looked up, she caught understanding on Tuesday's features.

Tuesday blew out a breath and started to tell Kelly the story of how she'd met and fallen in love with her former husband who'd died five years prior.

Tuesday leaned against the counter. "Things were fast with us. We clicked. He had dreadlocks back then. We were nineteen." Tuesday laughed.

"The next year we all decided to move into a big house together. Natalie and me and our other roommates. And Eric. We all went to school together, some of us worked together, we lived in the same house and we were a family. As we neared graduation, Eric asked me to marry him. Or I guess I should say he and I had this talk about life and the future and we decided to get married. He and I had plans. A path, and we were on it together. It was a really great time in my life. I'm telling you this stuff so you can understand what I'm going to say next a little better."

Kelly stilled, putting her phone down. The heat of a blush overtook her neck and face. Tuesday knew about the cheating. Kelly wasn't sure who'd told her, but it was pretty easy to tell where the story was heading.

"I found a letter. Not a love letter," Tuesday amended quickly. "It was a discussion about this thing they'd had while studying in Central America. It was like, hey I get it, I'd never say anything to her, I know you love her and I hope it works out."

A sick feeling washed through Kelly on her friend's behalf.

"I was planning our wedding, getting ready to move away from my hometown to Seattle, where Eric had a job. Boxing stuff up. I confronted him as he walked in the door. He confessed immediately. He begged my forgiveness. He said he loved me and wanted to be with me. He'd chosen me, deliberately, every single day of his life since he returned from that program he'd been in over two years before. I went home, because that's what you do. Anyway, my mom was awesome. She said love can start a marriage, but a commitment is what kept it together. Did I think Eric would do it again or did I think if I forgave him I could have a really wonderful life with a man who wasn't perfect but one who loved me? You listen to me, Kelly. Lots of people will say if he or she ever cheated I'd break up with them forever. And maybe you should, given the circumstances. Hell, you did. But it's how long ago now?"

There was no denying her fear of not only being left behind again, but also of people seeing it from the outside and thinking she was a doormat or stupid. She had left then, not so much because of that one incident, but that one last incident being all she could take, and his reaction only underlined why she left.

"Eight years. I served him with papers eight years ago."

"You're a different person now. Maybe he is, too." Tuesday shrugged. "Maybe not. But you get to think about it if you want to. Screw what anyone else says about it."

Kelly had come a long way in her life, but she wasn't quite sure she had that not-caring-about-what-anyone-else-thought part down yet.

"You were glad, then? That you gave him another chance?"

Tuesday nodded. "Yes. I never regretted it."

It had been a risk for her new friend to expose herself with that story and it had been exactly what Kelly had needed to hear. "Thanks for that. I needed to hear it. Can I say something else? Not about men or marriage."

Tuesday's expression turned curious. "Sure."

"I wasn't sure what I expected when you said you owned and ran a custom framing shop. But, Tuesday, this is so much more than that. This is a *gallery*. You should call it that." Tuesday had art living in her veins, that much was clear. It seemed a crime to call the shop anything but a gallery.

"I guess you weren't the only one who needed to hear something today. Thank you."

Kelly hugged her and left a few minutes later with a new piece of jewelry, so very glad she'd stopped by that day.

## CHAPTER THIRTEEN

"TOMORROW NIGHT IS the end-of-the-year festival at the elementary school. Are you ready for that?" Kelly asked Vaughan.

"Okay. Yeah." He smiled. "Yeah. Like what happens? What do we do?"

"There'll be a cakewalk and games and stuff to waste money on. Their teachers are there for the dunk tank and the pie-in-the-face stuff."

"Ah, okay. A carnival, then. We had those in school, too, back in the day. Didn't you?"

"No. I went to other types of festivals, though. Stuff at the base and then later, as I traveled for work, I did amusement parks and merry-go-rounds and Ferris wheels."

He stood next to her at the kitchen counter, looking out into the backyard where the girls played. He thought about a night a decade before where they'd taken a ride on the Eye in London.

"Remember London?"

Her laugh told him she did. "Hard to forget. I was hugely pregnant with Maddie. It was the last trip I took until after she was born."

That night they'd been alone in the carriage and he'd wedged in behind her, his hands on her belly as his daughter kicked and moved.

Their entire future had stretched out that night. He hadn't been terrified of it yet. Parenthood was still at the easy part when the baby was still inside Mom.

Silence hung between them for several long seconds. Not uncomfortable, but weighty. Important.

She dried her hands, clearing her throat. "Anyway. I bought you a ticket. It comes with a cookie and a juice box. Bring all your one-dollar bills. For all the games, not for your usual reason to carry a lot of small bills."

She had a smile that made him turn toward her to look better.

He cupped her cheek. "I missed being teased by you." He kissed her quickly, without thinking, and then remembered they stood in front of the window. Part of him hoped the girls had seen it.

Once he'd broken the kiss, they just looked at one another. Thank God Kelly didn't freeze up or push him away, but then the oven timer dinged and she went over to turn it off and take dinner out.

"The girls need to come in and wash up," she said as she turned back to him.

"How're we doing?" He'd told himself to wait for her to bring it up but he couldn't resist. "I'm sorry. I'm not trying to pressure you but I'd like to be more open about us around the girls. Around everyone. I want to take you on dates. I want to hold your hand when we're out." He'd been there three weeks and every moment it got more difficult not to touch her anytime he wanted—which turned out to be often— or kiss her, take her hand, whatever.

She opened her mouth to answer but instead a child came in, interrupting the moment. Instead of stepping in to tell Maddie what to do, Kelly turned and got back to work dealing with the food, leaving it to him.

"Maddie, wash up and get your sister inside, too, please."

Maddie turned around and screamed her sister's name, making him jump a few feet.

"Madeline!" Kelly's voice wasn't loud, but had that mom-command in it. "We've had a talk about that before. Daddy could have yelled for your sister, too. But he asked you to get your sister inside and you know what he meant."

Maddie's mouth turned down. "Sorry."

"It's okay. Your uncles and I still do that." Vaughan winked as Kensey came running in.

"You don't haveta yell," she told her big sister.

Dinner went well but as they were cleaning up, they hit another snag.

"Don't I need to sign something?" Kelly asked Maddie.

"I only have a few math problems left. I'll do them on the bus tomorrow morning."

"No, you won't. You'll go bring your homework down and do it here at the table. Then I'll go over it and sign it."

"It's two questions. They're easy. I still have to shower."

"None of those things you said are an answer to anything I told you to do."

"Daddy said it was okay."

Vaughan sat back in his chair. "I did?"

"Today. I showed you my work and said I had some

left and would do them tomorrow and you said that was fine."

"Do you think I'm ever going to find that an acceptable excuse?" Kelly shook her head.

"Aren't we supposed to obey our parents? He's my parent."

Vaughan knew his kids were strong-willed. It wasn't that they were always angels with him, either. But this day-to-day stuff was unexpected. Kelly seemed far more at ease dealing with it than he was.

Kelly sighed. "I'm so disappointed in you, Madeline. He didn't know the rules and you used that to get the answer you wanted. Now go get your homework and bring it down immediately. I'm seriously wondering if an end-of-school party is the best idea for you if this is your attitude."

Maddie burst into tears and threw her arms around Vaughan, babbling at him that she was sorry. He patted her shoulder, feeling like an ogre.

"It's okay, sweetheart. I did say that."

Kelly's posture went stiff and then she narrowed her gaze at him enough he knew he was in trouble.

"You do still need to obey your mother right now."

He kissed the top of Maddie's head before she left the room.

"I didn't know she wasn't allowed to do that."

Kelly's eyes went wide and then narrowed. "Wrong thing to apologize for. She knew you didn't know the rules. That's why she asked you instead of me. And then I called her out and told her it was disappointing. And you said hey no big, I said that thing you manipulated me into saying."

"I just wanted to give her the benefit of the doubt. We don't need to be so harsh."

"Oh, we don't? Your nearly three weeks of full-time parenting has made you a big enough expert to tell me the years I've put into helping them be better people is harsh?"

"That's not fair. I'm trying."

"I just gave you a gold star. It's invisible but I promise it's there. Now to the actual point instead of your hurt feelings. I'm trying to teach them how to understand that what they do impacts other people. It's a big-picture thing, Vaughan. She's in fifth grade, of course she doesn't want to do her homework. But she used someone else's ignorance to get away with breaking a rule. It's not the homework, it's the way she needs to have empathy. That's not harsh, that's our job as parents. They need to be adults someday. Adults who can stand by their words and deeds."

Like he hadn't. She didn't say it aloud, but he heard it anyway. And she'd been right.

"I'm sorry. I didn't think."

"You don't need to be sorry." Kelly shook her head. "We'll talk about this in private later."

He wanted to hash it out right then, but the girls were hovering, he knew. They'd get back to it that night.

ONCE KELLY HAD gotten all the homework handled, the showers done and the clothes laid out for the next day, it was time to put the girls down. Then Kensey got up because she *needed* a drink of water. The next time, ten minutes later, Kelly'd been walking down the hall toward her room when she caught Kensey with her headphones on, playing a video game.

It was after taking away the video game and headphones and tucking them into the time-out drawer that she realized something pretty important. Enough that it brought her to a complete stop.

Vaughan had been in their house for three weeks. And until very recently they'd treated him like a guest. But over the past several days there'd been a return to their usual behavior. On the whole, great kids, but they could act up like anyone else. And they did.

The girls were getting used to him being there. They'd stopped using their company manners and were giving their dad a taste of what day-to-day parenting felt like.

She walked to his room and tapped.

He opened up, holding the neck of his guitar. Then he got that grin and impossibly enough she wanted to kiss him and kick him in the junk at exactly the same time and in equal measure.

"Not even, sport. We've got *miles* to go before we're in that neighborhood. Kensey keeps getting up. I'm going to take a shower so I need you to put her butt back in bed when she gets up next."

"Oh. Okay. Sure."

She turned, leaving him to his fate and then came back. "Can I give you a tip about this thing with Kensey?"

He cocked his head. "What thing?"

He was so adorably clueless.

"She doesn't want to go to sleep. She wants to talk

and play. Don't let her con you. Be firm. Put her back in bed over and over and she'll quit it."

"Did she have a bad dream?" He leaned in very close. "Do you think she senses something between us and is acting out? See? We should tell them."

"Two separate issues. You and I will discuss telling the girls later on tonight. As for why Kensey is getting up a lot after she's supposed to be in bed? She's nine. That's what they do. Like Maddie's little snit earlier."

He looked sad so she took pity on him, brushing her fingers through his hair. "It's a good thing. Before they acted up in a different way. I call them company manners." She shrugged. "Now they get bratty around you. Also what they do. But they trust you to be themselves, bratty and all."

"Oh." She got the feeling he'd been waiting for something negative, but the smile he gave made her happy. He kissed her quickly. "Thank you for that."

"You're welcome. Now, like I said, I'm going to shower and you're on Kensey duty. She'll be up in the next ten minutes or so. Next up I'm going to guess she'll pester Maddie. Or have to go to the bathroom. She already has, by the way. Stay strong."

"When can I come to you?" He closed the distance remaining between them in one step. The heat of his skin dizzied her and she breathed him in.

"You'll know she's finally asleep after about half an hour or so after the last whatever it is she does." She took a step back and headed out.

By the time she'd walked into her bedroom she heard Kensey get up.

"What's up, sweetheart?" Vaughan called out and Kelly let herself leave their daughter in his hands.

SHE DID MOST of her best thinking in the shower and that night was no different. Kelly knew he was trying. Knew he hadn't thought of the issue with Maddie earlier in the same way she had.

She needed to cut him some slack. He was trying, which was what he'd promised. It wasn't so much that she was angry. More likely a trigger put there by being raised as a commodity instead of a person.

It wasn't really like you could untangle what stuff you had for a good reason and what stuff you had because of your damage, not when the outcome was something like raising your kids into responsible, whole adults.

It unsettled her to think of them being teenagers without a moral center. When you didn't, you could make not only bad choices, which everyone made, but also the kinds of choices and decisions that could mess a life up for years.

Ugh. Impossible to not see how much that was because she was thrust into a very adult world when she was only a little older than Maddie. It was sheer luck and the fact that other adults in that world had protected her instead of harming her that she'd gotten through it without the horror stories so many who started young in the fashion industry had.

She got out of the shower and as she brushed her teeth, put on lotion and got into some clothes, she thought about the way Vaughan had listened to her that night.

Before, he hadn't really looked at her with that much attention when it wasn't sex or something fun. He'd been too focused on being carefree to want to talk about anything heavy.

Another comparison, she realized, she'd made between how Vaughan was before and how he was now.

It made a difference that he'd changed.

"I FIND MYSELF thinking about you in terms of before and now," she announced to Vaughan as he came into her room half an hour later.

He started and then looked her way, a little wary.

But she wasn't mad so he got that sexy look, well, one of his approximately four thousand sexy faces, the one he wore when he knew he was going to sex her into a puddle of goo. One of her favorites.

But one that tended to make her forget everything, including things they really needed to talk about.

Not that she stopped him from sliding his arms around her and kissing her. She sighed, opening to him, tasting him. This connection between them sizzled and popped.

His tongue teased into her mouth and then retreated as the edge of his teeth slid over her bottom lip when he broke away.

"Now. Tell me about this before-and-now thing."

They got into her bed, still wearing clothes, legs crossed and facing one another. They'd moved from her sitting area to the bed days ago and hadn't bothered to go back.

"I was in the shower and thinking about you."

"Yeah? Did you masturbate while you did? And

if not, that's something I'd very much like to be in on if you choose to do so at another date. Or in five minutes."

Kelly couldn't stop her snort of laughter. "Stop. I was thinking about earlier tonight with Maddie and how when I told you why I disagreed with you, I had all your focus. You really listened to me. You thought about what I was saying and I felt respected."

That had meant a lot because sometimes with Ross she got the definite feeling he thought she was too lax with the girls.

His teasing grin shifted as tenderness replaced it. "I do respect you."

"Before, I don't know that you did."

He propelled from the mattress and started to pace. "That's not fair."

"I'm sorry." She shook her head, catching herself before she continued to apologize for speaking truly and honestly. "No, no, I'm not sorry for saying it, or for thinking it. That's the whole before-and-now distinction I was just making. Or trying."

He sighed, moving back to his place across from her.

"You and I have always had this deep physical and chemical attraction and connection. But before, you wouldn't have noticed I was upset earlier. You wouldn't have asked why. I probably wouldn't have contradicted you anyway. It's a chicken-and-egg thing, but that's an entirely different conversation."

"But it's not entirely different. It's connected, don't you think?"

"What I think is that when we were married this

entire conversation never would have happened. Because while we have amazing sex, we haven't been equals. I never insisted on it and you never made any real effort to pursue it."

"I've always respected you."

"If you could stop arguing with me for like five seconds I could pay you the fucking compliment I've been trying to pay you for the last ten minutes," she said, not feeling very complimentary.

He shut up.

"You came into this house and you said you'd changed and wanted me and the girls back. Tonight you showed me how much you've changed. And how much *I've* changed, too. You asked how we were doing, and I think I can say pretty good. Though you're very argumentative."

He leaned over to steal a kiss and settled again. "I had a lot of growing up to do. I'm trying. Thanks for noticing. How does this before-and-now thing work exactly? Outweighing the bad with the good?"

"Sort of, maybe? Let me back up a bit. Okay, so when I went to Hood River last week to see Tuesday, she and I had this conversation. Sort of about you and Ezra, sort of general." Kelly didn't want to reveal anything overly personal that Tuesday had told her, but the general stuff was important anyway.

"I'm not so much bothered by forgiveness. I forgive you. We had something and it broke apart. You weren't ready." She shrugged.

"Neither were you! You're the one who filed for divorce. I have my faults but you can't pretend you had no fault in this at all," Vaughan said quietly.

"Oh, eat a bag of dicks, Vaughan Hurley. If you think I'm *pretending* that I don't have flaws, you don't know me at all. Stop projecting your failures onto me." Kelly took a deep breath. "The moment they put Maddie on my chest I was ready. Before that? Hell no. I had no idea. But having her changed something fundamental and important in me. I wanted that. I wanted babies and a family. I wanted to give my kids better than what I'd had. And I've made mistakes because of that. But I was absolutely ready to have a family with you. *We* weren't enough for *you*."

The pain of that was something she thought she'd put away.

"I don't think our breakup was all you. Though fuck off if you think you don't hold ninety percent. I won't own your mistakes and if that's what you think trying to make yourself a place in our family means, you need to move out once Maddie is completely re-covered."

He winced, but he didn't argue.

"My biggest mistake—looking back now—was being willfully blind to the fact that you weren't ready. We'd been all high on baby talk after you'd been away and I let myself believe you'd settle down after we had two kids and a home. I got pregnant with Kensey but I knew in my heart you didn't want what I wanted."

"I don't regret our daughters."

"I don't think you do. How could you? They're perfect and ours. But you weren't ready to be a husband and a full-time father. And I was one of those women who had another baby to save the marriage that then broke up because nothing adds stress like a newborn and a toddler in a home."

She laughed because it had been like a fever dream, those first years. "You know what, though? I did it. I had a crappy upbringing and I'm determined not to let any of that touch them. I finished my degree and started my boutiques and businesses and I can support myself and my kids into the future. I was spineless before. And you were selfish. Now neither of us are those things."

Kelly paused, sucking in breath like she'd been under water and had surfaced. Her heart thundered in her chest as she realized the power of what she'd just set free.

She'd trusted him to say all that. To be angry at him and not have him walk away or deny what was real. She deserved him to own his mistakes so they could move forward. This was one of those make-or-break moments and no matter what happened, the *knowing* of it, the way she understood her culpability and more importantly, how far she'd come seemed to have lifted a huge weight off her as well as sent her reeling.

And then she burst into tears.

VAUGHAN, UTTERLY SHOCKED to see her crying, was struck still for long moments. He'd seen her cry, but never like this.

"I don't know what to do," he admitted, and her teary words quickly became unintelligible as she started to laugh at the same time.

She grabbed the hem of his shirt and blotted her

face with it and before long he was laughing, too, pulling her into a hug.

"You snotted up my shirt!" He kissed her temple.

"I did not. But I will when I do get snotty for real. So there."

"Are you mad at me? Or sad or…? This is one of those before-and-now moments. God, are we going to use that phrase a lot? Because it's weird."

"Was there a point somewhere in this monologue?" Kelly asked, her dry sense of humor returning.

"You're very snotty now. Not at the nose, but in the attitude."

"Am not." She smirked. "You just can't handle a Kelly who doesn't say she's sorry anytime anyone gets upset for any reason."

He set her back. "I want to be facing you for this. Also you're giving me a hard-on when you sit on my lap. That'd be rude."

"Wouldn't want that."

He flipped her off. "Okay, so *snotty* is a bad word. Saucy? But—" he shrugged "—maybe there's some truth to my being set off balance when you push back. The Kelly I was married to apologized more. Smoothed the way between us a lot more than I did. The woman you are now doesn't. You've never used tears to manipulate anyone, so the way you just cried startled me. It's not like I've never seen you cry."

"Show business people," she said as she rolled her eyes. An inside joke. Kelly's mother used to say those words with so much envy and rage in them anytime Kelly was overly emotional in any way.

"I still really hate your mother."

Kelly shrugged. "There's a national registry some-where you can sign up I'm sure. You won't even be in the top hundred, though. The tears were like one of those moments when you feel multiple things and some of them even conflict, but you feel it all so much and so hard you panic and burst into tears. Like that."

He nodded. The first night of the tour they'd just ended he'd had a gut-wrenching crying jag in the shower after the show. It had hit him, the elation of being out on the road and doing so well, their album selling far beyond what they'd expected and the thought that he was finally losing Kelly.

"I understand."

"To circle back, I don't have a checklist. I don't know when I won't have some worry because of something that happened before. I just know that I worry less about it today than I did yesterday."

He grinned. "Can we tell them?"

"You're like a kid at Christmas, Vaughan."

Laughing, he rolled her to the mattress, ending up on top. "I want to unwrap you every single day."

He wanted everyone to know they were together. That was the next step in this process and he craved it. Craved her trust to allow him back in that much more.

"You're using your charm on me."

He grinned, letting her have his full dimple. Yes, he knew she was helpless when he got very charm-ing. But it was genuine. He kissed her, teasing little nips and licks.

"I am. Is it working?"

She burst out laughing. "What am I getting my-self into?"

"Too late. You already let me see your boobs and now you'll never get rid of me." He stopped teasing. "I love you, Kel. I made mistakes. I'm sorry I hurt you and I fucked things up, but I'm here with you and that's where I want to be. Where I'm *supposed* to be."

She breathed out. "All right. But we don't need to announce it. Let's just continue to go slow and they'll see it when they're ready."

"Does that mean I can sleep in here with you so I can pounce on you when we wake up?"

"I get up at five to exercise. If you wake me before that, I'll cut you."

"Oooh. Yes, new Kelly makes me even hotter than old Kelly." He nibbled on her earlobe until she wrapped her calves around him, her fingers tunneling through his hair.

"Can I tell my family, too?"

"Why did you go and do that?" She pulled his hair.

He started laughing. "Ouch! Give them a chance."

"I can say the same of them."

That was something else he had to deal with. There was no way he wanted to have his wife—and that was the end goal here, to get her back all the way—ostracized by the Hurleys.

But before he could say any of that, she left a trail of hot, openmouthed kisses up his neck, undulating her hips, grinding against his cock until he stuttered a groan.

"Don't think I'm unaware you're using your body to change the subject," he whispered as he grazed his teeth over the shell of her ear, using his weight more fully to hold her in place.

Her answering gasp and the heat from her pussy told him she liked it as much as he did.

"Is it working?" She turned his earlier answer back at him.

One-handed, he managed to get his shirt up and off. "Always. But we'll be back to the Hurley topic later on."

"You have to make me come an extra time for making me talk about your family during sex."

There was something joyous about sex with Kelly that they hadn't shared before. He loved it, though. It made a difference. Added a layer of emotion they'd needed before but hadn't known it.

"Not like I'd argue with that any day, anywhere, anytime." He pressed a kiss to her forehead and stretched his muscles. Kelly's hands roamed over his bared skin, her nails digging in, urging him.

## CHAPTER FOURTEEN

KELLY WAS GOING to lose her mind over that thing he was doing with his tongue. This thought was one of the few coherent ones she'd had since he'd turned up the heat and she'd been busily melting into goo.

"Momma, whoa!"

The sound of a door hitting the wall called Kelly's attention to Maddie standing there with Kensey.

"Daddy's naked in your bed! Are you making a baby right now?" Kensey, apparently totally unaffected by this, bounded up onto the bed, Maddie on her heels.

"Nope! Not naked. Wearing pants." The panic in Vaughan's voice brought a laugh up from her belly.

"Kensey's singing in her room at the top of her lungs. I can't sleep and she knows it and she won't shut up."

Maddie *had* to say that first. Even though she was clearly surprised and as curious as Kensey she had to complain about her sister or explode. It made Kelly start laughing.

With a groan—of pain it sounded like—Vaughan moved off her, though he remained on his stomach. Kensey hopped on his back, chattering like a monkey about why it was important to sing when one was moved to do so.

The absurdity of it kept her laughing so hard, tears came from her eyes. Both girls were in bed by that point, asking Vaughan questions and laughing at the way their mom was giggling like a loon.

"You done yet?" Vaughan asked, amused.

"I'm sorry. Oh, goodness." Kelly wiped her eyes with the back of her hand and got the last of the aftershock giggles dealt with before she sat up, a pillow in her lap, and looked at her children.

*Their* children.

"I think we may have to rethink our earlier plan of not saying much and letting them figure it out," Kelly said to Vaughan.

"You think?" He grinned.

He was so fucking cute it never failed to work on her. Like human catnip. Or dark chocolate and sea salt on almonds. He'd wanted this all along anyway.

"Okay, then, you go on and explain it." Kelly waved a hand at him.

He moved to sit next to Kelly, mirroring her with a pillow on his lap. "When I started staying here it was to not only be a better dad, it was to also hopefully convince your mom that I'd changed from the terrible husband I was before. So she'd give me another chance, too. I want us to be a family, all of us."

Terrified, Kelly nodded. Agreeing. "I want that, too. We won't be making any babies, though." Not for some time, maybe not ever.

"Were you a terrible husband, Daddy?" Kensey asked.

He licked his lips and nodded. "Yes. I messed up a lot. Your mom deserved better. I'm that man now.

She's giving me another chance to prove I'll be the best I can be for all three of you. Will you guys?"

"We love you, Daddy," Kensey said, throwing her arms around his neck. "We like it that you're here. You pack good lunches and sing us songs while we make dinner."

"What's going to change?" Maddie's voice had a little fear in it. Kelly reached out to pat her leg. Her oldest daughter's eyes, so much like Vaughan's just then, were a little wide. "Are we going to live at the ranch? Will we have to change schools? All my friends are here!" Maddie looked back and forth between her parents.

Kelly wasn't anywhere near a place she could imagine living in such close quarters with her mother-in-law. She liked the house and the community here. They had roots and Kelly didn't want to rip them up to live on that ranch, away from the life she'd built over the past eight years.

*Her own life.* Not a life made by her mother, or driven by the necessities of remaining on track to hold her place in her modeling career. Eight years ago she'd been a single mom to two children under eighteen months old.

The most pride she'd ever felt was that she'd made a home here for her daughters. She had a way to support them all. A job and career she loved. It took a lot of tears to get that far.

Going to live at the ranch—at least at that point— would be a repudiation of all that pain. Kelly had been responsible for her own happiness for the first time in her entire life.

And despite the ups and downs of her life, she was happy. Happier right at that moment than she'd been in a very long time.

She didn't have to answer, though, because Vaughan did.

"No."

Vaughan's answer surprised Kelly. She'd figured his end goal was to have them all at Sweet Hollow Ranch.

"Your mom's boutique is in Portland. The commute would be awful from Hood River. And you girls have school here, your dance studio, friends. I can't see that your mom and I have any need to move. Especially during the school year."

Kelly thought about how much he *had* changed. The Vaughan she'd married wouldn't have even considered living anywhere else but Sweet Hollow Ranch. His home was custom. The band's studio was at the ranch. Ezra, his best friend and brother, was at the ranch.

"But we all have a house on there. We've got weekends and the summers and school breaks. I need to be there a lot more often during the harvests. So we'll have plenty of time in Hood River. Part of your heritage is that ranch."

Kelly realized how much she'd sort of forgotten that key point. Yes, she loved that his family was close with Maddie and Kensey. But they should be helping during harvest, too, as a way to show their love. They were Hurleys after all.

"We'll find a way to have you two help," Kelly said. "Your uncle Ezra has some great ideas, I bet."

Vaughan's smile made her so much more glad she'd made that offer.

They had to work together. Not her telling him what to do. Or him trying to figure out what she'd be happy with. That felt way too much like parenting. She needed a partner, a leader of their family team to stand beside her.

Kelly made a shooing motion. "Now, ladies. It's two hours past your bedtime. Tomorrow will get here pretty early so get moving back to your beds. Kensey, stop singing to annoy your sister."

She and Vaughan put them back to bed, tucked them in and kissed them good-night.

He took her hand as they walked down the hall, back to her room. "I can do that now. Cool."

"You might as well move your stuff in here," she said as they got to her door. "Okay, not your clothes. You can keep them in that room."

He pretended offense. "My clothes aren't good enough to live in that fantasy closet of yours?"

She shook her head. "My closet is sacrosanct."

He kissed her, clearly tickled that he could, which only charmed her more. "I can live with that. Be back momentarily."

Boy, oh, boy did she have a lot to tell Stacey the next day at lunch.

VAUGHAN STOOD IN the middle of his room. No, the guest room. And he smiled.

He grabbed his basics; he'd complete the full move the next day, wanting to get back to her as soon as he could while still giving her a bit of time to process.

The new Kelly needed that so the new Vaughan tried to give it to her before he was drawn back to her.

This feeling, utter joy and satisfaction, was one he really fucking loved. The ache that he could have had it all these years had become less sharp, though the dull ache of it kept him remembering it was his choice. A painful lesson for them all.

That part hurt the most, still. He loved his girls more than anything, but after three weeks of caring for them daily through school and dance classes and dinner and all that, he realized the connection between them all had deepened.

He'd never be able to get those years back.

Vaughan shook his head as he took his Dopp kit and a few other basics over to her—correction their—room.

"I cleared out a few drawers for you in that dresser." Kelly pointed to a tallboy-style dresser in a corner.

"I'm really not that bothered to have my clothes next door."

She looked up from where she'd been pulling things from a bedside table. "That dresser was pretty empty. I'd been working on it for eighteen months and only moved it up here in the early spring. I don't mind sharing that much."

He liked her grin. Easy. No sign of wariness.

"All right. Thanks. I'll keep the closet over there so yours can remain free of my boy cooties."

She laughed. "I haven't lived with anyone since you. I mean, the girls, but they have their own rooms.

I should probably tell you I'm totally selfish about some things like my closet."

No apology for it. That was a now Kelly thing, too.

EVERYONE NEEDED SOMETHING to be selfish about. He'd been too selfish and she hadn't been selfish enough. They could balance one another without tipping over. If they did it right.

"I should also tell you I've staked a claim on the apartment above the garage."

Instead of upset, she appeared to be happy. "Really? I'm glad. I knew you moved some stuff into it, but it's a relief you like the space."

"It's got great light. It's set far enough away from the house and all the surrounding properties that I can work out there and not get the cops called."

"Okay. Good. Yeah. I know you need a place to work. You'll also be able to work uninterrupted."

He'd have to work at the barn, the custom recording and practice studio on the ranch, when the band was ready to work on their next album. But that wouldn't be for another eighteen months or so at the earliest. Damien was about to be a father. Ezra was falling in big giant love, Paddy was skirting around proposing to Natalie. Everything was changing and each of them had to put their focus on their personal lives for a while.

"I want to do some solo stuff," he said quietly, testing the waters, "so I'm going to get the guy who made our space in Hood River out to get it customized."

"Solo? Wow, Vaughan, that's amazing." Kelly moved to him, sliding her arms around his waist.

"Well, I don't know about that. I've been writing

a lot lately. Some of it isn't going to fit in what Sweet Hollow Ranch does. And I'm cool with that."

He'd butted heads with Paddy over and over as they'd made their last album. Vaughan had ideas he wanted to pursue that he knew his older brother would always be trying to micromanage to change them.

He didn't want to change it. He did need to talk with his brothers about it. Vaughan had no plans to leave the band or even take a hiatus. But he had some bluesy country stuff in his head and he wanted to see what shook out.

They'd support him in this endeavor. It was who they were as brothers and as a band. And apparently Kelly did, too.

"All right. Let me know if you need anything. I'm…well, I'm excited for you. I'd really like to hear stuff. I miss that a lot."

He used to make music for her all the time. Always singing, playing guitar. He did that at his house and even with the girls, but he had a lot of music in his heart for this woman he looked at.

"Yeah?"

She nodded.

He kissed her. Speaking in between sips and tastes. "I miss it, too. I'll be sure to do it when I'm not deep inside you."

She gasped and he nipped her lips, pulling back so he could get her tank top over her head.

"Damn, these are spectacular. If I could walk around like this, with your breasts in my hands all day, I would."

"You're so full of shit."

BUT HER BLUSH was so pretty, he knew she was flattered and not serious.

"I am on many, many things. About how amazing your tits are? Never. That's stone-cold fact."

"This time, make sure the door is locked."

With a groan, he headed back to the door, which was indeed unlocked. "Sorry. I'm an amateur." Though he hated that *she* wasn't. Hated that Ross had been in that bed.

"We need a new mattress." He tossed his clothes and pulled the rest of hers off as he got her on the bed.

"Uh? Okay. Whatever. You want a new mattress, that's fine. Here I am naked on my bed with you over me. I don't even know how you do it. Like in a book where the guy turns into a werewolf and you can't quite see what happens when they shift?"

"You're twisted."

"I've always been twisted. I'm just better read now."

He kissed her, this time settling in. No one was going to barge in and ruin this.

Her neck was warm and soft as he slowly drifted down to the hollow of her throat and licked until she shivered.

"You taste so damned good."

Her rib cage was solid beneath his lips as he licked and kissed down her body and over to her right nipple.

"I'm not sure which one tastes better. I need a few tests." He licked several times and then blew over her nipple, watching as it tightened even more.

Then he switched to the left side, teasing, torturing. He wanted to gorge and gorge on her. So he did.

"Please!" she burst out after writhing against him,

her pussy against his cock. Bare. So hot he thought he might die from how good it felt.

She'd insisted on latex until they'd both been tested and retested. Only a week to go. Despite how much he yearned to slide himself inside her, claim her skin to skin, it would wait or he'd be spitting in the face of all the promises he'd made.

"Please?" he teased, swirling his tongue around the nipple he then left.

"In me or on me. Something! Anything!"

"I love it when you can't get it fast enough. Just a little bit of a flounce. So sexy."

He took pity on her, also because he wanted all those things, too. Her belly quivered as he kissed around her belly button, and her breath caught on a gasp when he used his shoulders to wedge her thighs wide.

All of her right there for him to look—taste and touch—his fill. Yes.

Her taste, sweet mercy, he did so much love not only the salt of her taste, but the way her back arched as he took a few licks.

Vaughan lost himself in her. Let himself leap into making her feel as much pleasure as he could.

He made her come once and then another time before he allowed himself to think about fucking her. But once he had, he was rolling a condom on.

"Turn over. Ass up, head down."

"What's the rush?" Kelly asked, drunk with pleasure tongue. "I haven't been able to return that favor yet."

She actually loved to go down on him. He was responsive and it was so sexy how hot she got him, that it was way more fun with him than it had been with anyone else.

But Vaughan liked to *fuck*. Once he was inside her, he'd take his time. Drawing things out for a nice long time, or he'd thrust hard and fast, beads of sweat on his forehead as he took her until she was boneless.

Not like that was a chore, either.

Sex with Vaughan was like a grab bag, but all the prizes were ones you really wanted.

Kelly rolled over as he'd asked, her knees still a little rubbery. Her fingers tangled in the sheets as he knelt behind her. The heat of his body blanketed her ass and thighs as she waited for him to touch her.

He brushed the head of his cock against her, teasing, teasing until she made a sound of annoyance.

"Yeah? All right, then." Vaughan pressed deep in one long thrust. Her answering moan had to be into the mattress or she'd wake up the girls and wouldn't that be fun? Nope.

He set a pace just shy of fast and hard. But he knew where he was going so she went along. Everything he did felt so damned good she had no argument.

THIS WAS DIFFERENT. This time he meant to claim her. She knew it. The way he touched her, took up space in her bed in a different way.

A way that scared her to her toes and yet, it felt right. It could be the two orgasms talking, and it probably was, but she'd keep thinking that way because it was better than being afraid and worried he'd walk away.

The room was quiet but for the slap of skin on skin

and her muffled sounds of pleasure. There was so much intense energy between them they didn't need words.

Each touch he gave her told her things. The scent of her body and his, of sex and love and lust all melding into something new. Something more.

VAUGHAN WASN'T SURE how much time had passed since he'd pressed himself deep. He only knew there was nowhere he'd rather be, no one else who'd ever be to him what this woman was. Never had been anyone but her.

A long twisty road but through Kelly and the beauty of second chances, there they were. And while he felt so fucking good he never wanted the moment to end, he drew closer and closer.

There was no way around the insane pleasure at the hot clasp of her body around his cock. It was so fantastically delicious he couldn't keep from coming so hard it was as if his entire body shot out his dick.

Wobbly kneed, he fell to the side, holding her close once he'd gotten the condom dealt with and returned.

"Well, that's better than a glass of wine to help me sleep."

STARTLED, HE LAUGHED and hugged her. "That's me. My cock is better than wine any day."

She pressed a kiss to his shoulder. "You should put that on the cover of your next album."

## CHAPTER FIFTEEN

THE NEXT MORNING, Vaughan got the call that the custom-built Harley Softail he'd been excitedly waiting on was finally done and ready to be his. The girls were in school and Kelly had headed out for Portland half an hour before so he had the time.

But he needed someone to go along with him to drive his car back. He dialed Ezra.

"Hey, stranger," Ezra replied as he picked up.

"Sorry about that. I didn't mean to disappear."

"Are you moving forward? Things are good with you and Kelly?" His brother didn't bother to rise to the bait and let Vaughan head down some guilt trip. Which, Vaughan supposed, was why Ezra had been his best friend since Vaughan had been old enough to crawl and toddle around following him.

"I have so much to tell you. The girls know about me and their mom. I moved into her bedroom last night. It's not totally fixed, not by any stretch. But it's going in a good direction. I wanted to see if you'd be available to go pick my Harley up. It's ready. On the way over you can fill me in on *your* love life."

"I wish I could. I'm leaving for a few days in the mountains. I have too much to get in place today to be gone that long. I'm sorry. We'll hang out when I get back."

"Mountains?"

"It's with Tuesday. For her birthday. Nat and Paddy are going, as well."

First, a stab of jealousy because he missed being around his brothers all the time. And then the realization all sorts of things were happening with Ezra and he was missing it came.

But not in greater measure than his happiness over this growing something special with Tuesday. Ezra deserved to be loved by someone amazing. "Ah, cool. Well, have a good time. But if you're so busy, I'll be over there within the hour to help. The girls are at school and then Kelly can get them from the bus stop. There's a carnival tonight but that's not until seven."

"Don't even think about it. Go get your bike. It's a sunny day. Have a nice ride, help with dinner and go to the carnival. I don't need you here. I'm working with Fletch." John Fletcher was the foreman of the ranch. Though Ezra ran things and their father was still active, as well, Fletch had been with Sweet Hollow Ranch since pretty much the beginning. He knew it as well as Ezra did.

"I won't keep you much longer because I know you're busy. Birthday trip to the mountains with another couple sounds like you and Tuesday are doing well."

"Yeah."

Vaughan heard the smile in his brother's tone.

"I like her. Kelly likes her, too. She talks to your girlfriend regularly. I dig that."

"I was thinking yesterday that Tuesday really likes Kelly and pretty much that's all it takes for Natalie to like Kelly. Mom sees that."

Vaughan ran a hand through his hair. He had to deal with his mother. It needed to be face-to-face and the past two times he'd been at the ranch he hadn't been able to catch up with her.

Time to stop farting around and just call her and arrange to have lunch or something.

He groaned. "I hope so. Regardless, I'm not going to be coming back to the ranch full-time. Not for the foreseeable future. I want to talk to Mom and get that past stuff about Kelly squared away before I let anyone know. So keep that one to yourself."

"You don't even need to ask that, asshole."

Vaughan snorted a laugh. "I didn't think you were going to take out an ad in the paper or anything. But you have a girlfriend now and she's friends with my… uh…with Kelly."

"Yeah, yeah, cone of silence about all this stuff with Kelly and Tuesday. I'll call you when I get back from this trip. All right?"

"Cool. Have a good time and stop worrying about the ranch while you're gone."

"So everyone keeps telling me. Talk to you later."

A long ride sounded really good. A way to maybe get some of his thoughts in order. Now that the weather was improving, he'd have a new bike to ride when their group did weekend trips in the summer and fall. He and his brothers had taken a few the year before with Adrian Brown and his brother Brody.

Maybe he'd get Kelly a bike, too, and they could ride together, just the two of them.

He called the car service he used sometimes for appearances and within the hour he was pulling his new bike up out front of Chameleon, Kelly's boutique.

Kelly had to laugh at the way everyone froze, wide-eyed at the sight of Vaughan Hurley coming into the store.

He had a helmet tucked under his arm and as he gave Kelly a smile that set everything south of her belly button to riot, he pulled off his sunglasses and stalked her way.

"We need to go camping," he said and then he kissed her.

Luckily it wasn't one of his long, sexy kisses, but even that brush of his mouth against hers had made her tingly.

"Right now?"

He smiled at her, tapping one of her earrings, setting it swinging. "This summer. You, me and the girls."

"You came all the way over here on a motorcycle I've never seen to tell me that?"

"I knew you saw me pull up."

She pointed. "You, sit over there. I'm helping someone."

He obeyed, but still wore that grin.

"Oh my God, is that yours?" her customer asked.

Kelly looked back over her shoulder. "Something like that, yeah."

"That's Vaughan Hurley, isn't it?"

"It is."

The woman shoved three dresses and a blouse at Kelly. "Damn. You get it."

That made Kelly laugh as she rang everything up. "I do. It's not overrated."

"I hope some of that rubs off on me."

Once she'd gotten the woman finished up and on her way, Kelly turned back to Vaughan. "You're a menace. She bought nearly eight hundred dollars' worth of clothes without blinking."

"I should hang out in your window all day, then, huh?"

"I'd never get anything done. Did you buy a motorcycle? Or is that an old one I never saw before?"

"I ordered it before we left on tour. I picked it up about fifteen minutes ago. You need one, too. Custom so it's comfortable for long rides. Or you could ride with me on the back. Yeah, that sounds even better."

"And this was before or after the camping idea?"

"Well, see, first I thought of you and I going on long rides together, maybe weekend trips here and there. And then I thought how awesome it would be to head out to Kalaloch and camp out at the beach with the girls."

"All right. I'd like that. I know they would, too." She cocked her head, looking at him. "Did you come here just to make my customers spend too much money and make me forget all about whatever I need to do later?"

"I like that compliment." He kissed her again. "I wasn't too far away and yeah, when I thought about going camping as a family it made me so happy I wanted to see your face."

It was the perfect thing for him to have said. She'd needed to hear it more than she'd realized.

"That makes *me* really happy," she said quietly, like she was telling a secret.

His expression was even better. Surprise, pride and then love. So much love that she found herself swallowing against a swell of emotion.

"And *that* makes me really happy."

He hugged her. "Are you here by yourself or can you have an early lunch with me?"

"I recently promoted one of my employees to manager. She starts at noon and handles closing." Kelly would be at the boutique less, which freed her time for Vaughan and the girls, but also for some print work modeling here and there as well as the non-storefront-related aspects of having two boutiques and keeping them successful. "But we can't go to lunch here."

"Why?"

"Because you're Vaughan Hurley and if we go to get pho three doors down you'll get recognized and I won't get to eat and you know that makes me cranky."

Again the devastating grin. "I am. And you're Kelly Hurley. People look at you all the time so you're one to talk. Also, I've been around when someone gets between you and your lunch. I don't want you to leave me bloody."

Most people didn't tease her about food. Not in a good way, in any case. Anytime someone didn't like her opinion she'd get *shut up and look pretty* comments. Her mother's attitude about food had nearly landed Kelly into a full-blown eating disorder. Heaven knew it was common enough in her world.

But she'd survived with only a few scars to her psyche—some weird obsessions she worked hard to control—and it didn't stop her from eating chocolate so Kelly considered that a win.

"Go for a ride. Meet me at home in an hour. I'll pick lunch up on the way."

"Can we have sex instead?"

"You just got a brand-new toy!"

He pulled her close. "You're my favorite toy of all time. I like to play with you every chance I get."

She kissed him and spun his body, aiming him at the door. "Go. Have fun. I'll see you in a while and if you eat all your veggies I might let you play with me."

With a quick one-armed hug, he jogged over to his bike. Kelly made no attempt to hide as she watched him sit astride and key the bike on. It gave her a shiver, the sound of the engine and the way he looked, all inked and badass.

It was impossible to wipe the smile off her face for some time after that.

VAUGHAN, ONE ARM around Kelly's shoulders, one hand holding Maddie's with Kensey holding Kelly's, knew he was probably having one of the best days ever.

He'd taken a nice long ride on his new bike, come back, had lunch with his woman, followed by excellent—and loud as the girls were gone—sex. And now he was at a school carnival.

With his family. This was why he saw men wear the expression he surely wore right at that moment. Beautiful woman at his side. Happy children. All was right in his world, no lie about that.

"I'm a lucky man," Vaughan said as he kissed Kelly's temple.

"You are," she teased. "So I'll allow you to buy me a shave ice in thanks."

Both girls thought this was a fine idea so they headed over to stand in line. Vaughan hadn't been to their school very many times. He'd attended a school conference and never missed a play or musical performance.

But this was different. He was a parent of students there. He belonged.

Once they'd procured their treats, they headed over to the giant bounce house thing where his children slipped through a little hole in the side and were gone to play.

"They're happy you're here." Kelly's tone said their girls weren't alone in that.

"I'm happy to be here. What about you?"

"Are you trying to get me to say something nice about you?" Her mouth continued to captivate him as she fought a smile.

He knew it, but he wanted her to say it, too. "Yes."

"I'm glad you're here."

He wanted to lay a kiss on her, but there were kids around and enough people looking that he didn't want to make a scene. But he kept an arm around her shoulders as he and Kelly finished their shave ice and hung out watching the kids play.

He got recognized a few times. Some of the parents waved, one or two said a hello as they passed. No one invaded their space or made a scene, respectful that he was there with his family and not as Vaughan Hurley, the musician.

After he realized that was going to be the case, he really relaxed in a way he only usually was able to do at the ranch, far away from everyone else.

"Not that corn dogs aren't a fine food option while on tour or a road trip, I'm going to suggest seeking an actual dinner after this. What do you say?" Vaughan asked her.

"A place without paper tablecloths and crayons? Doesn't have to be fancy, but I'd like something without *nugget* in the title."

Laughing, he pulled her closer. "Deal."

She stiffened a few minutes later and when he bent to ask her what was wrong, Vaughan caught sight of a tight-lipped woman coming their way, her attention lasered on Kelly.

"Who's the woman?" Vaughan asked.

"Ross's ex-wife."

Ross sure did have a type. His ex-wife was tall and blonde with blue eyes, just like Kelly. But where Kelly's beauty shone bright, like the sun and stars, this woman's pinched face and general attitude blunted her attractiveness.

She curled her lip at Kelly once she'd reached them. "I didn't expect to see you here."

"Okay, why is that?" Kelly kept an eye on the bouncy house, watching for their children, Vaughan knew.

"Haven't you done enough? Don't you have any shame?"

Vaughan wasn't going to tolerate anyone talking to

Kelly that way. "I don't know what your problem is, ma'am, but you're going to need to keep on walking. We don't want whatever you're selling."

"I *knew* it. I told Ross you were the reason she broke the engagement." Ross's ex looked Vaughan up and down, her lip curled.

Kelly stepped between them and Vaughan realized it was to defend him. His heart swelled. "I'm not happy I hurt Ross. I understand why you're in my face. But really, our relationship isn't any of your business. So, you got in your shots. People are staring, which I know you always adore. I'm inclined to let your little snit go, as my children are currently with *your* children, laughing and playing. But if your attitude affects them, you and I are going to have a problem."

"Are you threatening me?"

Kelly got very close to the other woman. "I'm *telling* you I won't allow you to harm my children. And if you get in between me and them, I'll make you understand why it was a mistake. So if you need that to be a threat, you go ahead on."

The ex turned, looking over her shoulder toward the bounce house where the girls were. "He's too good for you anyway. Here's a friendly tip, don't eat your feelings, Kelly. It's not good for your waistline."

"Have a nice day. Somewhere else." Vaughan made a shooing motion and walked around her, Kelly at his side. Her back was stiff, clearly related to all the hatred this woman slung her way.

He waved to Maddie, indicating she and Kensey come out.

He spoke quietly in Kelly's ear. "Now. We have

some rings to toss and some other various and sundry carnival action to attend to. Once we're done, I owe all my ladies dinner."

## CHAPTER SIXTEEN

STACEY FOUND KELLY in the tree house where she'd taken refuge.

Kelly sighed, moving her legs so her friend could come in. "Not that I'm unhappy to see you, but how is it everyone knows about my secret spot?"

Stacey rolled her eyes and settled in next to Kelly.

"I brought new chocolate back from my trip to San Francisco." Stacey held up several sleek, beautifully colored bars.

Kelly grabbed them quickly. "Okay, you can stay."

Stacey snickered. "Gee, thanks. Why are you hiding out here?"

Kelly examined the different bars, choosing pale blue. "If I share candy with you can we just avoid this whole conversation?"

"There's no *if* when it comes to chocolate. You will be sharing, that's a given. So go on and get your need to log this stuff handled so I can have some while you then tell me what's up."

"You're mean."

"Duh. I'm a lawyer, we're all mean."

Kelly tried very hard not to show any of her food or body image issues in front of her daughters. She never chided them about how many calories something had, though they learned about nutrition in school and she wanted them to be healthy.

What she didn't want them to do was log down every bite of chocolate like it was a confession of a sin.

She pulled out the mason jar and logged the chocolate. It had been a long time since she'd made an attempt to hide this sort of thing from Stacey. That was true trust, Kelly supposed. When your friends simply accepted your weird flaws and only called out the ones they thought were truly harmful.

"Ross told her about my food stuff."

"What? Ross told who?" Stacey asked.

Kelly handed over half the bar to Stacey before breaking off a small piece of her half, savoring it slowly.

Little flecks of toffee studded the chocolate. As it should. "Damn, this is so fucking good."

"You're welcome. I'm glad you chose that one because I originally bought you two, and then I ate one."

"Best-friend tax." Kelly shrugged. "Like when I steal fries from the girls. The price you pay."

"Indeed. Tell me."

"At the carnival on Friday, Ross's ex-wife was there. She was mainly stupid, but she made a crack about my weight and eating my feelings."

Stacey's gaze narrowed.

"People do when they find out I used to model. Sometimes people are asshats. But this was very specific." Kelly's voice wobbled a little. The betrayal still stung.

"You think she'd be dancing a jig. You only got in her way. But Ross? Damn. That's awful. I'm sorry. And I'd like to punch him in the throat."

There was the part of Kelly who knew all the stuff Ross's ex had said was bull. A slap meant to wound, not just with the insult, but the knowing. Ross had shared a secret part of Kelly. A part she'd revealed to him, trusting him to protect her from this sort of thing.

But he hadn't. And it had sent her reeling. Where she'd been all weekend long.

"Did you talk to Ross?"

"No. It only happened three days ago. Anyway, what's the point? I should be glad I have a reason other than me wanting someone else to break the engagement."

"Oh whatever. For fuck's sake, Kelly, you two weren't right for one another and this is just another example of why. I will gladly put poo in a bag and toss it, alight with flame, on doorsteps. I'll even drive so you can come along."

Kelly laughed, imagining that.

"You're not fat. You're not thin. You're you. And you're healthy. Sure, she looks similar to you. But she's not you. Which makes her bitter. I'm sorry she was a twat and I'm sorry Ross was a jerk."

"I'm glad you came over to bring me chocolate."

"Me too. Did you talk this over with Vaughan? Did he notice you were upset?"

"He just thought it was the interaction overall, not anything specific. I..." He knew some of her stuff, but not all. Not the hodgepodge of weird coping behaviors and bargains she'd made with her brain to let her have a seminormal life when it came to her body and to food.

"He's going to notice. And then what?"

"I'll be fine. I'm just wallowing a little. He won't need to notice."

Stacey sighed. "Keeping a food journal doesn't make you crazy."

Kelly echoed her friend's sigh. "I don't think I'm crazy. But I don't need to have this sort of detailed conversation about it with Vaughan. It would take more time and energy to explain and give him the backstory than the entire exchange did."

"I just think it's good to share this with him."

"He knows about some of the shit with my mother. But I really don't want to wallow."

Stacey waved a hand. "Yeah, I can tell."

"I didn't call you all over and then run out there weeping. I was *alone* and working through it."

"No, you're not the type. But you don't *have* to be alone to work through it. You have me. You even have Vaughan. I wasn't sure how he'd fare with this whole winning-you-back thing. But he's working. I can see it," Stacey said.

"He is." Which was why she didn't want to drag this stuff into that. She dusted her hands and looked back to Stacey. "Why did you come over?"

"I stopped by Chameleon and learned you were home today. So when I knocked and you weren't around but your car was here, I figured you were either out here or having sexytimes with Vaughan."

Kelly laughed, feeling better already. "Thanks for worrying." She sucked in a breath. "Sometimes I have like, I don't know, a flashback, maybe? Like I'll be with him, laughing about something, happy, and then a flash of what it felt to see his eyes that night. It wasn't the hand in his pants. I mean, I was angry and hurt about it, but what killed my marriage was that flash in his eyes. It was satisfaction. He wanted me to see it. Wanted me to be pushed away. He wanted that empty hand job in a hallway with some random person he didn't even bother to respect enough to get to know. More than me or our kids. And I saw it and knew it right to my very soul. There's never, ever been a moment in my life that hurt as much as that glimpse."

Kelly unbound the French knot at the base of her skull and then twisted her hair up into a loose ponytail. Stacey leaned against the trunk of the tree at her back. Listening.

"I'm happy. I have this life I'd written off as never happening with him. I could have had it with someone else, but it's him. It has always been him. And sometimes that terrifies me."

"When the ex got all bitchy and used something you'd trusted Ross with to hurt you, it underlined how much you're risking."

Kelly flipped Stacey off. "I wasted a few days of getting all emo and I really should have just called you instead."

"Ha. It's not so hard to see. You love him. And I tell you with total honesty that he loves you. You divorced a shitty, passive-aggressive boy. You're sharing your house with a man."

"But Ross is a man."

Stacey waved that away. "Apples and oranges. You were *not* in love with Ross. His telling the ex hurt you because you cared about him enough to trust him. Betrayal by a trusted confidant. Not the same as Vaughan not loving you the way you loved him."

"Ouch."

Chagrined, Stacey's features softened. "I'm sorry."

"Comes with the best friend being a divorce attorney. You disclosed up front," Kelly deadpanned as Stacey snickered. "Anyway, you get a weirdo who keeps track of how many squares of chocolate she eats per day. I think I got the better deal."

"You're a total weirdo but not because you exercise religiously and count your chocolate. The fact that you want a Doctor Who tattoo makes you weird. That and your unfortunate love of dance movies," Stacey said.

Kelly *loved* musicals and dance movies of all types and kinds. "Your sad, sad refusal to find the joy in all the *Step Up*s is a continual disappointment to me."

"I find joy in all those shiny abs. That's all you get. I even let you listen to the soundtracks when we're in the car. Those things fall in the realm of normal weirdness."

"Like when you yell at the television when people confess things on the stand in movies?" Kelly teased.

"Don't get me started by pushing my rage buttons, missy. You were abused. That you have managed to build the life you have is about you, not her."

It was an argument they'd had a few times since Kelly had originally disclosed the details of her life with Rebecca in charge. "She was a bad mother, but I wasn't abused. I had a place to live. Food on the table. Other kids didn't. She never hit me."

"You know very well there's more than one kind of scar. Does Vaughan know all of it?"

No one knew all of it. Only Kelly and that's how she planned to keep some of the very worst times. Those were buried under concrete. Far beneath the life she had now.

"He knows some. Back then, when we first met I self-medicated. Amphetamines are fantastic for keeping your appetite low and your energy high. And then I got pregnant and shaped my act up. The chocolate thing started then." Her midwife had casually suggested a therapist. Just to have someone to talk to because Kelly had been not only newly pregnant, but newly married, too, and stress was natural.

In retrospect, Kelly knew her midwife could see Kelly's panic at each pound she gained. Could see Kelly was on the edge and could use some help.

It had been that doctor who'd given Kelly the tools to deal with a lot of the problems Kelly had solved more destructively before. "I work really hard to be a good mother. To never be like her."

"You never have to defend yourself to me. I see you. I know what you do. I know how far you've come," Stacey said, her tone so fervent all Kelly could do was throw her arms around her best friend as she cried.

Over her life, Kelly had developed a thick skin to general criticism and commentary on her appearance. Kelly's first job had been a department-store children's-line catalog and marketing shoot. She'd been four. As they moved from base to base, country to country, her mother still managed to send her out on auditions and calls until they moved to New York so Kelly could pursue modeling and acting.

She'd been tossed into a very complicated economic, social and emotional hierarchy at an age she should have been doing algebra and going to dances. It toughened her up. Being judged usually didn't bother her because she had enough of a sense of value. She'd earned that much.

But she had her rage buttons, as Stacey called them. And being judged and found wanting when it came to her intelligence or her parenting really got to her.

Looks faded. What mattered was the true heart of a person and she considered her children her heart.

When she sat back, Stacey handed her a tissue and a smile. "If you apologize I'm going to be mad. You're a fantastic mom and the ex attacked that. I get it. I would kick her shin so hard and pretend it was an accident for you any day."

"You totally would. It's why I love you."

"Just think about it. Okay? Let him in a little. If he knows more, he can take more care."

Kelly knew Stacey was right. But she had no idea really how to go about sharing with him. "I'll wait until it comes up naturally. Or until like another week or two because it's not usually something that comes up naturally."

"Only if you're in hell."

"Yeah, well. You've met Rebecca."

"Only once. And I'd like to keep it that way. In any case, I have reservations for two at a superswank restaurant on Wednesday night. But my date has been sent to Rome for work and I no longer need them. So, I propose to come over here, hang out with my girls while you and Vaughan go and use that table and have an actual date-type thing."

Kelly really was lucky to have Stacey in her life. "Yeah? You're the best. I'm sorry about the cancellation. Is he the magazine writer?"

"No. This one is an international contracts attorney. I'm only using him for a penis that knows my every desire. I'm trying to keep it casual and shallow so I don't have to learn anything truly horrible about him until I'm ready to bolt."

With a snort, Kelly rolled her eyes. "So romantic."

"*Pragmatic.* Until the dude who makes me as goofy as Vaughan makes you shows up, a girl still has needs."

Laughing, Stacey lured Kelly from her tree house and they headed inside.

## CHAPTER SEVENTEEN

It wasn't that Vaughan disliked Stacey. She had an easy, genuine affection for his daughters, which he approved of mightily. She and Kelly were close, like sisters. And, as Vaughan knew the power of that sort of connection, he approved of that, too.

But Stacey knew all his dirty laundry. And it was hard not to feel embarrassed about it every time he saw her. She'd sat across from him and his attorney during their divorce and as the ugliness of the entire situation got worse and more of what he'd done came out, his attorney had gone on the attack and things had been said that Vaughan very much regretted.

That it happened in full view of Kelly's best friend, that the knowledge of his smallest moments was in her gaze sometimes, was hard to get past.

But she was part of this family, a family he was also working to be part of, so it meant trying to get to know this person who was so important to his kids and to Kelly.

And she'd given him a chance to romance Kelly and came over to babysit the kids while he did it.

"I really appreciate your doing this," he said to Stacey as they got ready to leave.

"It's never a chore to hang out with Miss Madness and her partner in crime, Master K."

Kensey and Maddie thought this hilarious as they hugged Stacey.

"What movie are we going to watch?" Maddie asked.

"First there's homework to check, I hear. Then we watch movies. None of them will be *Frozen*."

"Aww, why not?" Kensey asked.

"Because I've seen it with you guys about eight thousand times already. I'm good with Elsa and Anna for like, the next forty years or so."

"Or until you have kids," Kelly said as she entered the room. "There'll always be a *Frozen* of some sort."

*Damn.*

Vaughan couldn't do more than stand there and stare at Kelly, who looked fantastic in a short dress in all sorts of blues. Long, long legs showed, ending with sparkling stilettos.

It wasn't as if he forgot what she looked like. But when she pulled out all the stops getting dressed up it could be like looking at the sun.

"You look beautiful," he said, trying not to appear as stunned as he was.

She blushed. "Thanks. You, too. Always did clean up nice, Hurley." Kelly winked and he offered his arm.

"You two have fun. Yes, I'll put them to bed at nine." Stacey's look made Kelly laugh.

They kissed their daughters and headed out on their first date in a decade.

Or, they would have if his mother hadn't been on the front doorstep, her hand raised to knock.

"Mom." Vaughan hugged her. "What's up? Is everything okay?"

Sharon held up some bags. "A few things for the girls. I was out shopping for the baby." Her smile went so deep and happy. Vaughan missed seeing her more often. "You don't think I'd forget my girls, do you?"

Kelly stepped aside, motioning his mother into the house. "Hi, Sharon. They're in the living room with Stacey. They'll love seeing you. Go on through."

"Oh. Are you going out? I figured that you'd be home because it was a school night."

Kelly stiffened and Vaughan sighed. "Yes, we're going out to dinner."

"I gave them my dinner reservations at a lovely, dark, romantic restaurant. These two need time alone." Stacey's smile was pleasant enough as she came through to the entry where he and Kelly had been standing with Sharon.

But she came to a halt next to Kelly, clearly there to defend. Things were tense and he hated it.

"I like to spend all the time I can with my goddaughters. They just ran upstairs to put their homework away." Stacey gave Kelly a little push out the door. "See you two later on. Don't be late for dinner. Have fun, now. Sharon and I will be just fine with spaghetti."

Kelly shook her head. "It's fine. You can take your reservation back. You have time. I have a closet full of clothes."

No way was he giving up dinner alone with Kelly. She'd taken time with her outfit. He wanted to look nice, too. Wanted to have this romantic few hours.

She'd been a little withdrawn over the weekend after that scene at the carnival.

"That would be totally silly." Stacey pushed herself past Vaughan and Sharon and led Kelly out into the driveway. Vaughan took that opportunity to steer his mother farther into the house.

"Why is she upset *now*?" Sharon turned on him, keeping her voice low.

"Why are you so dead set on disliking her? What's with the crack about school nights?"

"How is that a crack? I asked a question."

"If your mother-in-law said something like that to you, how would you have taken it?"

"I'm not her mother-in-law anymore. Unless you've done something stupid without telling anyone. Have you?"

"Marrying Kelly again wouldn't be stupid."

His mother's right eyebrow slid up. He hadn't seen that expression in years. "There's a lot going on you haven't talked to your family about. You want to correct that?" she asked.

He heard the thunder of feet as the girls made their way across the second-floor gallery, heading to the stairs. "I can't do this right now. Maddie and Kensey are coming back downstairs and if they had any idea of this situation between you and their mother they'd be really upset. We need to talk. I haven't always…" He stopped himself. Now wasn't the time to confess anything. He had a pissed off ex-wife in the driveway and his mother in his hall with two kids under twelve about to flip out with excitement that not only was Stacey there, but Nana was, too.

Sharon sighed and patted his arm. "Come to the ranch next week. We'll talk. I'm sorry if I upset anyone. I didn't mean it as an attack."

"I love her, Mom. I need you to figure out how to be all right with that."

"You don't know a damned thing, Vaughan. But we'll talk later. Go, take her to dinner. Be a shame to waste all that dressing up. You two look nice." With an annoyed sniff, she headed away, calling for the girls as she did.

"I don't want to go anywhere. I don't want her in my house when I'm not here," Kelly whispered as she and Stacey headed outside. "She clearly thinks I'm a terrible mother for going to dinner with Vaughan on a school night."

Stacey waved a careless hand. "Who cares if she does? Look, Shurley has issues. But *Vaughan* needs to deal with that. You will go to dinner. You will let Vaughan make this up to you with jewelry or a trip or whatever. I'll be so pissed at you if you let this ruin your night. I'm here with the girls. Whatever her faults, she loves them to death."

Kelly's biggest worry right then was that he wouldn't deal with it. That he'd just let his mother get away with stuff rather than tell her to stop. Rather than reveal to her all his worst things.

Stacey made an *X* over her heart. "I'm not going to poison her. Or make a thing. Especially in front of the girls. But she's not all bad. There has to be a part of her who knows this is silly and wants to make things better."

"I can't think about it anymore or I won't go. If

Vaughan doesn't come out here in the next two minutes you and I are going out to dinner." Kelly frowned.

"Oh, so you're mad now?"

"Why does it feel like you wanted that?"

"You're better mad than sad." Stacey shrugged.

Vaughan came outside, a smile pasted on. "See you later, Stacey. Thanks again. If she gets… If it goes…"

"I can handle this. Have a great dinner." Stacey turned and went back inside, the sound of the locks being thrown an underline to her dismissal.

Vaughan pointed to his car. "Ready to go?"

"What the heck? Where did this one come from?"

He opened the door of the sleek, black sports car. "I've had it a year or so. I don't get to drive it as much as I want. Not a family car. But I figure, it's a take-my-best-girl-to-dinner car."

Kelly made a noncommittal sound as she got in. He shut her door and went around to the driver's side.

They drove to the restaurant and he walked her inside, a hand at her elbow after giving the valet a look when he helped Kelly from the car. There was no mistaking the claim, the way he stood close, as if he dared anyone not to see he was with her.

He used to be jealous, which considering his behavior was ridiculous. And he was blatantly holding himself out as her man as they approached the hostess. But it wasn't scary or gross.

It was nice.

The hostess stared. Their server flirted with Kelly and after they'd ordered and were enjoying a drink, he took her hand. "Should we talk about the thing with my mom?"

They'd avoided the topic in the car and she'd let him because she had some thinking of her own to do.

Ugh. She'd rather avoid it and pretend it never happened. But years of that had gotten them where they were right then. So Kelly pulled up her big-girl panties and acted like a grown-up. "No. But let's anyway."

He smiled and looked so handsome her heart stuttered just a beat or two. "She apologized, by the way. She didn't mean anything by the school-night comment."

"Not to me."

He sucked in a breath. "Fair enough. To me, and I said it to you."

"It's an apology to you to pass on to me. Not the same."

"You're going to have to give a little, too."

She tried to pull her hand free but he kept it and she let him. "Oh, I am?" She knew her laugh had that slightly hysterical edge to it and she let him hear it. "Here's the thing. I can accept that explanation. It didn't *have* to be a negative comment. I don't normally go out on school nights, as it happens. I can even be the bigger person and accept a half-assed apology given to a third party. But for you or anyone else to insinuate I haven't *given* when it comes to the Hurleys infuriates me."

It really did. This was a big deal. Sharon was going to be showing up on the doorstep and if they stayed together there'd be holidays and gatherings and all that Hurley stuff.

This situation with Shurley had to be handled or they'd never make it. Kelly realized that was a truth she had to face. Not long-term. They were a close family and did things together all the time. If Vaughan had to choose, Kelly realized he'd choose her and the girls. But part of him would wither and over time he'd resent her.

"Even before we split it was clear I'd never be rugged enough or whatever it is everyone else has but I lack. For years I tried until it was just a relief I didn't have to deal with any of you except for visitation."

He winced. "Ouch."

"I tried for years. I stayed here instead of Manhattan where at that time my professional life was centered. I never, ever get in your way when you want to see the girls. They're with you on holidays. I took them to your parents while you were on tour, for God's sake. So kindly take your suggestion that I give a little and shove it up your ass."

Vaughan, clearly stunned, just stared at her. And she didn't even feel the need, not for a moment, to apologize.

"You're right. I'm sorry. You did make sacrifices. You have made an effort to keep the girls near my family. They see that, too, and totally appreciate it, Kelly." He sighed, but kept their fingers linked. "None of us are who we were eight years ago. Ezra has gone through hell and fought his way back. Damien fell in love, got married, he's going to be a dad in a month or so. Paddy was totally blindsided by Natalie but I fully expect him to be proposing soon. They *all* like you. They've *all* told me to get you back. My dad's given me some pretty freaking great advice. They want us—you, me and the girls—to be a family. One hundred and ten percent, they're all behind me, wanting us to work out. Truly."

"You know, here's a thing. None of us are who we were, that's true. But you want to keep glossing over the seeds of this entire mess. Not just the years after we split. But the way your mother has been to me since day one. This isn't about my sacrifices. That's parenting, Vaughan. This is about the shitty attitude your mother has had since the moment she met me. She thinks I'm a gold-digging whore and she thinks that because *you never told her the truth.* That makes me sort of ragey right now, come to think of it."

"I'm going to see her next week at the ranch to talk to her. About everything. And to tell her she has to welcome you the way she has Mary, Natalie and Tuesday. It can't work any other way. Thing is, and I'm not defending her, but I think she's been trying to find a way to admit she might like you for a few years now."

"I already let you put your penis in me, stop lying."

He burst out laughing, bringing her hand to his mouth to kiss her fingertips. "Not lying! I swear. She's a mom. She sees you and no one can look at the job you do and deny how great you are at raising our girls. We'll talk. I'll explain and yeah, confess. And we'll all move forward. You, Maddie and Kensey are my priority. Do you believe me?"

She didn't hesitate before nodding. She just hoped he kept them his priority and didn't run off when it got hard.

The truth was, yes, they all had changed. Heaven knew she wasn't the same, either. She wanted to fit with the Hurleys, too. Wanted to feel like more than an outsider who brought the kids over to see them.

"There's no moving forward until she hears the truth and reacts appropriately."

"All right. I'm sorry this happened. I wanted tonight to be special and romantic." Vaughan had realized, when Kelly told him about what Stacey had done for them, that other than sleeping and sex and parenting stuff, he hadn't been paying enough attention to the romance, that intimacy they needed to keep building and renewing. Strengthening them like a shield from whatever storms came along.

He raised his glass and touched it to hers. "To second chances."

"Redemption."

He drank and then took a while to watch the candlelight glinting against the gold of her hair, the sparkle of her earrings, the gloss of her nails. So exquisite but she made it look effortless.

"You look so gorgeous. I want to get out a spoon and eat you up in three bites."

Her smile drew him closer.

"That's a nice thing to say."

"I forget sometimes how stunning you are. And then you get all dressed up, or I see you in some fantastic outfit for work and I remember. I remember sitting, watching you get your makeup done for a show. I remember what you look like, that walk of yours, as you owned that runway. Boom. Boom."

"My agent has me come in to teach the newbs how to walk. Twice a year. Like orientation with Aunt Kelly. God, they're all so young. Fresh-faced off the bus from nowhere, USA. I see them a year later, the ones who make it anyway, and all that fresh-faced stuff is fading."

"Along with the supermodel thing, I forget sometimes that you didn't have much of a normal life as a kid."

"Says the rock-star rancher." But her tone wasn't angry or upset. Just amused. "We were in the Philippines when I was Kensey's age. Then we lived in Turkey. I'll give Rebecca credit, she found every freaking casting call she could, no matter the location. After that is when Rebecca left him, taking me with her. When we got back to the United States she put me in classes and about a year later I was picked up by Exclusive. Still with them, actually. Twenty years in July."

He'd seen the photos of her, a fourteen-year-old walking on the runway. She'd been part of a new wave of models at the time. The all-star team, so to speak.

He wanted to know more about her life. Back when they'd been together she'd told him some, but he hadn't pressed for more than she'd given. Probably a mistake. In any case, one he didn't want to repeat. "Do you see your mother much? Or your father?"

"He died three years ago. He's buried in Tacoma. I found out a few months after."

"I'm sorry." He was. He couldn't imagine the pain of having one of his parents just walk away like her father had.

She shrugged. "People die. He drank too much and it killed him. Or so I'm told. I haven't seen him or spoken to him since before we met."

"You never told me the whole story."

"Dinner out with a gorgeous man is not the time for that shit."

"It's part of you. I want to know. How can I understand you if I don't?"

"Maybe. But not right now. Call me selfish, but I just want a nice night without drama."

"I bet you never had drama with Ross." Vaughan heard the petulant quality in his tone but he couldn't be embarrassed by it even though he had no one to blame but himself.

"Are you jealous?" Her tone was incredulous and he wanted to laugh. Of course he was jealous, for God's sake!

"Yes. He was going to marry you. Be a father to my daughters. You loved him. And not me."

Their appetizers arrived and she was quiet for a time.

"I never stopped loving you. As for Ross? I loved him. But as Stacey points out to me all the time, I wasn't *in* love with him. And I'm not marrying him. I've been married once, Vaughan, and that was to you."

"He took care of you when I should have."

"*I* took care of me. I don't need a keeper."

No, she didn't. She'd always been independent. But this version was grown-up and he wasn't a part of it. Not in any positive sense.

"We didn't have drama. Though his mother—" she rolled her eyes "—is a huge part of his life, too. He's not a dramatic person. He's solid. I used to think he was reliable."

"Used to?"

She tried to wave it away but he wasn't going to be swayed. Something had come up and he wanted to know what it was.

"Please. Tell me."

"It's not even a thing."

"Then it won't be a problem for you to tell me what it is."

Kelly's annoyed growl made him hide a smile.

"Fine. I think he told her, the ex, about some of my food stuff."

"How do you…? Oh shit, the comment she made at the carnival?" He felt sick on her behalf.

Kelly nodded.

"I'm sorry. That's fucked up."

Her bottom lip wobbled, just a bit, and he ached to make that pain go away.

"I'm trying really hard, you know. Trying to not break your heart, or hurt your feelings. I have. Before. But I don't get him. I figured he had more on the ball than that."

"Everyone does stupid shit when they're hurting, I suppose."

"Did you confront him?" Vaughan didn't know how to feel about it if she had.

"I thought about it over the weekend. But I realized there's nothing to be gained in doing that. It's over. I feel less bad about breaking the engagement now, so there's that."

His heart lightened at her joke.

"I guess I expected him to be hurt and even angry. But he took something that was private, something he only knew about because he was allowed into my life, and he told someone else and she used it to hurt me. I hate to think he knew that would happen, but it might have. It could even have been a random comment because she's a bitch. Whatever it is, nothing good can come of me confronting him. The strongest reply I can give is to not let it show that I was hurt."

It shouldn't have to be, though.

"Is it cool that I want to punch him for making you sad?"

She snickered and then sighed happily when their entrées arrived. "Sure. That's cool."

They had a long, leisurely dinner and drinks and by the time they walked back to the valet stand, his life was about a thousand times better, and it was already really amazing.

Once they pulled out, he headed away from the freeway.

"Scenic route?" Kelly asked.

"I have a hotel key. We have a babysitter for several more hours. I was thinking, loud hotel sex might make tonight even better."

"My. You're going to earn that merit badge early if you keep this up."

KELLY TURNED SLOWLY as she tossed her bag on a chair. "Some view for a quickie," she told Vaughan, who prowled around her, getting her all flustered and tingly.

"Paddy brings Natalie here from time to time. He said it was romantic. You in my hotel room, ready for me to sex up one side and back down the other is a million times better."

He moved close and then dropped to his knees. She sucked in a breath, her hands gripping his shoulders for a moment.

"Mmm." He pressed his face into her, the vibration of that hum of satisfaction echoing to her clit. "Been some time since I've looked at you from this angle."

His hands slid down the curve of her calves, down to her ankle where he slid first one shoe off, and then the other.

Kelly gave in and tunneled her fingers through his hair, messing it up. "You look like a pirate this way."

Those green/brown eyes of his locked on her mouth for so long she tightened her fingers, tugging.

"Legs, I'm kind of in the middle of something right now. But I'll pirate it up. Pillage you extra hard."

"Promise?"

The teasing light in his eyes faded. All laughter was gone, replaced by white-hot need. He pulled at her dress, impatient.

Kelly pushed his hands away, moving to do it herself, far more carefully.

"I want you naked," he said, going back to grab the hem of her dress.

"I'm happy to make that happen, but if you rip this dress I will hurt you." A quick unclasping of the neck and it fell away, leaving her in a pair of tiny panties and nothing else.

"Best. Day. Ever."

"It's about to get a lot better."

She slowly unbuttoned the front of his shirt, sliding her hands all over his bared skin as she freed his arms, putting the shirt with her dress. Then the belt, unbuttoned the pants and it was her turn to drop to her knees.

"I was doing something."

She yanked his pants down and helped him step from them, along with his boxers.

"Yeah?" Kelly rubbed her cheek along his cock and he hissed but didn't argue any further. Which was good because she liked where she was and had no plans to let him get her all addled and take over again. Not just yet.

"Go on, then. Swallow it."

She did nearly choke because the rough, dirty words went straight to her solar plexus and points south.

Dirty talk was new and she liked it.

Enough to comply, taking him as deeply as she could before pulling back and doing it again.

This time it was *his* hands on her shoulders to keep his feet. That pleased Kelly nearly as much as the power of bringing him so much pleasure.

The muscles in his thighs bunched as he locked his knees and she hummed, delighted.

Vaughan swore under his breath, his fingers on her shoulders tightening until one hand let go, reaching to caress her hair and the side of her face and throat. The heat of him flowed against her cheeks and chest.

Each time she took him as deeply as possible, the coarse hair on his legs brushed her nipples. The slow build of pleasure began to saturate each one of her cells, warming in its wake.

This was connection. Not just a blow job, but the deepest trust she'd felt with him since he'd moved in.

The tenderness in his touch rocked her to her foundations.

"Still the most beautiful creature I've ever seen," he said quietly and she opened her eyes so she could see his face.

He gasped when she did, the shock of the intensity of that depth of connection seemed to snap into place.

She didn't have to tell him she understood. That she felt it, too. He could see it in her gaze, she knew.

"So close," he whispered.

Kelly scored her fingernails up the backs of his calves and gripped the base of his cock with one hand and cupped his balls with the other. He let out a string of curses and then came on a snarl of her name.

Kelly barely had the time to kiss the head before he'd pulled her to her feet and crushed his mouth to hers, taking a kiss that seared her.

"But you mess with the goods, doll, and you gotta pay."

"Jesus, Pretenders lyrics snarled at me by a naked rock star with ink and piercings. I may have just come."

He swept her up and tossed her to the bed, falling with her, rolling on top. "*May* have? Well, we should be sure. For science."

Her laugh died as he took a nipple between his teeth, flicking his tongue against it hard and fast. Licks of heat flowed through her. He reared up enough to touch her everywhere he could as he moved to the other nipple.

He was going to kill her. At some point she was going to explode into flame and there'd be only ash left.

Which was her last really coherent thought as he shifted down, kissing and licking over her belly, to her hips where he paid attention to her most sensitive spots until she was ready to roll him back over and jump on his cock herself.

"*Now*, I think we're ready to conduct our first scientific trial."

"Get to it!" Kelly was pretty sure she sounded a smidgen panicked.

He laughed as he used his thumbs to spread her open and blew against her pussy right before he began to lick and suck at her clit as he kept her wide with palms that seemed so very big all of a sudden.

White lights shone against her closed eyelids as she came with a very loud moan. He kept at it until she pushed him back, a hand on his head as she shifted up the bed.

She heard the crinkle of a condom wrapper and started, eyes wide as she realized he was already hard and ready.

"A girl could get used to this kind of recovery time."

He stayed on his knees between her thighs, her back on the bed. Then he grabbed her, pulled her up his thighs, sliding into her while she wrapped her calves around his waist.

In this position he controlled how deep, how hard; he kept the pace as he thrust, settling in.

"Good to know as I have no plans to let you get used to me not being around."

She hoped so. Now that he was around again, she'd gotten used to him, and not just in bed.

Vaughan took his sweet time, drawing her so very close to climax and then easing back, slowing only to incite her again just a few strokes later.

Then he wet his fingers in his mouth and used them on her clit. With all the teasing it was pretty much all she needed to get that last bit of sensation and spiral into climax, arching her back, holding him close with her legs.

He groaned, grabbing her hips and holding her against him as he rocked deep. Kelly watched his features as orgasm claimed him, felt the pulse of his cock inside her as a few smaller orgasms skittered through her system until he pulled out and fell back to the bed, gasping for air.

He got up, returning just moments later, rolling a cart in that she hadn't even seen when they'd first come into the room.

"I think we've solved the problem of whether or not you came."

"So smug." Kelly laughed.

He grinned, kissing her hard. "I am. What man in my position wouldn't be smug?"

"As long as you keep making me come like that, I agree to your smugness."

"Not even done yet. We have another hour or two so I say we have some champagne and then go for another round."

"You have a deal."

## CHAPTER EIGHTEEN

"DADDY, WILL YOU sing with me?" Maddie asked as she got off the bus the next afternoon.

He took her hand and Kensey's on the other side as they walked back toward the house.

"I will always sing with you, baby. Name the time." The sky overhead was deep blue, white marshmallow-fluff clouds dotted it. Kids streamed down the sidewalks, played in the park as they walked past. And his children loved music as much as he did.

Not much better than that.

"You know, Mommy's birthday is in two weeks. I want to give her a song."

He stopped, kneeling to face his oldest. "That's a great idea. She'd love it. Do you have a song in mind?"

Maddie nodded. "Patty Griffin's 'Let Him Fly.' It's her favorite."

"I'm not sure I know that one. I love what I've heard for this birthday present, though." He stood, continuing to walk back home. "Sing me some."

Maddie began to sing it. Her voice was already strong. She had the same depth her uncle Ezra had.

And as he listened to the lyrics, Vaughan realized it was a song about a woman loving a man and letting him go. Vain as it might be, he assumed it was about him.

Once they'd gotten home, he was already formulating a plan.

"I have an idea. Kensey, do you want to be part of this birthday present for Mommy?"

"Heck yeah! I can dance. She likes my dancing."

"Course she does. I think that's perfect. You two want to go to the ranch? I need to pick up a few things." Now that his work space was coming together above the garage, he wanted to bring one of his smaller amps and some of his stands over.

He texted Kelly to let her know he was going to take the girls over to see his parents and would be sure they got fed, did their homework and were home by nine. Then he called his parents to make sure they were around and up to company. They both sounded thrilled at the chance to see their granddaughters so he loaded everyone into the car and they headed off to Hood River.

"Do you miss living here, Daddy?" Maddie asked as they waited for the big iron gate to open leading up the drive to Sweet Hollow Ranch.

"I've been gone on tour longer than the time I've lived with you guys." He rolled his window down, loving the smell of the fields, of clean air and green things. "I love this land. It's part of me, and part of you two, as well. But it's not too far so when I need to be here to help your uncle Ezra and Poppa work the land, that's good, too."

"Mommy should be here, too. Will she now?" Kensey asked as they pulled into his parents' driveway.

"I'd like that, too, sweetie. It's complicated adult stuff. But that's the hope, yes."

Minnie—the dog that was technically his and the girls' but who'd defected to his parents—ran out at his father's side on her teeny little corgi legs.

The girls had plenty of love for Grandpa and the dog and when Sharon came out, they ran over to hug her, as well.

Vaughan hugged his parents, too, and they all headed into the large kitchen and dining room.

"How about pizza? Poppa can go pick it up, along with some chocolate milk," Sharon asked.

"You two can do your homework while you wait and then it'll be done so you can hang out with your grandparents and eat without that hanging over you."

They didn't argue, but eyes were rolled. He let it pass because heaven knew he and homework didn't have much of a relationship. They did well in school, which thrilled him. They could eye roll here and there as long as that kept up.

"I need to grab a few things from my place," Vaughan told them.

"Your brothers are all over at Ezra's," his father called out. "Have dinner with them so we don't have to share Maddie and Kensey with you."

"You can have the dog, though. She's antsy and all the walking will tire her out," his mother said.

Vaughan loved how his mom pretended she wasn't talking in baby voices to the dog and feeding her peanut butter sandwiches when he wasn't around. "You want to go see Loopy and the pig?" Vaughan asked Minnie, who danced around, barking excitedly.

"Okay, then." He bent to kiss the girls. "Behave for your grandparents. I'll be back in a bit."

Normally they'd have asked to come along, or at the very least gotten up to walk him out. This time they just nodded and said they'd see him later and that was all the thought they gave him.

It wasn't until he was standing in his studio at home that he had an epiphany. He was no longer an unusual quantity for his children. They took him for granted the way they did Kelly. Their assumption was that he would be back and get them home by nine. Their assumption was that even though they'd just seen their grandmother the day before, she was still a rarer sight than Vaughan.

"What do you know, Minnie? I think I've unlocked a dubious and yet totally normal parenting achievement."

He loaded his stuff into the car before heading over to Ezra's to see what was up.

WHEN VAUGHAN WALKED into his brother's house, it was to hear his other brothers, Damien and Paddy, giving Ezra shit over a statement that Ezra craved Tuesday and was uncomfortable with it.

Well, a guy turned his back for a month and he had to jump back into everyone's life at full speed.

Ezra was a control freak. He'd been out of control and his entire life had burned to the ground. Ever since he got out of rehab all those years ago, he'd re-built that life with a patient and yet firm hand.

At the same time, Vaughan knew the shame of what he'd been like when he'd been a drug addict still hung around Ezra's neck like a weight. A weight of his own choosing as the rest of the family had long since forgiven Ezra's sins.

If Ezra was throwing around words like *crave* it meant he was still using it to keep Tuesday from getting too close.

"I think it's interesting you use the word *crave*," Vaughan said as he fully entered the room. If he could help it in any way, Vaughan would push his brother into making the right choice. And he thought Tuesday was that right choice.

"The prodigal Hurley returns. Pull up a plate and something to drink. We're poking Ezra about his love life," Paddy said.

Vaughan headed to the kitchen where food was laid out. One of the things he missed the most about living at the ranch was getting to eat his sister-in-law Mary's excellent food.

They'd come a long way from those barely-out-of-school shitheads with some instruments, a van and some dreams. Still, those early days weren't all bad.

"It's times like these I miss getting drunk, fighting a bunch of assholes in an alley behind a crappy little dive and crashing with a black eye and blood on my shirt in bed as the sun came up. Life was simpler back then."

No one spoke for long, tense moments and Vaughan started to feel bad that he'd dropped a bomb into a nice dinner. But then Ezra started to laugh. A deep belly laugh and everyone relaxed.

Ezra flipped Vaughan off and then tipped his chin at Paddy and Damien. "It's okay to laugh, you know. I'm not going to run out and buy heroin because Vaughan brings up our storied and violent past. But if I do you can blame him in therapy. I will."

Ezra gave Vaughan a one-armed hug as he walked past, grabbed some more food and headed into the living room. Paddy continued to poke at Ezra about the whole crave thing and Ezra clearly tried to tune him out but it didn't work. Everyone knew one another's weak points and how to get a rise from their sibling.

Finally, Ezra just blurted out, "Needing something on that level isn't stable ground for a junkie."

Paddy nodded. "Fair enough. Do you see the situations as similar?"

"I know the difference between a woman and drugs."

Vaughan heard the defensiveness in Ezra's voice, but it was Damien who addressed it before anyone else could.

"Stop being such a defensive dick. I might even agree if you *were* a junkie. But you aren't. You used to be. Now you're just a grumpy asshole who could be getting laid a lot more regularly but would rather punish himself by holding what he *needs* away to prove some sort of point that does not matter. You kicked heroin. Tuesday is not drugs. She's not an addiction. You're not out of control for liking a woman a lot," Damien said.

Ezra growled as Damien kept sneaking food from his plate to the two kittens who owned Ezra. Ezra barked at Damien to stop feeding the cats; Damien ignored him.

Essentially, a day that ended in a *Y*, then, for the Hurley brothers. It wasn't his house that he missed, but this sort of camaraderie.

"I'm going to spoil the fuck out of all your goddamn kids. Know that right now," Ezra grumbled like it was a threat.

Vaughan snorted. "Too late. My girls already have more shit than they need and it's got Hurley written all over it. Kelly's family are assholes, but you people send my kids so much stuff. I had no idea how much stuff until I was at their house on a daily basis."

"Yeah, so what's going on with that?" Ezra leaned forward, taking the opportunity to change the subject.

But Vaughan was smarter than that. "Nope. I'm here to talk about you. And to pick up mail and some clothes. The girls are up with Mom and Dad having pizza and when that's over, I'm taking them home because they have school and Kelly will punch me in the throat if they're back after nine."

"Are you living there now?" Damien asked.

He started to tell them the whole story, but he also realized Ezra wanted that. Wanted the attention off him and on Vaughan. And if anyone needed pushing to get what they needed from life, it was Ezra.

He'd share soon enough. "In the guest room. But again, first we talk about Ezra and then I'll talk about what's going on in Gresham."

Ezra frowned, but gave in, answering. "There's not much more to say. I have what I guess you'd describe as a girlfriend. It's far more serious than anything I've done before and I'm mainly okay with that. It's not like no one knows about it. Hell, Paddy and his girlfriend just spent four days with me and Tuesday last weekend. I'm done talking about it. Thank you for being concerned."

Paddy flipped Ezra off. "I'm more nosy than concerned. I figure you two have it handled. She's got as much dark, tragic backstory as you do but she's strong. She doesn't take your shit, which I like."

Vaughan hooted, ignoring his sadness that he'd missed seeing this firsthand. "Ha! Do tell."

Which they did. Filling Vaughan in and then also updating him with news from their lives, too. Mary was getting irritable and ready to give birth. Paddy was considering asking Natalie to move in with him, and Tuesday was going to relaunch her business as an art gallery.

"Now you. We've told you about our lives. What's happening in yours?" Paddy demanded.

"I'm working on some solo stuff."

Each of his brothers reacted a little differently, but none of them seemed upset or angry.

"You leaving the band?" Damien asked.

"Hell no. I just have some material and I don't think it's our sound."

"But if it's your sound, it's our sound," Paddy argued.

"No. If it's our sound, you'll want to change it. Make it yours. Make it Sweet Hollow Ranch. And I don't want that. I love the band. I love making music with you. But this is different."

Ezra nodded, petting a cat while the other one had fallen asleep in the small space between Ezra and the chair arm. "Okay, tell us about it."

But it was nearly eight and he had to get moving.

"Next time. I'll be over here next week. Having lunch with Mom. I need to tell her everything. She has misgivings about Kelly that aren't based in truth. And I've let that remain the case for years. Time to pay up. I want you all to understand what Kelly did and didn't do after the divorce. She doesn't feel welcome here and I get why."

Vaughan stood to go.

"Natalie and Mary were talking about this the other day. I think we all misjudged her and that's not cool. I'd be really upset if you guys did that to Mary," Damien said.

"All I ask is that you get to know Kelly and give her a chance. And I can't do that if she doesn't feel like anyone wants to know her at all." He had this family. This support. They loved Mary and Natalie and Tuesday, so why the hell not Kelly?

"Fair enough," Paddy said as they all walked Vaughan over to his car. "I want to hear your stuff. Just because you're doing it solo doesn't mean we won't all be there for you. To help if you want it."

Hearing that from Paddy—the brother also known as Make-It-Perfect-Paddy—meant a lot. They'd clashed on the making of the last album over Vaughan's approach to the material. He respected Paddy immensely and it had frustrated him, made him feel as if he'd never measure up. But this was so much better.

And what he'd needed.

He said his goodbyes, grabbed the girls, dropped off the dog and headed back home. Where he wanted to be more than anything else.

## CHAPTER NINETEEN

"I NEED TO make a trip to New York," Kelly said as she finished up her last stretch and headed to her water bottle.

The sun had been up awhile, but it was still that pale morning light and it lent their room a pretty glow.

Not at all hurt by the gorgeous man in nothing more than pajama bottoms and a naughty look on his mouth, either. Watching Kelly do yoga was one of Vaughan's favorite activities, it seemed. He'd lounge in the nearby chair reading, dealing with his own business stuff or writing. He never bothered her or made noise and she'd grown to like having his energy around.

"Can I come?"

"Really?" She was so afraid to hope, afraid he'd make light of it or not take it seriously.

"Yeah. I'd love to go back with you. I can hang with the girls while you're working and then when you have the time we can do family stuff. Maddie was a baby the last time I was in New York City with her."

His smile was so wonderful, so full of love and happiness that it made it hard to breathe for a few moments. She loved him so much, so fiercely, it had marked her to the core. There was never *not* loving him.

Even before Kensey had been born she'd begun

to miss him. It wasn't that he was working and she was home. Kelly had loved being home with Maddie.

It was that he had a whole other life when he left the door. And he liked that.

So his absence in her life had been a low-level ache for a very long time. One she figured would never leave her. Because despite all that, she'd never been able to not love him. She'd tried. God knew she'd tried right up to planning to marry someone else.

Vaughan *wanting* a family with her had been all she'd ever desired when they'd divorced. And it remained her chief wish. That expression he wore was enough to untie several knots she'd had in her belly for a long time.

And she let herself believe a little more.

"If we left Friday after school and take a red-eye, we can stay through Wednesday. I don't want to miss the grand opening of Tuesday's gallery the following week."

"Friday to Wednesday is totally doable. Let me check in with Ez, just to be sure he won't need me. Since the girls will be out of school by week's end, I thought it'd be a good idea to put our idea of having them more involved in the land into practice. Bring them out a few times a week."

He'd made it a point to insist the girls be home with them over the summer break and she hadn't argued. They had plenty of fun when they headed over to the ranch. Vaughan had a pool there. There were horses to ride and all that land to run and play on. Plus their uncle Ezra had all sorts of animals he'd let Maddie and Kensey name. Naturally all the goats were named Marshmallow.

"Good. They need it. They'll have a cousin soon so that'll be fun for them, too. Just remember to give yourself time for your music. You need that."

He stood, pulling her into a hug. He was warm and smelled of sleep in their bed.

"What's that for?" Kelly asked.

"I'm working on the solo project I told you about."

She took his hands. "You didn't say much then. Will you tell me about it now? Maybe play something for me?"

He nodded. "Yeah. I'd like that. Later? I've got something to do first. I'm headed to the ranch this morning. I'm having a late breakfast with my parents."

"Okay. I can't wait to hear the details. I'm excited for you. Proud." And a little concerned he might be separating himself from them. As awkward as it was to be around his family, she never wanted him to cut himself off. She understood how important they all were to one another, and as a unit. As much as she wished she was included in it, she'd never want him or their children to cut that off.

"I was planning to walk them to the bus stop this morning anyway and to pick them up and take Maddie to piano and Kensey to ballet. If you left now you could miss traffic and spend the day. I know you miss them, Vaughan. It's one of the best things about you. I'd never ask you to give that up. It's as much a part of you as the color of your eyes."

"You think so? Even with all the shit between you and them?"

"I've thought about this over the years. About why your family and I never clicked. Most of it is about how I came around. They didn't know me at all and there I was, young and pregnant and your wife. And there was no prenup."

Oh, Sharon had shit the bed over that. It had been the biggest weapon in her arsenal during the divorce and the year or so after when things were at the very worst.

"She had no right to do or say any of that."

"No, she didn't. And it was *your* job to tell her that. But you didn't. So you both failed." Kelly cleared her throat as the shock passed over Vaughan's face. She'd never tell him, but Kelly had wanted to say that for years and now that she had, another layer of weight lifted and the space between them wasn't bigger at all.

Just the opposite.

He *listened* to her, which was why he'd reacted the way he had. Regret replaced the surprise.

Kelly let out a long breath. "That's in the past for me. I needed to say that. And now that I have, it's gone. I told myself I'd forgiven you, but I hadn't. Not until right now."

He hugged her again and she let herself believe he'd changed. Let herself believe *she'd* changed, too.

"Thank you," he murmured as she stepped back.

"As I was saying. First impressions are important and mine was not good. Not that there was anything wrong with me and they should have tried to get past their preconceptions." That needed to be said, too. "But you come from a good family. A strong family. That family loves our children and even if I'm never

as liked as anyone else, I want that for them. Don't
cut yourself off from that over me."

"WELL, I DON'T want my daughters to grow up seeing
their mother not welcomed by their father's family."
Vaughan shoved a hand through his hair, beginning
to pace.

"There's no way our relationship will work if they
don't welcome you. Not if I stay close with them." He
knew that with utter certainty. "You'd resent me if I
didn't stand up for you."

She nodded. "Yeah. I did. And I would. I'm not sure
how we get around that, but I'd like to try to work out
our differences and be nicer to each other if for no
other reason than Maddie and Kensey. And I admit
it, I want them to like me."

Vaughan took her hands. There she was, putting
herself to the side for someone else and he was done
seeing that happen.

"I failed you before. You're totally right. But you're
also right that my family is a good family. And because of that, I think we can fix this." Vaughan didn't
believe his mother wanted this tension between them
to continue and after his dinner with his brothers at
the ranch the week before, he believed they all would
welcome Kelly happily.

"I won't lose you again. I'm not just going over
there to eat and then hang out or help Ezra. I'm going
to talk to my mom and dad about you. About us. And
I'm going to be sure they know the truth I've been
dodging for a long time." In just a few days he'd have
been staying with them for five weeks. So much had

changed. Enough to give him the strength and will to do the right thing.

Kelly's features lit and he reversed his pacing and moved back to her.

"I broke us. I cheated and betrayed you and then I let my family think the worst of you because I was too weak to bear the weight of what I'd done. I'm sorry, Kelly."

She sniffled a little and he was glad he'd said it. Sorry that he hadn't before.

"So, this morning I'll walk the girls to the bus along with you like we do every morning. And tonight is taco night, so I'll be back because it's my turn to pick the food up when you call to say you've got Maddie and are on the way home like you did last week and the week before."

The wonder of that hadn't gone away yet. The way he and Kelly had begun to work with one another to keep their family running. She trusted him with a little more each week and it was a gift each time.

He'd have tacos with his ladies at six that night just like he did every Tuesday night.

"Okay, then." She went to her tiptoes to kiss him.

He cupped her cheeks, so pleased she'd let him in so much more. Touched that she'd insisted he continued his relationship with his family. Determined to fix the mess he'd made.

He followed her into the bathroom. "We've got about fifteen extra minutes. Any idea what we could do with it?"

The shirt she tossed over her shoulder answered

his question and he laughed, quickening his pace to catch up.

"Make sure the door is locked," she called out as he made to grab her.

"Oops." He turned around to do that and when he'd come back, she was naked and getting into the shower.

He locked the bathroom door, too, and joined her.

"Now you're learning," she teased.

He shucked his pants and joined her, already hard, always wanting her.

This kiss took him deep. He wanted every moment they had, wanted to fill each of them with pleasure, greedy as always.

She slid herself against him, squirting some liquid soap between their bodies until they got nice and slippery.

"Mmm. Taking showers is so much more fun when you live here."

He laughed, kissing down her neck as he shifted to slide his cock between her thighs and pushed closer, not entering her body, but stroking the head and length of himself against her, hot, wet and oh so welcoming.

She sucked in a shaky breath and he nipped her earlobe. "Feels so good. Everything with you is hotter than the last time."

She scored her nails down his back as her breathing hitched. As he continued to thrust, taking them both closer and closer to climax, he soaped over her ass and then up, around her hips until he took her breasts in his hands, tugging her nipples the way he knew she liked best.

Her pussy grew impossibly hotter against him as

he continued to stroke through the notch between her thighs, taking care to angle the flare of the crown of his cock against her clit, just so.

Her teeth sank into his shoulder as she came. The unexpected edge of pain, the fraying of her control, sent him into orgasm right along with her.

"Better than a cup of coffee any day," he said as he kissed her.

Laughing, she finished her shower.

## CHAPTER TWENTY

AFTER A QUICK knock on his parents' front door, he let himself in, calling out that he'd arrived.

He followed the smell of food and his father's hail through to the kitchen where his mom was cooking and his dad had clearly just come inside from the fields. The alfalfa was coming in the following week or so. The ranch was abuzz with activity and had been for hours.

Michael Hurley loved being outside. Loved the land and making things grow. He and Ezra were very much alike in that way. Vaughan loved that the ranch was their land, but not anywhere near the level they did.

He waved a hand at Vaughan. "Hey, son."

Vaughan hugged both his parents and then got himself a cup of coffee.

"How's it going? Alfalfa still on track for next week?"

"It is."

"Kelly and I are taking the girls to New York, but we'll be back Wednesday. I'll stay here for a few days to help then."

"Bring the biscuits to the table, Michael," his mother said. "Vaughan, grab the butter and jam from the fridge."

Once all the food had been laid out, they sat down to eat. Minnie camped her fat little belly over Vaughan's feet, just in case he might drop some food.

"What are you doing in Gresham, Vaughan?" his mother asked as she spooned up some eggs onto her plate.

"I'm getting my family back. Or, maybe that's not right. I'm earning them, I guess. Yeah, that's what I'm doing," Vaughan said.

"Why now? She left you eight years ago. Why does she suddenly want you back?"

"Sharon, honey." Michael patted his wife's hand and she gave him a scary look. Vaughan's father ignored it. "Ease back, now. Your Southern is showing."

"That girl showed up, made him love her and then stole his children and his money. You tell me why I shouldn't be outraged by that."

Vaughan and his father both stared, stunned, mouths agape at her words.

This was a bigger mess than he'd assumed. There was a lot of emotion there and it was misplaced. For so long Vaughan had let this stew and now... "This is totally my fault." Vaughan ate awhile as he tried to get his words together.

"What is?" Sharon eyed him carefully.

"I should have pushed harder to bring her into the family. We should have welcomed her instead of suspecting her. I was away a lot. Distracted. I didn't want to make waves and she tolerated it."

"Tolerated?"

"How can you be so smart about so many things and so, so deluded when it comes to Kelly? What is it about her more than Natalie, Mary or Tuesday that makes you react so vehemently against her?"

"She broke your heart! She stole your children when you were still reeling from that and then she used you for money. She's got her fancy house here and her multimillion-dollar condo. Her stores. All paid for by my son. Who she hurt."

"Mom," Vaughan began but Sharon held a hand up.

"I'm not done, boy. Hold your tongue until I am."

"I'm going to let that happen. But I'm telling you now, tread carefully." Vaughan clamped his lips together.

"That was years ago. She was young and I can understand why she latched on to you. Army brat with a stage mother who pushed her into show business to pay the bills. And you come along. Keep it shut," she warned him when Vaughan began to argue.

He nodded and his father gave him an approving look. Vaughan knew his father supported his getting Kelly back so that expression said Vaughan was on the right track to let Sharon speak.

"But then, she stayed here. Your daughters are wonderful children. Bright, affectionate, artistic. She encourages that but doesn't seem to want to exploit their talent. I've been a mother with kids who were artists. I know what it takes and so maybe I don't hate her anymore. Maybe I even appreciate the way she keeps them in our life."

"I appreciate that you feel better about her and all, but nothing you felt about her until now has been fair. It's based on a lie. More than one lie. I told her to file for divorce. More than once when she confronted me about my behavior. It was a way to shut her up and keep her off my back. The last time, well, she listened to me. The truth is, I didn't want to be married."

Vaughan's father put his hand on top of his wife's to stay her response. She was pissed off, that much was clear.

"*Kelly* wanted it. Wanted kids and picket fences. She wanted welcome mats with dogs in Christmas sweaters on them. I wanted *her*. But she wanted to be an us." He put his face in his hands for long moments.

He'd never said any of this out loud. Not even to her on the occasions he'd apologized. It seemed too cruel to say. Too shameful that he'd thrown away a decade because he'd been a dick.

But he'd made a promise to stand up for her and they needed to know everything.

"She caught me in a compromising situation with someone else."

His mother's face, if he lived to be a hundred he'd never forget what it felt like to watch her anger fade into disappointment. In him.

"Don't you sit at this table and use pretty words for what it really was. Tell me what *compromising* means." His father's tone went very sharp and Vaughan winced.

"I cheated on her. She stumbled in on me with a hand that wasn't my own in my pants." It was awful, so awful to disappoint them this way. He hadn't been a good man and then he'd allowed them to think ill of Kelly for years rather than own up to his mistakes.

"'Stumbled in' isn't actually fair. I knew she was coming. She was pregnant with Kensey, had a toddler at home and she came all the way out to see me on tour because I asked her to. Part of me wanted that final push, I guess. That night wasn't the first time I'd told her to file for divorce if she didn't like what I did. But she'd always backed down, apologized. But not that time."

"Obviously not." His father's reaction told Vaughan he'd known far more of the truth than he'd let on. Which only made him feel worse.

"I didn't fight it. I walked away. I love my kids, and I loved them then, too. But she didn't use them to get money from me and she certainly didn't steal them from me. Come on, Mom. I left her the work of raising them while I lived my life. If I gave her the apartment in Manhattan and money to finish school it's because I knew I was wrong. And because she was giving up her career to do my job." Vaughan scrubbed hands over his face. "In my estimation it was a fair thing to do, even if she did have her own money. You're going to tell me it's cheap to raise a kid? Or that it isn't my responsibility to support them financially? They could be in a place she owned in Manhattan right now. I'd see them three or four times a year. You guys even less. She gave that up to come here and settle. So those girls could see their family more often. She gave up her career and I never even gave throwing money at her a second thought."

Vaughan wanted to throw up. He'd held all that in for so long and it had weighed his heart.

"I should never have let this go on this long." His voice caught. Shame burned his cheeks. "I wasn't a good person. I hurt her and I was selfish and missed out on things I'll never get back. I make them pancakes before school every Monday. I check homework and listen to a thousand stories about stuff that is incomprehensible to me about dolls and characters and books and singers and games and their friends. I sing with them after dinner and tuck them in every night. I have a family now."

His father leaned across the table to squeeze Vaughan's hand. "Shame is an entirely appropriate emotion in this case. I'm disappointed to hear the details. Disappointed in you and your lack of honor. Disappointed you allowed your mother and I to have a very bad opinion of Kelly so all these years there's been tension. No, you weren't a good man and I want to kick your behind for what you did to her and to your children."

Vaughan hadn't been this close to crying while getting a stern talking-to from his father in a decade or so.

"But," Michael continued, "you *are* a good man now. You're owning up to your mistakes and you're fighting to get back what you threw away. *That* I can be proud of."

It helped a little. Enough that he could continue. "I'm trying. I know I screwed up. A lot. It kills me sometimes when I think about how much. My daughters are getting old enough to know when something is wrong. They see Mary here. They see how much you guys love and support Damien's family. And you should. It's important. They've come to know Natalie. I expect she'll be joining our crazy group sooner or later. This is their legacy. All the land we can see from the porch. They love getting dirty and riding out to the fields with Ezra. This is part of them like it's part of me."

His mother had remained silent but she was working on something. Vaughan could see the wheels turning and it wasn't another moment before she finally spoke.

"Then why are you there in Gresham, away from us? If this land is so important, why are you living there instead of here?" she asked.

"Why would I be? Kelly isn't welcome here." Vaughan adjusted his tone. He loved his family so much and he wanted things to be better. At the same time, he promised Kelly he'd stand up for her and that's what needed to happen.

"I'm there and not here because I can't imagine anything crueler for me to do than to expect her to sit home while everyone else is welcomed here. You both have opened your hearts and the Hurley family to Natalie, Mary and Tuesday. Kelly can see that. It's not a very nice feeling and I just can't tolerate it, especially if my daughters could see. They need to see me respecting her and backing her up. That's what they need in a partner when they're adults. It's what you and Dad do."

He wasn't so worked up that he needed to miss that biscuit before it got too cold.

After he gobbled it down in three bites he went back to the subject.

"Eight years ago *I* chose a life of me and not us. Yes, we were young. But it was me who was immature. But I'm making a family with her now. I love her. She's given me another chance. Even after all the junk I pulled before."

Vaughan looked back and forth between his parents. "I wasn't ready then. I was selfish. And the cost… I aim to marry Kelly again. This time with all our friends and family present. I want you to see the Kelly I know and I want my family to be respected and welcomed as it is. Which means with Kelly."

His mother put some more ham on her plate as she eyed Vaughan carefully.

"Are you moving to Gresham permanently, then?" she asked at last. "We'll see you and the girls even less?"

"Let me answer the second question first. How often you see me and the girls is up to you. I want to bring them here. They want to come here. Kelly thinks it's important they grow up with a sense of connection to this ranch and to this family. She told me my love for you all was one of the best things about me. And that's why I can finally stop farting around and get my act together. I'm doing my best to be a person worthy of all three females I live with. That means we'll split our time between the house in Gresham and the house here around school schedules, dance and music classes, Kelly's business stuff, the busiest times of year on the ranch and working with the band."

He ate some more, sipped his coffee. "I didn't protect her before. I let her take the blame when it was me. I should have, but I didn't. So I'm doing it now. I'm all for making this work for everyone. But not at Kelly's expense. Not ever again. I nearly lost her. Another man could have raised my kids. He wanted to adopt them. Wanted her to yank them from me, cut me out and raise them as his own. That's when she broke the engagement. She told him she'd never separate them from me or my family and that she couldn't marry someone who thought she should. She doesn't know I heard it."

"Well, there are a few issues here, Vaughan Michael Hurley." His mother got up and went to sit on the couch. "You can clear the table and clean up the dishes when I'm done. But that won't be for a bit. Put your behind on that couch." She pointed and Vaughan moved quickly to obey.

His father muttered, "In for it now, boy," as he passed.

"Let me tell you something. My baby shows up on my doorstep with this, this blonde bombshell who barely spoke and looked at you like you were everything. You tell me you met a few months earlier, got the girl knocked up and got married. I knew nothing about her, or your marriage or the baby until that precise moment. You think that was a good way to start?"

"I think it was how it happened, Mom. What do you want from me?" Vaughan asked.

"I don't want to have been a person who called Kelly a gold-digging whore with more looks than brains. You *lied* to me and then you let me act like a bitch to your ex-wife," his mother said.

"You were a bitch to her before I lied."

His father's face darkened. "Do not speak to your mother in that tone or I will make sure it never happens again."

Vaughan sighed. "I apologize. I'm not going out of

my way to be disrespectful. I'm trying to make this a place I can bring my family. And right now I can't."

"Which is your own fault," his father said.

"Most of it, yes. And it doesn't even matter because the damage has been done and I'm here asking you if you can make an effort to be kind to Kelly so I can bring her back and make her a part of this life, too."

"You made me into the shrewish mother-in-law." His mom shook her head slowly. "She was the first and maybe I didn't react well." She snorted. "No 'maybe' about it. I was defensive and I jumped to conclusions and then when you split it let me project all that at her instead of you. You were a terrible husband, Vaughan. Which means that I was a terrible mother."

"What?" This was why he'd avoided this topic for so long. He was making everyone upset now. "This isn't about you being a terrible mother. I'm not saying that. I never would say that. You're a great mother. But you misjudged her and I let it go on and now that has made a big problem."

"She hates us."

"The thing is, Mom, I don't think so at all. She wants to belong. I can't do it all, though. Damien, Paddy and Ezra are trying, which is great. But I really need you and Dad to open the ranch and your hearts to her the way you have everyone else. I know it won't be instant, but it needs to happen or I can't be here. Do you understand?"

"She'd make you choose?"

"I'm choosing. Me. I'm trying to be a better husband. If you make me choose between Kelly and this family, I'll choose Kelly and the girls. I don't want to.

I love you. I love this place. I want to raise my kids on this land and with their cousins. But I can't if my wife is treated differently. Especially over something she never did."

"You don't have to choose. We were wrong. We know that. But a lot of things have happened over the years. It's not going to be immediate, or easy," his mother said. "Damn it, boy. You know how much I hate being wrong."

Vaughan wisely did not smile. She hated having to eat crow and she was going to. He'd have to deal with a payment for it, he knew.

But right then she was saying everything he could have hoped for. "It won't be easy, no. But she wants it. Just give her a chance."

"Why don't the four of you come over for dinner the night of Tuesday's gallery launch? As a first step it's not too big, but it's a first step."

There was hope in his heart. Like this could actually be resolved and get better. "I'll talk to her. Be sure it works with the schedule, but I think it's doable. Thanks, Mom."

"Don't thank me yet. Just a reminder that I'm going to have to apologize. You know I hate that part." She glared at him.

"Yeah, me too, Mom, me too."

## CHAPTER TWENTY-ONE

KELLY HAD LOVED New York City from the first. She'd been young, but not naive. By that point in her life she'd lived in three countries and several states so it hadn't been as daunting as it might have been for someone else.

It was all color and noise. Smells of the very best on earth and their polar opposite. The subway gave her freedom and she'd taken it. Taken it to escape Rebecca's constant scrutiny and judgment as Kelly had wandered all over.

And she'd loved this condo from the moment she and Vaughan had stepped from the elevator into the foyer. Walls of windows looked out over Central Park. A silly extravagance it had felt at the time. Certainly an extravagance given its cost. But he'd given it to her as a wedding present.

And during the divorce, he'd signed it over to her. At the time it had felt more like a repudiation of what they'd had together, but now, years later, she could see it differently.

Maddie and Kensey had learned to walk and crawl on the hardwood floors. Despite her sadness at her divorce, this home had always given her happy memories.

She waved at the doorman as they entered the lobby.

"Hello there, Hurley family!"

"Andrew, how are you tonight?" Kelly asked as she waited for him to check the box where she may have mail or packages. And she had both.

Vaughan took them.

"Andrew, this is Vaughan. He's Maddie and Kensey's dad. He'll be with us this week. Vaughan, this is Andrew. He's amazing and knows where all the best hole-in-the-wall restaurants are in the city. If you're nice to him, he shares his wisdom."

Andrew blushed after Vaughan shook his hand hello. "Ah now, Ms. Hurley. Stop. Always glad to have you and your girls in the house. All that pretty makes everyone a little kinder." He winked at Kensey, who gave him a high five.

They headed up, Vaughan smiling, making her wonder just what he was up to.

Once the doors opened and they stepped into the front entry, Vaughan sucked in a breath and walked into the main living space.

"You've really made this place into a showcase," he said.

"It's a comfortable house with a spectacular view in a fantastic neighborhood. I can't complain in any way." She didn't thank him, because she'd long since given him credit for it. Sure his money bought it, but after that, he wandered off and did his own thing. This was her home. Ridiculously luxurious or not.

But she liked him in it.

It had always felt as if he needed to be there. And

as she put her things down and the girls headed to their room, Kelly watched Vaughan move around in the space.

"Come on up to the bedroom. I'll give you some space in the dresser and closet."

He took her hand and grabbed the overnight bag she'd carried upstairs. "Oh, so you'll share with me here? I must be a pretty fantastic lay for you to share your closet space," he said in an undertone.

"You do all right." She winked.

They went up as she called out to Kensey and Maddie to change into pajamas.

"They make this trip often enough they have it down." Kelly pushed open the double doors leading to the master suite. A room she often escaped to at the end of long workdays.

"Wow. This is magazine worthy."

"I did a campaign for Sensei Ross. He included design services in my payment. This was all him and his partner."

The room was laid out in blacks, whites and grays with the occasional pop of blues and greens.

She pointed to the closet. "There were dressers built in when we bought the place, remember? You can take the tall set of drawers. Right now it's mainly empty."

She kicked off her shoes and changed from her flying clothes into pajamas of her own.

The girls came in, launching themselves into her bed and she joined them, snuggling as they waited for Vaughan.

"Holy cow, we've been invaded!" Vaughan came

to join them and the sweetness, the *rightness*, made tears threaten.

"I'm hungry," Kensey said.

"I think we can probably fix that." Kelly rolled from her bed and they all headed to the kitchen.

VAUGHAN HAD TAKEN Maddie and Kensey to Central Park and then to lunch while Kelly had handled some stuff at the store and then went off to a series of meetings.

They were due to reconnect with her in just a few minutes so he and the girls had cabbed over to her at the boutique, and that's when he realized the little chameleon set into the bags and other store wrapping was the same one from her tattoo.

It wasn't an entirely pleasant thing because it meant he'd underestimated her on pretty much every level. She worked damned hard to build a business that would support her and their daughters. And she did it successfully.

And gave their daughters a great example of what you could do if you put your mind to it and kept at it.

He'd been texting his parents pictures all day, wanting them to see Kelly and what she did through the lens of what they already knew. How fantastic their granddaughters were. That was the key, he felt, to bringing his mother around.

Mother to mother.

When he'd left the ranch the day before, he'd had a very strong sense that his mother would really think about everything he'd said. His mom was fierce, hell yes. Always in defense of her family. Kelly had triggered that—rightly or wrongly—from the start.

His mother was also, to her core, loving. Smart. Vaughan trusted she'd find a way to make things right.

In the meantime, he'd continue to have his brothers and their women in his and Kelly's life. The fact that she was already friends with Tuesday was a positive. It gave them opportunities to hang out and get more comfortable.

He hadn't had the opportunity to talk to Kelly in detail about any of the stuff that had happened the day before but he'd spoken with the girls and had arranged for their regular sitter to come over that night so he could take Kelly out to dinner.

"Can I help you?" One of the employees came over. He smiled, flirting an automatic reaction.

"Thanks, but no. I'm waiting for Kelly. We're supposed to meet her here." He tipped his chin to Maddie and Kensey.

The look she'd been wearing cooled immediately. "Oh. You're him. She's here. Just came in through the back."

He laughed. "I don't know if I should be flattered or insulted."

She gave him a long up and down and then shrugged. "Little of both. You do make pretty kids, though."

"We really do."

"Mommy! We had so many dumplings at lunchtime." Maddie ran over to Kelly, who emerged from the back.

Vaughan froze in place at the sight.

The woman he'd been talking to snorted a laugh. "You dumped that. Damn, that must suck."

Kelly had been working so she looked every inch the part. Model, businesswoman, lover of fashion.

He'd gotten used to her in a ponytail, or even how she dressed when she worked at her Portland store. Put together and beautiful, definitely. Sexy as fuck the night they'd gone out to dinner.

This version was pretty similar to the one he'd first seen.

"The first time I saw her she wore a dress a lot like the one she has on." This time, too, she showed a great deal of leg. Which was good because she had fantastic legs.

She caught sight of Vaughan and smiled. "I did a resort wear thing for sunglasses and sandals. Got to keep the clothes."

Her hair had been pulled from her face, but was free in the back and hung in a riot of curls.

"Did you get the curls, too? Will those stay?" Kensey petted Kelly's hair.

"No, baby. Sorry. They made this with curlers, a ton of product and then a curling rod. I felt bad for the hair people because it took so long."

"I like it." Vaughan managed to tear himself free and join them. "You and I have a dinner date. The sitter will arrive in about ninety minutes so we should get going."

Her smile brightened about a hundredfold. "Sounds good. I still have the car they sent for me earlier. It's circling around." Kelly said her goodbyes and they headed back to the apartment.

KELLY WAS GLAD her makeup looked so fantastic because it suited the dress Kami had given her just a few hours prior. She switched out the headband for a set of pretty pins with red enamel accents.

The dress was done in various tones of gold with the tiniest oxblood-red thread accent at the waist. It wasn't a dress that played coy at all. The front had a keyhole neckline that dipped low enough that a bra would be impractical. Thank heavens the dress was made for her specifically, because on anyone else, a wrong twist might mean a wardrobe malfunction.

On Kelly, though, it was perfect. Sexy. It showed a great deal of skin, but they'd done some sort of rub-on tan stuff earlier that day so her skin tone was warm and worked with the shades of gold in the dress.

The shoes were the same red as the pins. She might be eleven years older than when she first met him, but she wanted him to always have that look he'd had earlier in her boutique.

This entire outfit was her way of saying to him, *don't you ever forget this is what you have.*

Of course, when she got back downstairs as they were getting ready to leave, he'd come down wearing a fucking suit and looking good enough to eat right then and there.

"You guys look so pretty you could be on a book!" Kensey slid past in her socks.

His hair had been tamed back on the sides, but it threatened to do whatever it wanted. She knew in an hour or so it would be messy and yet look utterly calculated by some three-hundred-dollar haircut.

Kelly slid a hand down his tie. "Wow. So this is your A-game, huh?"

He grinned. "How'd I do, Legs?"

"Love this suit. Did you have it in your suitcase?"

"I have a place here, too. We stopped over to grab some of my clothes. You look gorgeous. For real."

Kelly smiled, warmed by the compliment. It was weird that he had a place in town and she didn't really think about it until right then. But really nice he'd put his things in the closet.

They kissed the girls and headed out.

"What brought all this on?" she asked as they finally arrived at the restaurant.

"When we went out to dinner and had dessert in the hotel afterward the other week, I realized I had put all this energy into the kids and our family, but not enough on Vaughan and Kelly when I'm not deep inside you."

"You're saying all this to get me hot, aren't you?" It was working.

They went through a side door where Vaughan's name was on a list. The host led them to an elevator and sent them up to the top after sliding a key card through a slot.

Once they began to climb, Vaughan slid his arm around her waist, holding her close. "Did I? Get you hot?"

Kelly kept her gaze on their reflection in the elevator doors. "The answer to that question is going to be yes in at least ninety-eight percent of the situations I'd be presented with."

A smile hitched his mouth up at the left. "Then that's just a very positive by-product."

They were led to a table on a rooftop deck, surrounded by overflowing planters of flowers and herbs. Votive candles sat in hanging jars, dotting the space like fireflies.

Once they'd been left alone and were perusing the menu, Vaughan spoke again. "Mary's the one who told me about this place. She said it was quiet, private and romantic and had great food I'm supposed to take pictures for her. I wanted us to have something special. Just Kelly and Vaughan."

"She's a foodie? Should have guessed, naturally when she brought like forty-five amazing dishes to the house that day."

"She ran a supper club for a few years. She's done a few cookbooks now. Has a web series in development. *Foodie* is probably a lightweight word for it. But yes."

"She's very sweet to the kids. And she was nice at the house."

"They're a little busy just now. She's due next month. But she's told me she wants us all to come over for dinner. You'll like her."

They ordered a bottle of champagne and the appetizers their server had recommended.

Vaughan looked her over carefully. "Are you all right? There's something you want to eat on the menu, right?"

"Pretty much all of it. You need to get something different than I do so I can try yours. Otherwise I'll have menu remorse. You know when you order something and like three minutes later you wish you'd ordered something else?" Kelly turned her attention from her menu to Vaughan's face. "Why do you ask?"

"You just looked a little hesitant. Like you didn't really want anything."

Kelly shrugged. "I have an appearance tomorrow and several important business meetings so I have to think about everything I put in my mouth. I was doing calorie math."

"You look great. You're in fantastic shape. You can have dinner without worrying."

*Oh, she could?* How nice of him to give her permission.

He didn't mean anything he'd said to be anything but complimentary. She tried to remember that. She didn't want to fight with him. It was nice to be there in the evening as summer was ready to push spring out of the way.

It was sweet of him to have brought her there. The place was one of those well-kept secrets so she didn't need to deal with lines of fans outside with grabbing hands and all the temptation they represented.

He was trying really hard and she needed to do the same and get the hell out of her own way.

"So, tell me about your solo project," Kelly asked him as a jazz trio played Cole Porter across the rooftop.

"THIS PLACE IS like a scene from a movie," Vaughan said. He definitely needed to thank Mary for the suggestion and his manager Jeremy for the favor he called in to get them this table.

"Thank you for making this happen."

"My solo stuff. I've had some ideas for a few years. I've tried to bring them into Sweet Hollow Ranch. This last album was an education for me. I pushed hard on things I felt strongly about. Some of it made a difference and it was good for me to learn how to step up and be more active in our creative process."

Food arrived, they ordered dinner and he spoke again.

"And then the tour ended and I landed in your guest room. And all this change hit me. I started writing as a way to get it out. Like free writing, I guess. And then they were lyrics and songs."

"I'm thrilled for you. I hope you'll let me hear it."

"I seem to recall a certain naked model sprawled in my bed as I played guitar and serenaded her more than once."

"I love hearing you sing. Why not do this with Sweet Hollow Ranch?"

"It's not our sound. It's my sound. I want to sing these songs. I want to produce them how I want them. I told Paddy, if it's a band thing, I have to compromise. I don't want to. This is mine. I want it how I want it."

"All right."

"Just like that?" Vaughan asked her.

"You have a talent. A gift. I support you doing whatever the hell you want with it." She shrugged. "You're an artist. That process isn't always predictable and sometimes you need to flip the script and do something totally new. That's exciting."

"Thank you for supporting me." It meant a lot to him. "I spoke to my brothers about it. They're all behind me. I figure given all the major stuff going on in their lives, the band won't be back in the studio for a year or two. Now's my time. I have the place to work. The time to work and so much fucking joy and terror and amazement in my life right now I feel like if I don't use it when it's clearly pushing so hard to be done, I'd be turning my back on it."

"I get it. If you need to be at the ranch more while you work, that's fine. We can make it happen."

"I just got that apartment above the garage just right. The soundproofing has been installed. I've got my boards there. Most of my guitars and other equipment. I'm good. There's something about that view out the windows, over the neighborhood, the trees and roofs here and there. Maddie suggested window boxes and I think I agreed to go flower shopping with her sometime soon."

"She's really good at making people bend to her will. Like her dad."

"Thank God for it. Here I am, across the table from the most beautiful woman in the world, rocking a dress that makes my mouth water. You look at me, see past all the bullshit and you love me. I'm pouring all that into this new material."

"I'm glad, too. I'd love to hear it when you're ready to share."

He caught movement from the corner of his vision and turned. Two women at the bar across the way had recognized him and were taking what they thought were surreptitious cell phone pictures of him.

Kelly turned, caught sight of it and sighed. "I guess it was too good to be true. Bound to happen sooner or later. Hopefully we won't see nipples or have to deal with propositions."

"Let's just see if it gets worse or if they've done all they plan to." He took her hand. "Don't let it ruin our romantic date."

Fame had brought many advantages to his life. A lot of power. Certainly a lot of money. Those things in turn brought opportunity.

But there was another side to it. People camped out on the lawn. Heightened security concerns. He'd had Kelly's house completely rewired and updated for security. If he was going to draw attention to his family, he wanted to be sure they were safe.

And there was the in-between. Being recognized all the time. Some days it made him paranoid. Mostly he'd learned to ignore it. People were usually just excited to see him.

It made having a quiet, intimate dinner with his woman a lot harder, though.

"You asked me about the brunch with my parents and we got interrupted and even when we were alone there was nakedness. I told them the truth. All of it. Including that I'd be living in Gresham."

Kelly sat back a little, but to his great relief, that wariness she'd had for weeks didn't return. "What was their reaction?" She sipped her champagne and waited for him to continue.

"I didn't do my job with you before. On every level. They understand now. They know…my *mom* knows she was wrong about you."

She pushed the sweet potato puffs at him. He looked

at them and she snickered. "Think of them like tater tots. I promise. They're really good."

"Would you have said that to Ross?" It was important to know.

Kelly made a face and then shrugged. "Ross would eat a tater tot of any kind. As would any sane person who wasn't allergic to them. It should be unnecessary to *encourage* someone to eat a tater tot. I have to tell you, there were years when my diet consisted of three leftover bites of cold mac and cheese, a few tater tots and a grape or two."

Her sense of humor had become more self-deprecating, but not in a loathing sense. Kelly was more comfortable with herself and it only made her more alluring.

"I like them as much as the next person. But I do notice you're not eating very many."

She snorted, rolling her eyes. "Do you really think I'd try to fool you into eating them like you're one of our children?"

He had to be the luckiest man in the world to be loved by this woman. "I am so fucking happy right now. I love you and I'm glad to be with you under the stars. I'm happy you tease me."

Kelly had a slight reserve with most people. She was cordial but she didn't let very many close to her. Into the place in her life where she exposed that softer side. Where she trusted you enough to tease.

He kissed her palm. He'd thrown it away once but she'd given it to him again. He meant to do a better job with this opportunity. "Thank you for letting me back in."

Her smile in response made it a little uncomfortable in his pants. Unguarded.

He tried one of the sweet potato things and they were really good, especially with the spicy stuff to dip them in. "Okay, those really are fantastic. This didn't seem like the fried-potatoes-and-stuff-to-dip-them-in sort of place. I could make a meal from them alone."

He took pictures and then Kelly took a few of him eating them so he could send them to Mary.

"I sent one of them to the girls, too," Kelly said as she handed the phone back.

When it buzzed moments later, he slid it unlocked to see a picture of their daughters making faces. Vaughan held it for her to see. "Guess that explains the selfie."

"They love it when you send them pictures. When you're on tour it's like they're with you a little bit. It's a very cool thing you do. I never thanked you for that."

Their next courses came out.

"The pictures they send back help me get through. Especially at the point on tour when I am done. I'm rubbed raw and exposed and I just want to be home and know I'm safe. I see their faces and I can do another show and kick ass because they're home waiting for me. And they're safe."

Kelly swallowed hard, continuing to eat slowly. "What did your parents say?" she blurted.

He didn't need her to clarify. He knew she meant how did they react after he'd told them the whole truth. "They're pissed off at me. Worse, they're disappointed. My dad told me I should be ashamed. He said I hadn't been a good man. But then he said I was now. That meant something. My mom? Well, she was *so* pissed. At me for, as she put it, making her act like a bitchy mother-in-law. Kelly, I know things have been hard for you and that this whole thing with me and my family only made it worse. But after my parents yelled at me and my mom made sure I knew she planned to make me pay for having to apologize for being so awful, they invited us all to dinner at their house on the night of the gallery launch. They were wrong. They know it and I'm hoping you give them another chance."

"Your being a good man means something to me, too. I wanted to believe your promises at the beginning. But I was afraid to. I'm a lot less scared now. And a lot happier," Kelly said.

"I can't make it all better." There was too much damage for him to ever expect he could erase it all. "But I'm trying and I want you to know you make me glad I do. Every day. They're going to make this right. I told them that was necessary."

She groaned. "Great. I told you not to do that. Now they're going to think I put you up to it and made you choose. I'm the Yoko of Sweet Hollow Ranch."

"I already chose. I'm here. With you and our daughters. You're my family. Everyone got off to a rocky start but we're all older and wiser now. I honestly believe this is going to be just fine. There's so much amazing stuff happening for all of us right now, there's no other way but to be a big loving family."

"If you say so. I'm in if they are."

They had a lovely, long dinner, though she didn't

eat enough for his liking and he told her so as they got up to leave.

Kelly gave him a glare. "Look, I told you. This is part of my life. I have to think about how many calories I take in each day. I have to think about what might make me look bloated. What might make my skin look worse. Sometimes I need to be far more conscientious and in control than others. When I have work in front of the camera, that's one of those times."

"Vaughan? Can we get your autograph and a picture with you, please?" The two women from the bar cut them off at the elevator.

"And this is yours." Kelly stepped out of the way, but he could tell she was agitated. This had been a sore point for them while they'd been married and then, well, he'd given her a reason to be suspicious and wary of his interactions with female fans.

He took some pictures and signed a menu.

"Do you two want some company?" one of them asked him.

"Fuck off, skank." Kelly walked into the elevator and he followed quickly. The host downstairs told Vaughan the car had been called and was at the curb.

But just a few feet from the door two photographers stood, taking shots of Vaughan with his arm around Kelly. They called his name then one of them recognized Kelly.

Shouting her name, they got in closer but Vaughan hustled to the car where the driver held the paps back while Vaughan got Kelly inside.

"Sorry about that, Mr. Hurley. They just showed up," the driver said as he got behind the wheel.

"I think they got a tip from someone inside that I was there. Not your fault."

"You need to think about a guard. If you're out with your wife and kids…" The driver met Vaughan's gaze in the rearview mirror. He didn't need to say any more.

Being with them made it more dangerous than not being with them. He'd call Jeremy the following day and get some ideas. He'd hired plenty of drivers and guides and there was security at the venue, but a bodyguard wasn't something he'd wanted to be hindered by.

But now that he had his family around, it was a necessity apparently.

They headed home; the tension between him and Kelly had begun to rise once more. But it was more a build of energy than anger. There were dark and twisty memories littering their history.

But it wasn't anger. Or resentment. Since they'd moved into the same bedroom the bitterness of their split had melted away. Day by day. Each time they resolved some problem the ghosts of all that'd remained unsaid for so long had rested a little more.

## CHAPTER TWENTY-TWO

"I'D FORGOTTEN," KELLY said once they'd gotten into the elevator heading up to her place.

"About what?"

Her fingers twisted with his and where once she'd have felt divided from him, the monster of his fame always ready to spring, this problem was one that felt as if they faced it *together*.

But the reality of it had been dulled in the past six weeks. He was at home. In their neighborhood. The houses were on large lots so they had a lot of privacy. Even at the carnival, though he'd been recognized, the other parents had been pretty good about being appropriate.

The moment they'd arrived at the airport she'd had to remember. They'd waited until the last minute to board but even at that, on the flight they'd been disturbed more than once.

And then the constant stream of women angling for his attention. Chicks in restaurants offering group sex like it was something normal to do. Camera flash as people shouted her name, a reminder from the driver about a bodyguard.

This was what being with him entailed. The flip side to the beauty of the music he created. The celebrity that formed a bubble of unreality around a person for a lot of good as well as bad.

"I wanted to go for drinks," he said. "I'm sorry about that scene. I should have chosen better."

"It wasn't the restaurant that was the problem. It was a small, private place. It wasn't a celebrity haunt."

They had to stop discussing it until after they'd paid the sitter and had locked up for the night.

"We can change and have a drink out on the deck."

He pulled her close once they got changed.

"You looked so gorgeous and sexy in that outfit. I'm sorry to see it go. But you're so beautiful and perfect sometimes it's like I can't look at you straight on or risk blindness."

No one gave compliments like he did.

She kissed him. "I have closetsful of clothes. I'll dress up for you again. Especially if you wear a suit more often."

They headed out to the deck outside the bedroom.

"This looks better than I remembered." Vaughan settled next to her on the outdoor couch.

"About five years ago I had a garden architect over for dinner." His brow arched and she rolled her eyes. "My agent's husband, who attended with his wife and about eight other people."

"I'm trying not to be a dick. I can't control my face sometimes. I know it's my fault I wasn't around. I just see how men look at you and react to you everywhere we go. It makes me all weird."

"You were born weird, Vaughan. Anyway, this garden design was his idea. I just told him how I wanted it to feel and went back to Oregon. Three months later

I returned and fell in love instantly. This is one of my favorite places to be at the end of a long day."

"Plenty of privacy out here, too. I remember that's why we loved it out here so much."

"It really is spectacular how you can associate just about anything to a sexual memory."

"What can I say?" He grinned. "You're memorable." He sobered. "I'm going to call Jeremy tomorrow to arrange for security when we travel."

"At least you know he takes this sort of thing seriously." Kelly frowned as she recalled the murder of Jeremy's young daughter and the kidnapping and assault of his wife, who'd been a very high-profile musician at the time.

The price of fame was something people liked to joke about, or to say celebrities somehow deserved to have their lives torn apart simply because they made music or films.

Fame had been one of the temptations in her own marriage's demise. Vaughan's oldest brother had lost years of his life and success because of addiction.

Kelly's kind of fame had been relatively faceless. A silly thing when you thought about her job. But most people didn't recognize her on the street, especially if she was dressed like a normal person.

"I already had the security updated at the house. It's as safe as we can be without living behind walls with guards in towers."

"I don't want that." There were things she'd given in to, like the private school with good security. The extra precautions she'd taken when the house had been built, including a panic room Vaughan had insisted on.

Kelly continued, "I've given Maddie and Kensey as much of a normal life as I can. As normal as you can get with a rock star for a father, rock stars for uncles and a mom who was a model. They have privilege. But they have friends and dance classes and they don't have to live in a house with a moat."

"What if we found a house in Gresham that's on more acreage? We could have a gate, but it would be less like a house with a moat? We could build it to our specifications."

"I live in a house that was built to my specifications. It's on three quarters of an acre as it is. It's not like the house is unsafe. Acreage isn't why those women sidled up to you tonight after tipping off the paps that we were there."

"You're very stubborn."

"I refuse to do useless things to pretend away the real problem. I've given up enough of my life and freedom to your goddamn fame. I don't want your daughters' lives to be upended. I worked nonstop to give them an existence where they're not responsible for paying my bills or making me relevant. They don't have to perform for a roof over their heads and they won't be doing lines in the bathroom at fifteen because that's what everyone else in their lives does."

His mouth had been open, getting ready to argue with her, but then he stopped abruptly. Instead he reached out, pulling her into his lap to face him. Between his thin sleep pants and hers, all that hardness and heat reacted immediately.

His hands were in her hair, tugging to expose her neck and breasts to his mouth. He tormented her, licking, biting and sucking her nipples through the material of her tank top.

Her nails dug into his back after she'd yanked his shirt off.

He let out a string of curses as he shoved his pants down to free his cock and then yanked her shorts and panties to the side, sliding into her hard and fast.

And naked. She gasped at the feel of him and then at the expression he wore as he held her still, his hands at her hips squeezing just shy of pain.

"We good?" He managed to speak, though his gaze had gone blurry and sex-glazed.

They'd been tested and then tested again but she hadn't been able to go in and get an IUD yet.

"I'm not on any birth control other than condoms. As good as this feels…" She had to pause to writhe when he moved slightly and it sent a ripple of sensation outward from her pussy. "I'm not going to play with fire. I had a baby to save a relationship before. It doesn't work." Two kids was enough. Maybe forever. But certainly until they were much further along in their relationship.

He ground his teeth but pulled out. She dashed inside, grabbed a condom and they were back in business within the space of a minute.

"Love it when you're on top," he said as he rained kisses over her cheeks and eyelids. "I can touch all my favorite parts."

He underlined that by dancing the tip of his finger over her clit until she went all warm and boneless.

Vaughan did that. Touched her and made her forget everything. This was different. He still touched her in all the right ways, but now there was no forgetting. But a knowing that had changed.

They'd taken another step. Perilous though it might be, surviving it, turning to one another instead of away was a new process for them. And when it happened as a matter of course, it meant everything.

He came hard and fast on the heels of her climax, holding her close, continuing a slow and easy stroke for long moments after that. "Better than drinks out at a fancy bar."

Standing, he managed to keep her in his arms as they headed inside.

"And you don't even need bottle service to have the best seat in the house."

"Not our patio, Legs. Deep inside you. That's the best seat in the house. And it's all mine."

As she fell asleep, she let the words sink in. Allowed herself to be happy as she lay sheltered in his arms.

## *CHAPTER TWENTY-THREE*

TWO DAYS LATER, Kelly, Vaughan and the girls, returning from a quick trip to the market to grab supplies for dinner, nearly made it to the elevator when she heard a voice and it sent a shiver up her spine.

"Take them upstairs," she told Vaughan, planting herself between her family and her mother.

"Why? Who is that?" He peered closer and swore under his breath as he recognized Rebecca. "What's she doing here?"

"I don't want the girls exposed to her. Please."

"I'm coming right back down." He headed into the elevator with the girls, who'd begun to notice something was going on and had started to ask questions. Kelly just wanted those doors to close so she could deal with the trouble on her heels outside the view of her daughters.

"They wouldn't let me upstairs. I said you had me on the list. They said I needed a key card."

Kelly led her mother away from the elevator and back to the front doors. "Why are you here?"

"Ms. Hurley, is everything all right?" the daytime doorman asked.

They never should have let Rebecca in. Her mother wasn't allowed in the apartment. She didn't have a key card on purpose. But Rebecca had a way. She most likely freaked the guy out into letting her inside.

"It should be." Kelly turned back to her mother. "Not going to ask again. Speak or get out."

"I knew it. I saw those pictures and your rep and his were totally silent. I *knew* then that you'd let that bastard back into your life. What's wrong with you? Didn't he embarrass you enough the first time? How can you do this? Are you going to quit even the few jobs you do take now to be home at his beck and call?"

"Don't worry, it has nothing to do with your bank account."

"You need to think. With your head and not what's between your legs. A man will always steal your vitality," Rebecca hissed, bitterness flowing from her. "You let him *ruin* you before. Are you so desperate for love you have to do this again? What sorts of jobs can you get when people think of you as rejected goods? You were young the first time. Still vibrant." Her mother looked Kelly up and down, clearly displeased with what she saw.

Kelly started to fall back into that place where she felt fat, ugly and not good enough. And then she caught the look on her mother's face that said it had been her intention to push that insecurity.

Ugh. Twisty, crafty bitch. "Shut up. I know I asked you to speak, but that was a mistake. Shut your mouth. You've registered your opinion. I've given it the weight it deserves. Don't come here again. Or to the store. If you want my money to keep your lifestyle up, you will shut up and leave me alone."

"I'm your mother. I made you!"

"Thank God I survived it. My children are upstairs. Where I'm going. Don't come back. Don't talk to the media. I'll continue to put money in your account but if you start shit I will cut you off for real this time."

"After all I've done for you? You ungrateful bitch. Always have been lazy. If I hadn't pushed you where would you be?" Her mother used a patented Rebecca move, grabbing Kelly by her upper arms to shake her.

"Take your hands off her. Now." Vaughan had returned, full of rage.

"You! I don't—" Rebecca cut off in midrant as Vaughan pushed himself between them until her mother had no choice but to let go.

Vaughan pulled out some money from his wallet and shoved it at her. "Cab fare." Without moving his body, he turned his head to get the attention of the doorman. "Can you please hail her a cab?"

"Right away, Mr. Hurley."

Vaughan moved to give the guy a tip and Kelly heard him also say that Rebecca was not to be allowed back inside for any reason.

Kelly looked at her mother, shaking her head. This was what the woman brought to her life. Dread and negativity. There was no way she'd let her kids be exposed to this creature.

Sharon might be toxic in her own way, but this was hatred, pure and simple. She was there because she couldn't deal with the idea of Kelly being happy.

Again Rebecca and her superfast violence struck, her mother grabbing her arm and yanking in a way that felt far too familiar.

Kelly righted herself and pulled free as Vaughan rushed over. "You can't hurt me into compliance anymore. I'm bigger than you are now. Get out of here before I reconsider my generous offer and call the police instead."

"Get out, Rebecca. Don't think of harming my family again. You're done now," Vaughan said.

"Or what? You gonna hit me, big man?" Rebecca taunted.

Vaughan's smile was not joyous in any way. "I don't need to use my fists to beat the hell out of you. Understand that. Money and power are far more painful and far less trouble for me to use to shove you out the air lock of Kelly's life."

Kelly wanted to hug him, weeping. He'd protected her. Not just physically, but he'd made it totally clear he'd fuck Rebecca up if she kept on.

Rebecca saw that, too, and stepped back. "Don't come running to me when he dumps you. Again."

"I only run *from* you, Rebecca."

Rebecca yelled one last volley of insults before heading outside.

On the way back up, Vaughan took her hand. "We have a lot to talk about. But it can wait until you're ready."

"How about never? It's bad. She's awful. She's gone. The end."

He didn't say any more because the girls needed to be distracted when they got back. She'd shielded the girls from Rebecca for many years and planned to keep it that way.

VAUGHAN WAITED UNTIL after they'd gotten the girls down and then after an interview she did, before he circled back to the scene in the lobby earlier that day.

She came into their room, paused to drop a kiss on the top of his head and that's when he moved fast, bringing her into his lap. "My evil plan worked."

"Oh yeah? Is this where the pillaging comes into play?"

"Tell me about Rebecca."

"Thank you, Vaughan."

"For asking about your fucked-up mother?"

"For protecting me." Her voice broke and she hated that weakness. "You got between us. You made her leave." Not many people would have done that for her. It left her off balance.

"Legs." Vaughan blew out a breath. "I should have a long time ago. She's an awful person and the way she handled you tonight makes me want to punch things. I'm here now. I will protect you." He kissed her quickly. "So, tell me about her."

"What is there to tell? You know she was awful when I was young. I send her money and she usually behaves herself and keeps out of my life. She showed up at the store here a while back. She causes a scene and demands free things. I told her to knock it off. I send her clothes all the time. It's not enough. It's never enough. That's why I keep a continent between us when I can. Because when I don't, stuff like what happened earlier happens again."

"She's why you count your calories and freak out about food. I hate that. How old were you when she started that stuff?"

"Being a model is why I count my calories. But—" Kelly paused, heaved a sigh and kept going "—I can't recall a time it wasn't done. She had a little book she always kept tucked in her purse that listed calories for everything you could imagine."

Kelly stopped and tried to change the subject with a wiggle of herself over his cock.

"Not going to work."

She laughed because he was hard. "I beg to differ. Seems like it's working pretty fine from where I'm sitting."

"Ha. That part always works when you're around. But I'm not changing the subject."

"What do you want, Vaughan?" Her tone went a little thready, just a breath. "For me to tell you she was a horrible mother? That she's cruel and self-centered? She was. She *is*."

"I already knew she was a terrible mother. I got that from our first meeting." His new mother-in-law had been derisive of entertainment money and *show people*. And when Kelly had announced she was going to take off some time when she had Maddie, that had been an ugly scene.

Vaughan would never forget hearing Rebecca tell her daughter that it was bad enough she was ruining her body with childbirth, but that the clock was ticking and Kelly only had so much time to wring value from her looks before she turned into an old hag.

"Can't we please change the subject? I'm working to keep her away from the girls. She hasn't seen Maddie since she was two. She has no relationship with them. I don't send her pictures or have the girls make her pottery."

"But you do for my mom." Yeah, another thing he'd

taken for granted was how much she did even in the face of hostility from his family.

"They love your mom. She loves them. It makes everyone happy. But my mother wouldn't appreciate it. Eventually she'd do something to hurt them or scar them and for what? They miss nothing by not having her in their lives." Kelly shrugged.

He slid his thumb over her bottom lip. "What about you? What do *you* miss?"

She shook her head. "*Nothing.* I don't miss a thing. The only reason I pay her is out of some sense of responsibility. If I keep her housed and taken care of in the Hamptons, she's not trying to stay with me in Oregon. She has other things to do besides deciding now is the time to get interested in her granddaughters as a way to get something from me. It's only money. I have it, thank goodness. And I'd rather spend it on keeping her away than bags or cars."

Kelly's gaze went far away for a bit, and then she spoke again. "I can't risk her telling Maddie she's fat. Or trying to bribe Kensey into performing with treats she'd then berate her for eating later. Rebecca would see those beautiful little girls and start taking them to auditions the moment my back was turned. There's no letting her into my life. Not remaining sane and healthy after. She would take our children and strip them of their sense of beauty and joy and she'd twist it. She'd make them hate their bodies and their looks."

In his zeal to get her to reveal this to him, he'd forgotten how tender she was. Stupid for him to forget, when he saw a dozen times every day just how strong she was.

"I know I'm fucked up with food. And even when I'm not modeling it's still there. But I will die before I'd let the girls see it, or before I'd let them grow up in a home with a mother who hates her body. There was never a single time in my house when my mother wasn't on a diet. No fad went untried. She's the one who taught me that amphetamines suppressed your appetite and gave you energy you didn't have because you were starving yourself."

"Hey." Vaughan took her cheeks between his hands. "I know you're protecting the girls. I know you do the right thing for their sake. I'd like you to do it for your sake, too. Because you're worth it."

"Don't try to fix me. It's not that simple. I do the best I can. This is the healthiest I've been my whole life. I've constructed enough rules for myself that I have the control I need but I'm not obsessive. I exercise and when I'm not on a job I eat a pretty normal diet. I like myself. I'm not just saying it because it's what you want to hear."

She exercised every single morning for an hour. Sometimes he joined her. On her yoga days he liked to watch her as she moved. Sensuous. Lithe. Powerful. But at the same time, there was a sort of ritual to it that he understood better now.

He hated that she had to fight off stuff her mother had ingrained. What sort of person did that to a kid? He said it out loud, not meaning to.

"I don't think she ever really thought of herself as responsible for someone else. My grandmother was a very severe woman. She picked at my mother nonstop when we were around. Which wasn't that often. When

I think back on the times we saw her, I realized how much she browbeat my mom about her looks and what she ate. She got married pretty young. I'm betting it was to get away from home. But he wasn't enough for Rebecca. Hell, we weren't enough for *him*."

The father who'd walked away without bothering to look back.

"I don't know that you can take responsibility for that, Kel."

Kelly rolled her eyes, ignoring him. "My mother sees everyone in terms of what they can do for her. I was pretty and learned fast so she pushed me into modeling. Once it looked like it could be a real thing for me, she tossed him aside and we moved to New York. In her mind, she sees all the stuff she did when I grew up, the heavy physical discipline, the rationing of food and affection to get me to do what she wanted, as good mothering. She gave me a career. And she did. But the cost, huh?"

"Did you get therapy? I mean, that's a personal question and you don't have to answer. But you've done a lot of work and you've done it to protect our daughters. It's a pretty amazing place you've ended up in with your mother and your childhood."

"I started going when I was pregnant with Maddie."

"I never knew." How could that have happened? He was still married to her then. "Why didn't you tell me?"

"You wouldn't have cared. Not then. I know you think you would have. And I know the man who just threw himself between a crazy stage mother and her meal ticket certainly does. But you just… I needed someone solid."

Defensiveness rose in him. "That's unfair."

"Oh, is it? It was pretty unfair from my end, too. And yet, it needed doing and no one was there to lean on so I handled it." Her anger wisped away and she sighed. "I was freaked about the weight and the changes in my body. I saw her for several years. I still call her up from time to time when I need it. But mainly, I'm better."

It wasn't as if he hadn't loved her back then. But the shame of her being right about how he just wouldn't have given it the importance it deserved hit hard. "How did I not see? I mean, I knew you were concerned about your weight in general. I knew about the speed before Maddie. And even the chocolate counting. But I had no idea of the entirety of this. I'm sorry I didn't pay enough attention. So fucking sorry. Again."

Her gaze roved over his features; the light in her eyes was affectionate. "I think you should see this in a positive way. I'm done looking back. You *weren't* ready for a family. I didn't have the tools to deal with that or fix it then. After fruitless years, I left because there was no other choice if I wanted to respect myself. But I don't want this past stuff to be something you have to beat yourself up over time and again. You asked me and I told you because I trusted you enough to share. *That's* the point. Don't miss it."

He hugged her, knowing how lucky he was even as he hated that he hadn't before. "All right. Thanks for sharing. And thanks for giving me a real chance. I love you."

"I love you, too. But I'm so glad to be going home tomorrow."

Harvest would start Thursday and Jeremy was going to be in town so he'd have to deal with some band stuff. He wouldn't be around as much because of it so he wasn't as excited as she to be leaving.

He'd gotten spoiled, spending all his time with them. He had to split that attention and he wasn't looking forward to it. Now that he understood the joy of family with his women, he was loath to leave it even for just a short time.

"Come to bed." She kissed him. Teasing.

"Always."

# CHAPTER TWENTY-FOUR

"YOUR MOTHER IS HANDLED." Stacey settled onto the couch next to Kelly. "She'll behave. I spoke with her about the importance of boundaries. And that yours needed to be respected. Essentially I told her to back the fuck off or she'd be a lot poorer."

"Thank you so much. You should have seen her in the lobby of my building. I wanted the ground to swallow me up," Kelly said. "But Vaughan was so protective. He got between us and made her go."

"She told me about how he *threatened* to ruin her."

Kelly shrugged. "He underlined that it wasn't about his fists, but he'd make her pay with his money and power if she fucked with me again. I've been half expecting her to try to charge him with assault or something."

"I've impressed upon her that she's to operate as if there's a protection order in place. She needs to avoid your building and your boutiques. I'm having some papers drawn up. An agreement that should she violate your rules she'll be waiving all future financial support. That'll do the trick."

Her friend had urged Kelly to do something like an agreement with her mother for years. Stacey didn't like it that Kelly paid her mother at all, but if she was going to, Stacey had told Kelly to at the very least cover her ass so she could use it to keep her mother in line and out of Kelly's life.

It was long past time so the moment she arrived back in Gresham three days prior, Kelly had contacted Stacey to get her working on a legal framework to protect her family from Rebecca.

Stacey's nose wrinkled. "She's a piece of work. I'll give her that. She's outraged that you're back with Vaughan and look so happy. I'm glad I wasn't there or I might have punched her."

Kelly laughed. "That's what she wants. Then she could shake you down for a settlement."

"I'm very happy to hear Vaughan protected you. That's what we needed to see! After the scene how was he?" Stacey asked.

"I told him a lot about my childhood. About her and the food stuff. He was pretty cool. You were right. I should have before now. He also told his parents the whole truth. And we're going over there for dinner this coming Wednesday before the gallery opening."

"Wow. How does all that make you feel?"

"Valued. It makes me feel like I matter to him. That he listened and did the hard thing. He whined about how mad they got at him. But only a little." Her father hadn't ever stood between Rebecca and Kelly to protect her. Vaughan hadn't with his mother, either.

But now he'd changed and was trying. Which didn't necessarily mean she was going to hang out at the ranch with them for a week. Not at that point.

"The house is quiet when the kids are gone, huh?" Stacey asked.

"It's not like they've never spent time over at the ranch." Kelly shrugged. He'd taken Maddie and Kensey to help with harvest. Really they rode horses and played cards with Sharon and their aunt Mary, but they loved every minute and because Kelly had a bunch of stuff to handle at the Portland shop, she'd stayed behind.

She'd gone from sleeping at his side every night after putting the girls to bed to sleeping all alone in a silent house for the past three nights.

"I used to sort of like the first few days of their time with him. Being alone, not having anyone to answer to or be responsible for. I could sleep in and watch whatever I wanted on television. But I'm used to it now. I get up to work out and Vaughan isn't here. The girls don't come get in bed with us and demand breakfast. I keep waking up because it's so quiet and I'm worried." Kelly snorted.

"Anyway, he's bringing them home tomorrow afternoon. Their manager comes into town first thing tomorrow so they go from harvest to band stuff. I told him to just stay out at the ranch. Jeremy, their manager, can stay with Vaughan and they can work. I don't want him coming back here at three in the morning. Or having the girls sleeping at his parents' because he's out late with his brothers."

"That's good with you for real?" Stacey asked.

Kelly blew out a breath. "What am I going to do? Supervise him at all times? I can't live that way. Having to follow his every move to keep him faithful and from making a mistake? He wants us or he doesn't. I'm not his mother. He has to police himself. I look at all those women I knew when Vaughan and I were married and the only ones still together with their musician husbands are the couples who make one another their priority. I can't *make* him do that. He has to be a big boy and monitor himself. I'm raising two kids. I don't need to raise him, too. Anyway, I'd end up hating myself and him as well if I tried to accept anything less."

Kelly twisted one of her rings as she thought about how true that was. Another thing she never wanted her daughters to see was their mother not being treated well by their father.

"But I'm still scared sometimes. I'd forgotten what it was like to have your man openly hit on right in front of you. I can't offer him secret squirrel restaurants and all that exciting nightlife. I'm not exciting like that. I'm not twenty-two. My boobs haven't been in twenty-two territory in a really long time. My God, have you seen twenty-two-year-old boobs? They're fucking spectacular. All gravity-defying and taut. I'm not taut."

"You're heading into a full-blown shame spiral. Stop. Need I remind you that you're one of the genetically gifted? Stop with the *woe is me, my stunning tits aren't as stunning as they were before I had two kids* stuff. Otherwise I'll be forced to slam your head in the fridge like in an action movie."

Kelly sputtered a laugh. "You're feeling sassy tonight."

"I'm saying he knows you and he seems to like your boobs just fine. I get why you don't want to have to monitor him. I think that's wise. Couples who need that sort of time together to keep one of them out of trouble rarely last."

"I miss him. But it's a few days. I don't think he's pretending to be harvesting alfalfa as a cover for banging random chicks."

"That's not what you're afraid of anyway," Stacey said.

"No. It's all of it. This life isn't a thrill a minute. This life has dentist appointments and tantrums and teacher conferences. This life has laundry and toilets that need plunging."

"Fuck that. It also has a supermodel as the mother of his children. You're gorgeous and smart and you run your own business. You've raised two great kids. You're worried that's not as enticing as an easy lay with tits still up at twenties geography?" Stacey pointed at her chest at a spot a good bra could still get near.

"Your selfish, dumb-ass psycho of a mother didn't know her own worth so she torpedoed yours, too, so she wouldn't be alone. You're not her. Not ever. Stop trying to argue your way out of your happy ending."

VAUGHAN'S MUSCLES HADN'T been this tired in a long time. How Ezra managed to do this on a regular basis was always a source of amazement to him. He'd worked on the harvest, in and around showing the girls how things were done and when he dropped into bed every night he'd pretty much passed out.

Now that he'd taken a more active role in their day-to-day lives, they were bolder about coming to him for assistance.

That had been a painful realization. When they

stayed at the ranch in the past they were just as likely to go to his mother for something as they were him.

But that had changed. As proud as it made him, it also was another thing he'd fucked up and couldn't go back to fix.

And it underlined just how much Kelly did. Traveling with them in a nonvacation fashion had been far more exhausting than he'd imagined. They were already pros at what to do at the airport. But they needed constant surveillance and guidance. Kelly seemed to have inborn radar. If either child got a certain distance away, her attention snapped to and she wrangled her little ducklings back once more.

She made it look easy. Just two months ago he'd imagined he was just as involved and able to multitask when it came to his daughters and their care as Kelly was.

It was a wonder that Kelly hadn't hit him with a shovel.

Vaughan smiled as he thought of her, missing her more than he could have imagined.

The girls had missed her, too, and the past four nights he'd ended up with two kids and a corgi in bed with him instead of his woman.

The night before he'd waited until the girls had conked out and he snuck out of bed to FaceTime with her.

"Did I wake you?" he asked when she answered. She was in bed, but clearly not sleeping.

"I was waiting for you to call."

All that connection filled him when he saw that

smile. "I want to share something. I got some more done on a song today. Wanna hear it?"

"Yes, very much so." The happiness in her voice made him feel better and even more glad he'd called.

He set his tablet up so she could see him play and swung his guitar into his lap.

And then he sang her a song about a woman who did more than most people knew, a remarkable woman who filled his heart and his life. He wanted to sing that to her, not have Paddy sing it. That was another reason he was doing this on his own.

The look she always wore when he sang or played music settled back into his stomach. He realized that while it had only been a few days, he'd missed this.

He missed the way she listened to him. Missed her laugh. How he survived years without it was hard to imagine. It seemed to fuel him, fortify and anchor him.

She clapped when he'd finished. "I love it. This is so fantastic. You're doing something wonderful and I'm so proud."

Exactly what he'd needed to hear.

They'd talked for a few minutes more before he headed back to bed.

Vaughan wanted to talk to Ezra about it, but his brother had a whole lot of his own stuff going on just then. He worked himself to exhaustion. More even than his usual insane levels.

The oldest Hurley brother was in love with Tuesday. Anyone looking at Ezra could see the change in him. It was a good thing. Beautiful. But even after all these years of being there for his family, of turning his life around, Ezra wasn't entirely sure he deserved to be happy. And until he figured that out, he'd never allow himself to believe he was worth it.

And, as Vaughan loaded Kensey and Maddie into his car to take them to Gresham so they could eat an early dinner and head off to dance and piano classes, he realized he didn't want to be alone in the house at the ranch. He wanted to be with his family in his *home*.

But Jeremy was set to arrive within the next few hours and despite missing Kelly, it was always nice to see their friend and manager and it would really only be one more night until he got back home anyway.

So he headed out to Gresham, frowning when he saw Ross's BMW in the driveway.

Since the girls were with him, he didn't yank the other man out of his house and toss him into the street. But it was a close thing when, upon going inside, he noted Ross's angry expression and Kelly's body language. She'd put a table between herself and her ex-fiancé and that didn't please Vaughan one bit.

"Mommy!" Maddie and Kensey hugged Kelly, said hello to Ross and then headed upstairs.

"Ross was just leaving," Kelly said, taking Vaughan's hand.

Vaughan put himself between Kelly and Ross. "All right, then. Goodbye, Ross. I pulled into the garage so I didn't park you in."

"Actually, I wasn't quite done. Vaughan, if you could give us a moment in private," Ross said.

*As if.* Vaughan made a face and then looked to Kelly. If she'd given him a sign, Vaughan would have gone into the kitchen while they finished up. But she didn't and she didn't let go of his hand, so he stayed.

Vaughan shook his head and wished he had a reason to punch the other man's face. "I don't think that's necessary. Kelly and I are back together. I'm sure she's explained that. I'm sorry it happened this way."

"You have nothing to do with this," Ross insisted.

"With ejecting you from my house? You're wrong about that."

"Ross, just go. You've said what you needed to say." Kelly clearly didn't want to start something. Vaughan understood that, but Ross was treading on some thin ice.

Ross threw his hands up, frustrated. "He's going to leave you again. He can't want this life. And then what? You think I'll be waiting around?"

"Ross, please. I told you already." Kelly kept her voice low. "Even if I wasn't with Vaughan, I'd have broken the engagement one way or another. We weren't right. I'm sorry I hurt you. I really am."

Ross stormed out and she just sighed, giving Vaughan a look. "So that happened."

He hugged her, loving the way she felt. "I can't believe how fast I got used to the way you feel against me again." Vaughan looked at her face carefully. "Did he scare you?"

"No. His ex told him what she'd said. He came over to apologize. He admitted telling her that when he was angry at me."

"He said he wanted you back, didn't he?"

Kelly shrugged. "Doesn't matter. I'm already taken.

Thanks for bringing the girls home. Are you heading straight back?"

He'd thought about it. But now he didn't want to go. He wanted more time with her. "I was thinking we could have dinner and then I'll go. Does that work for you?"

Her smile made everything better.

"Yes. That would be great."

He hugged her once more and then went to lock the front door carefully. "He didn't use his key, did he?" Vaughan asked as he found Kelly in the kitchen.

"No. I changed the locks anyway when I first broke things off, remember? But he knocked. It was fine. We dated two years. He's not having an easy time of it and it's my fault. I hurt him."

"You said your apologies. You gonna feel bad forever because you didn't marry someone you didn't love?"

"Not forever. But I've had my heart broken. I know what it feels like. I don't hate him. I just hate the way he acted at the very end. But he was good to the girls. He was good to me. I wanted him to feel better for venting." She brushed her hands off. "Now that's over."

"Why doesn't he get back with the ex? She clearly still digs him."

Kelly laughed and laughed. "She doesn't dig him as a partner. He's tall and he's handy and it's easier than hiring out when something breaks. She wants a nonsex husband."

"Ew. The worst kind." He shuddered.

"Harvest go okay?" She changed the subject and he let her.

"Yeah. Good crop this year. Everyone pitched in, including your daughters. They also made sure Mary had plenty to drink and probably helped her with the realization having kids means never being uninterrupted again."

"Ha. Well, glad they could be of service. She's all right?"

"She's uncomfortable and hot. But the baby is good and so is the pregnancy. She asked about you, wanted me to reiterate the invitation to their house."

"All right."

"Is it too weird?"

"What?"

"Finally being welcomed by my family."

"Well, that's a pretty big way to describe something that hasn't happened yet. I'm glad to be invited. Glad that they're trying to take a step in the right direction. But that's all it is right now. I do hope they will welcome me at some point, truly. But I appreciate this step." Her smile was wary a moment, and then bloomed. "How'd that sound?"

He hugged her. Things would be just fine. They had to be.

"That sounds just right. And totally true. How'd inventory go?"

"It went fine. Tuesday came in today for a dress to wear to her grand opening day after tomorrow. She's going to turn some heads in it."

"Did she talk about Ezra at all?" His brother had been pretty quiet about Tuesday, using the burst of work the harvest brought with it to keep busy. Vaughan knew Ez was well and truly freaked out by the depth of feeling Tuesday evoked in him.

Every small thing his brother revealed was intensely personal and though he wanted to bounce a few ideas off Kelly, he tried not to share anything he thought Ezra might not want shared. Considering how private Ezra was, that pretty much meant everything.

"Sure she did. He's her boyfriend." Kelly's smile was coy.

"Oh, is that how this is going to be?" He sidled up to her, pulling her close again.

"They're private people, which is why you aren't giving me all the details, either. They're both clearly going through some stuff. But she cares for him, deeply." Kelly hesitated and licked her lips. "Second chances are important. Tuesday and I share that in common."

Humility rushed through Vaughan's system. Standing in a house he considered home, not just because of the people in it, but because he liked it, too. He felt truly welcome each time he came in.

He wanted her. Wanted to lay her back and love every inch of her. But two human birth control pills stomped around upstairs, already bickering about something that would no doubt spill down to them soon enough.

And like a weirdo, he loved it. He loved how it made him feel. Full. Satisfied. He'd had a good life before he moved into Kelly's guest room nearly two months before.

But this? This was everything. He understood the

way Damien always got drawn back to Mary whenever they were apart.

"I don't want to go back tonight. I'll sleep here and then go over first thing. I haven't slept next to you in forever."

She made a face. "Four days isn't forever. Jeremy is in town and staying in your house. You want to hang out with him. You're the one who gave that little push to see if you could help Ezra and Jeremy get their friendship back! Of course you want to see that happening. Plus, you just finished your harvest so you and the rest of your brothers are going to want to celebrate. Have dinner with us and then go to the ranch. I figured it would be just the girls so they're having chicken, mac and cheese and broccoli." She winked.

"The holy kid trinity. In my house it was fish sticks, mac and cheese and broccoli."

"We like to switch it up. Sometimes we have rice pilaf instead or corn on the cob when it's fresh. We're zany that way."

"I missed this. My house with my family, with my singing, dancing, bickering children. My woman being the heart of it all."

When he talked like that, all her doubts fell away. All her loneliness from his being gone seemed silly.

"I missed you, too. I've gotten used to you being around." She pulled a few things from the fridge. "We'll be here tomorrow. And the day after."

Kelly said the words, but she had to admit when he was gone she wondered if he realized his life was way more fun without a woman and two kids in it. But that seemed stupid, like all her other doubts when he stood there so open and loving. So genuine.

"Speaking of the day after tomorrow. Don't forget we're having dinner with my parents before the gallery opening on Wednesday."

Sharon was trying with this dinner invitation. Kelly had plenty of misgivings about dinner with her former in-laws. In Sharon's lair. But she'd agreed and tried to give the situation the benefit of the doubt. Having them know the truth was a relief. But it wasn't as if after all the time and things had been done and said between them it'd be effortless. But if they both thought Vaughan was worth it, Kelly figured at the very least they could reach a place where they could all be around one another without any tension.

Kelly already worried they'd blame her for Vaughan's doing a solo project. He assured her otherwise, but she worried about it coming back to bite her.

But she was thrilled he was doing this solo project because Kelly had watched him gain confidence in himself as he began to work on the songs in earnest. He had a confidence in the work that seemed to grow daily. They could blame her if they chose, but she hoped they'd see this growth and artistic expression as an amazing thing.

"I was just thinking about the song you sang for me on the phone last night." Kelly shook herself free of the memory.

"You were? It looked like panic at having ham with Sharon and Michael Hurley."

Kelly held up a hand, went over to the stairs and called up to tell the girls to wash up for dinner.

"I remember dinner. Everything is fine. I really was thinking about that song." She didn't want to talk any more about the dinner or to make him feel bad or anxious.

He was only going to be there for a little while and she wanted to enjoy it.

Ten minutes later she was buttering bread and passing the salt and pepper as the girls told her all about their own special boots to wear out in the fields.

"I had a pair when I was your age, too," Vaughan said. "Not purple ones, though. They only had green ones."

"Purple boots? That's so cool," Kelly said.

"Uncle Damien got them for us. He got a tiny pair with caterpillars on them for the baby to wear when he comes out," Maddie said.

"Babies can't even stand. What's that baby gonna do with boots?" Kensey was clearly dubious of the whole situation and Kelly tried not to laugh.

"It'll look cute." Maddie's voice had that pretending-to-be-patient tone. "People just dress babies like dolls."

Kensey gave a long-suffering sigh. "Baby toes are cute. You don't need to cover them up with boots. But they might fit my American Girl doll so I asked if I could have them once the baby was done and Aunt Mary said sure. And then I explained to her all about American Girl dolls. She told me she had a few friends with little babies who'd be growing up to want dolls so she was excited to know about them so she could make sure them other kids get some dolls and stuff. I told her she could call Mommy to get the address of the store we went to."

"That's very helpful. I'm sure the baby will be very happy to have such wonderful cousins who know all the good stuff already." Vaughan winked, amused. Probably because the girls had pestered Damien, which would have amused him.

"Remember Damien and Mary are going to need quiet so use your indoor voices and don't make a pest out of yourself when you're at the ranch."

"Uncle Damien says we can come over anytime."

"That was said the first day we arrived," Vaughan said, also meaning that might be different after several days with their chatty girls.

But he looked amused. The way the brothers seemed to enjoy nothing more than fighting with one another was mediated by the intense love and connection they all shared.

"Uncle Damien needs some experience. We're just helping." Vaughan's expression was mischievous.

"Vaughan Hurley, you troublemaker, you."

He laughed, as did their daughters, who loved it when Mommy and Daddy teased one another.

HE STAYED UNTIL it was time for Kelly to leave to get the girls to dance class. He hugged them all, saving Kelly for last.

"I'll see you tomorrow. Sweet dreams. And make sure everything is locked up tight." Vaughan said the last quietly, making sure the girls didn't overhear. "Don't let him inside again, all right? Not without me here."

Kelly didn't think Ross would ever hurt her. He rarely even raised his voice when he got angry. But her interaction with him earlier had left her skittish. She nodded. "Okay. Drive safe and have a good time."

"Hey, Legs, I sure love you."

She blushed and he kissed each cheek and then her mouth. There was giggling from the car.

"I love you, too."

"Take care of my girls."

"Always."

He watched them drive away and Kelly shoved all her fears as far down as she could.

After she deposited the girls at their classes, she headed to the coffee shop she hung out in until class was finished. She had some tea and looked over things usually, handled her email and that sort of thing. But before she could, her phone rang.

"Hello?" The number was from the same area code as the ranch but it wasn't Vaughan.

"Kelly, it's Sharon Hurley. I just wanted to call to touch base about dinner. Make sure you aren't allergic to anything."

Kelly looked at her screen again, just to be sure, but it really was Sharon.

"I'm not allergic to anything. But thank you for asking and for the invitation."

"I should have invited you myself. I realized that after Vaughan left. It was rude. Not the only rude thing I've done over the years. We'll talk more when you're here. It's not an over-the-phone thing."

"All right."

"See you and the girls on Wednesday, then."

"We'll bring wine and something nonalcoholic to drink," Kelly surprised herself by saying.

"Yes, that would be nice. Thank you."

Moments later after she'd hung up, Kelly was still looking at her phone as if it might bite. But Sharon had sounded sincere. Even a little friendly.

It was the first time since she'd met Sharon that the other woman had ever admitted her behavior had been rude.

Could it actually be that this might work after all?

## CHAPTER TWENTY-FIVE

VAUGHAN, KNOWING HE had to bow to the inevitable, called Kelly. He was supposed to go home that night but it was looking iffy.

"Hey you."

He smiled at the sound of her voice as she answered. "Hey. I'm still in a meeting. Once this one is over, we have another one with marketing. I'll be here at least three more hours."

"Oh." He heard the disappointment in her tone. "All right. It's already seven, though. You should stay at the ranch instead of driving back so late."

He knew he should, but he didn't want that.

"Don't miss me yet?"

She was quiet awhile. "I miss you enough to scare myself here and there. But that doesn't matter. What matters is that you'll have lots of times when you need to be away because of the band, or the ranch, or whatever."

"Scared?"

"I got used to you being gone. I remember what it feels like to be left by you. It's not a place I want to go back. And now I'm used to you being around again and I'm afraid of never feeling it again. Which is why you need to stay there tonight."

"I'm not leaving you."

"Most of my brain knows that. I also know that since we're making a go of this, we have to deal with your work. I can't worry about it all the time. What's the point of being with you if I had to do that? Anyway, that's just a stupid worry. Mainly I miss the way you smell when you first wake up. Your skin is all warm and you're snuggly. The sex part that follows is also something I miss. I'll get both when you come home tomorrow. Which you will because I'm not driving over to your parents' for dinner without you."

She made him laugh, which made him want her more.

"She called last night. Your mom."

Surprised, Vaughan paused a moment. "And everything is okay?"

"Surprisingly yes. It's not fixed by any means, but having her call means something to me. It felt like she was trying."

Relieved he didn't need to bail anyone out of jail or go yell at his mother, he spoke again. "I'm glad to hear it." And holy shit, he was.

"I'll see you tomorrow. Go on. Finish your meeting. Have fun with your brothers."

"I love you, Kel. Remember to lock up."

"Already done. I love you, too."

He hung up and headed back inside where Paddy and Damien were arguing over something that was most likely stupid, so Vaughan stayed out of it and seated himself between Ezra and Jeremy.

"Should I ask?" Vaughan tipped his chin toward the argument.

Ezra snorted. "No. If it gets too violent I'll toss them outside before they break anything important. Your tiny-ass dog thinks it's hilarious to bark when the yelling starts."

"More and more like Mom every day." Vaughan laughed and his brother joined him.

"Everything cool with Kelly?" Ezra asked.

"She told me to sleep over here tonight if we went late."

"So why are you anxious?" Ezra knew him well enough that Vaughan didn't bother to evade.

"When I was married to her I liked being with her. I always have. But if I was gone weeks or months I missed the sex, but I never felt an overwhelming need to rush to her. Now? I hear her voice and I want to go to her. All the stuff I know I have to do, the people I know I want to hang out with, you're all great, but it's her I *need*. I've lived in this house for years. I love it. But when I walk into the house from the garage in Gresham I'm *home*. I have this thing that is so... I don't even know how to put it. I didn't even know it was possible to feel this way. These are my kids and I was married to Kelly before and this time it's different. I sound like a total cock, but I just didn't know. And now that I do, I can't un-know it. I want it because it feels good. I sleep better with her around."

"You are soppy full-on in love with Kelly. Wow." Damien pushed Paddy from the way and stole his chair at the last minute. Paddy smacked him upside the head and Damien tripped Paddy, who nearly fell face-first into the edge of the table.

"Knock it off, assholes. I have too much shit to do

and zero time for emergency room visits for stitches," Ezra said.

"Nine stitches." Vaughan touched the scar at the side of his neck, at the hairline where he'd cut it open on a jagged piece of lumber with a nail sticking out of it. "I had to get shots for that."

He and Paddy had gotten into a shoving match that had slipped into punching when Vaughan had lost his footing, slipped and fallen off the porch.

"Mom literally kicked my ass," Paddy said as he picked up Minnie and started talking to her. "Then she kicked Vaughan's for getting hurt and Ezra's for not stopping the fight."

Ezra gave them both a dark look. "Even though I wasn't even there. You guys are really dicks sometimes."

Damien rolled his eyes. "You guys are such babies. As I was saying about Vaughan and Kelly. Tuesday really digs Kelly. So she talks to Nats about it. Then Natalie comes to our house and tells Mary and then it's all, *hey why are you guys not camping out on Kelly's lawn to tell her you were wrong?*"

"So why aren't you?" Jeremy asked.

Vaughan shook his head. "Kelly would hate it, first of all. She's sensitive about all that stuff. She knows what people thought of her before. That would only remind her of something I'm trying hard to get us both past. If you could not be morons when we're around, that's a start. We're having dinner here with Mom and Dad tomorrow night before the gallery opening."

"Mom's on a quest. She got on my ass earlier about Tuesday when I was trying to work out. I nearly threw her at you and Kelly, but I'm not that cruel. I did try to send her to Mary and Damien's place, reminding her about contractions, but then she said Mary's contractions were the practice kind. Whatever that means," Ezra said.

Vaughan fed one of the kittens a little bit of potato chip. "What I want is for everyone to just chill and give her a chance. I don't need you to get her name inked on your biceps. But she's my family. Like Natalie is Paddy's. This is the mother of my children and the woman I plan to be with for the rest of my life. A chance. That's it."

"Goddamn it! I told you guys to stop feeding the cats," Ezra griped.

The kitten stood on Vaughan's shoulder, head butting his ear, purring so hard it vibrated through his bones.

"I had to be fair. I already gave the dog some pizza and the other cat, the one with the crazy eyes, a grape. Dude, what kind of cat eats grapes?" Vaughan asked just to watch Ezra's vein bulge a little.

"You're an asshole."

"I learned my craft from you, old man." Vaughan waggled his brows at Ezra, who flipped him off.

"We're all giving her a chance, Vaughan. Honestly," Paddy said. "Nats and Tuesday are having lunch and drinks with her on Saturday in Portland after Tuesday finishes work."

Everyone looked to him. Vaughan hadn't known that and neither had Ezra.

Paddy looked smug. "Oh, that's right. My lady talks to me about stuff. They planned to include Mary but she and Damien are hosting her family this coming weekend."

"Okay, everyone, get something to drink and take a bathroom break. We have a call with the European label people in ten minutes," Jeremy said, getting them back on track.

Minnie gave him a look until he picked her up and kept her in his lap. The girls had loved being with her, and the little dog seemed to miss them, too. Vaughan knew the feeling.

"Vaughan." Jeremy kept his voice low. "Don't let this go. Be the best father and husband you can. You'll never regret it. It feels great because it's what you're meant to do. I had that once."

Jeremy paused, probably remembering, as Vaughan had, his little girl who'd died and the wife who was someone else's now.

"Thanks."

"If it were me, and I felt up to it, I'd drive home to sleep next to my woman with my babies safe under my roof." Jeremy raised a shoulder.

Before Vaughan could respond, Paddy and Damien came back into the room with the laser pointer and a furry mass of barking and scampering fur. Minnie jumped from Vaughan's lap and ran toward her brethren, barking right along with them.

Ezra came in, trying to get the animals to calm down and when that didn't happen, he lunged at Paddy to get the pointer and they crashed into the wall near the back doors.

Vaughan darted between them to open them both

so his brothers could spill out into the night before they broke a window or someone really got hurt.

"Come the hell on. We have this call to handle and then I want to go home to my bed with my woman in it. I'm sure Damien and probably Paddy can attest to this. Ezra could, too, if he'd stop pretending he had to stay away from Tuesday to prove some sort of stupid point."

"The fuck you know about it?" Ezra swung and Vaughan narrowly avoided his brother's king-size fist headed toward his nose.

Jeremy sighed and then whistled really loudly as he banged two large copper garden pots together.

"Jesus. I thought Erin and Adrian Brown were bad. You four have given me gray hair. Get inside so we can be there and ready to make some money when the call comes in." Jeremy turned and went back into the house.

With a few last elbow jabs and muttered insults, the four of them helped one another up from the ground, dusting off and putting things back where they'd been knocked away by the brawl as it passed by.

"I miss your dumb ass," Paddy said, as he headed back into the house.

Ezra laughed as they followed. Damien had to take the call with a bag of frozen corn on his lip. He'd split it when he'd rolled—or been pushed—from the back deck to the ground a few feet below.

"It's probably going to save your pretty face if you're in Gresham most of the time," Damien said.

"That would be a gift to the world." Vaughan pretended to buff his nails on his shirt. "Anyway, it's less than an hour from here. I don't know what the long-term future holds, but our house in Gresham has plenty of extra bedrooms and Kelly might share her tree house with you if you're nice. Seriously, she's got a sweet little setup out there. Weekends, if I can get Mom and Kelly on track, would be spent here a lot. And summer vacation. All that stuff. My point is, I don't need to be living half a mile away to be around. Things are changing for all of us. But we're Hurley. We got this."

"You're sappy now that you're in looooove," Damien sang quietly as the call went through.

KELLY PUT ON her headphones, hit Play and smiled as the beginning of Beyoncé's "Flawless" came on. Now that the girls had been asleep awhile, Kelly opened the big windows in her bedroom and scrambled atop the little built-in couch.

Lights off, no one to see her, she lit a cigarette and started to dance in the moonlight in her panties and a tank top. For Kelly, *this* was illicit and wild.

Technically, she'd stopped smoking the day she found out she was pregnant, but every once in a while, when she got particularly stressed out, Kelly gave in and let herself have a cigarette.

She laughed as she danced. Illicitly smoking and blowing it out her window like a teenager.

When she hit the *I woke up like 'dis* part, she had one fist pumped in the air as she silently shouted, jumping up and down on the couch, and as the song ended she opened her eyes to find Vaughan standing in the room.

She shrieked and fell off the couch. Luckily he'd rushed to her and saved her from a big fall.

"A guy turns his back for a minute and comes back to find his woman smoking cigarettes and dancing, half-naked, through her bedroom. It's like a collision between every single great teen movie I've ever seen."

Laughing, Kelly threw her arms around him and then withdrew, getting rid of the evidence and listening to see if she'd woken the girls up when he'd surprised her. Maddie would never, ever let her hear the end of it if she saw Kelly smoking.

And rightfully so. There wasn't any *only those three times a year when I'm about to lose my mind* when it came to a kid's view of the world.

"I told you to stay at the ranch tonight." Man was she glad he hadn't listened. She nibbled on his earlobe and pretty much rubbed all over him like a cat.

"We finished the last meeting and I hightailed it out of there. *This* is where I wanted to be. I'll go back tomorrow. But for now, I'm here. With you. You in tiny panties and a threadbare tank top looking like a wet dream come to life." Vaughan slid his hands underneath her shirt to do all this magic stuff on her breasts and nipples. Tracing little patterns with his fingertips, tugging her nipples, all while his scruff abraded her neck where he'd been kissing.

"No one can see in here. There's no house in the line of sight from the window seat."

"Mmm. Too bad for them. Because you're quite the sight." He kissed her slowly and she hugged him, not wanting him to let go. *He came back.*

"Everything is okay?"

"Yes." He pulled her shirt up and off. "Even better now."

"Door locked?" Kelly asked.

"Shit." He darted away to lock the door before he came back to her. He stopped a foot or two away, staring at her. "Strong and fragile all at the same time. I missed you, Legs."

"I missed you, too. It's nice you never listen to me. Sometimes."

"I'm not superhuman. You're standing there in nothing but moonlight and a scrap of cotton. How can I possibly focus on anything but the way you are, just for me?"

Her breath caught in her throat. "I am. Here just for you." Like she'd been meant just for him. No one else fit her the way he did.

He got rid of his clothes as he backed her to the window seat she'd just been on.

"I haven't had you here yet. We should rectify that. Put your hands on the side there. Bend forward. Yes. Yes indeed."

She did as he asked, turning away to grip the arm of the back of the seat. Vaughan dropped to his knees, nipped the backs of her thighs as he parted her pussy with fingers and then his mouth. A shock of pleasure went through her.

"No one and nothing else tastes like you," he said against her skin but it felt as if he said it in her head. As if he lived inside her.

Kelly had lots of people to talk to. All day long, as it happened. But not a lot of people she could *really* share with. The man touching her right then hadn't always been one of them, either. But that had changed.

Letting Vaughan put his cock inside her wasn't half as intimate as the way he texted her at two in the morning just a few days before to share a lyrical snippet. He'd gotten in and he wasn't going to let go.

"I suppose I can tell you now my IUD is working. We're all good to go." Not the most romantic thing ever to say, but he surged to his feet, pressing at her, the bead of his bare cock nudging her open.

"Today keeps getting better and better," he murmured. He turned them both, sitting, bringing her astride him, facing away.

"I want you to ride me, Kelly."

He held himself at the root as she slowly circled herself above him and lowered herself down, bit by bit.

"I missed this, not just because of how you feel when I'm in you, but because no one else makes me feel it but you." Vaughan pressed kisses along her shoulders and back as she slid down him and pulled back up. Over and over.

She was glad she faced away. Glad he couldn't see her face as he said such things to her.

Vaughan reached around, slowly stroking a finger over her clit as she gripped his forearm so hard she hoped she didn't do any damage.

"It's a lot harder to make myself wait when I'm in you like this."

His free hand slid up her chest, in between her breasts to her throat. He cupped her there. Not hurting, but so, so unbelievably hot, shivers ran riot over her skin.

She undulated a little, rolling her hips. This felt so ridiculously good she wanted to melt into a puddle. But puddles probably couldn't come so she decided against that and chose climax instead.

Once the first wave hit her, she let it go, let it crash over her and suck her down. Dimly, she knew he'd joined her but she was more aware of the way he held her—her back to his front—as he remained deep inside, one arm now around her waist and the other still banded up her chest.

He muttered a curse and lurched them both over to the bed, where they crawled beneath the blankets. Kelly found a shirt and her panties to pull back on as Vaughan pulled her into a hug.

"Going without this part sucks. I'm glad to be home."

"I'm glad, too," Kelly said, smiling in the dark.

# CHAPTER TWENTY-SIX

"OH MY GOD, Stacey, I don't know what the hell I was thinking." Kelly paced in her closet, looking at all her clothes, not finding any of them suitable.

Stacey was on the phone because she was currently visiting her mom, who lived down in Eugene.

"I know your mom just had hip replacement but really, is that more important than being here to help me choose an outfit for this dinner? Selfish. Tell her I said that," Kelly teased. Mainly.

After she finished laughing, Stacey adjusted her screen and gave her best scary lawyer face. "I need you to take a deep breath. Think of this as something you'd solve for someone who came into the boutique. A dinner and then stopping by a gallery opening. The kids will be with you at both, so there's that. What's on the menu?"

"Ham. It's one of her specialties, I'm told."

"Navy. It's a good color on you. Understated and classic. Twist your hair back."

"Pop of color." Kelly found a pretty navy fit-and-flare dress. A good length. Flattering. No excessive cleavage. To go with, Kelly chose cute tangerine pumps. Not too high. And she had a bag that would go well. After showing Stacey everything—thank goodness for video calls—and getting approval, Kelly got ready to hang up.

"Thanks for talking me off the ledge."

"You want her to like you. It's okay, you know. She should like you. You're wonderful. If she still doesn't she can suck an egg."

"Suck an egg, huh? Your mom must be nearby," Kelly said.

"Yes indeed. You're going to be great. You're awesome. Vaughan loves you, your daughters love you. How can Shurley resist?"

"We'll see. I'll talk to you later." Kelly hung up and got dressed. It felt like a job interview, which seemed stupid, but it did anyway.

She didn't want to wish Sharon liked her. For years her former mother-in-law had been so unpleasant, Kelly had gotten to a place where she'd gone numb. But when she'd seen how Sharon was with Tuesday, Mary and Natalie, Kelly couldn't deny that she was hurt.

She wanted that, too. Wanted Sharon to look at her with the same warmth she looked at the others with. Sure it'd be nice for the girls to have their mom and grandmother friendly, but it was more than that.

Kelly wanted the other woman to like her. To finally believe—to see—how much Kelly cared about Vaughan and their family.

It made Kelly feel weak, to want that sort of relationship with Sharon. But she wanted it just the same. And the call Shurley had made would have seemed a small thing to an outsider, but it was huge. Which was what gave Kelly the strength to keep hoping things would work out.

Despite her nervousness, things were going well. Vaughan was showing her his commitment. Every day. Being there.

He'd come home to her that night before. He'd wanted her and sought her out and it wasn't just the sex. It was that he wanted to be home. Where she and the girls were.

That put a bounce in her step.

And when she got downstairs to find both girls still clean, their hair still in place, Kelly knew it was Vaughan and his guitar that had kept them calm.

"Is that some of your new material?" she asked as she came into the room.

"Yep. You ready?"

"Sure." Kelly smiled brightly. The girls ran to gather their things and they were off shortly after that.

She tried not to think on all the ways that night could go wrong and instead sang along with the radio with everyone else.

Vaughan knew Kelly was nervous but he let her pretend she wasn't. What could he say? Kelly and his mother had a complicated relationship and now that his mom knew the whole story, Vaughan believed she'd come around.

But the damage had been done. Years' worth of it. He just needed to find a way to mediate, to keep himself between Kelly and anyone who'd harm her. He knew she expected him to protect her should his mother go on the attack.

And he would. He sure as hell hoped that wouldn't

happen. He didn't think it would, actually. But if it did, he had to choose Kelly or everything they'd worked to rebuild over the past two months would go to hell.

Once he'd pulled into his parents' driveway, they got out and Kelly paused to take in the view. The sky was beginning to get pink as the sun got ready to set.

"This is so pretty. I have always loved this spot."

He kissed her temple. "This is going to be just fine," he said quietly. "I got your back if there's a problem."

"Let's hope that won't be tested."

Minnie came racing down the front porch but instead of running to Maddie and Kensey, she leaped at Kelly, who grabbed her and stood.

"Hey there, Minnie," Kelly said.

His mother, yelling the dog's name, came outside but when she saw them, she lost her annoyance.

"Hello, my loves! Come on inside." After hugs for their grandmother, they ran in, off to search for their grandfather.

Minnie didn't want Kelly to put her down. When Kelly tried the dog just looked up at her with those big eyes and waited.

"I think she likes you," Sharon said. "She ate one of my slippers today so she's been keeping a low profile. Come on." She waved them inside. "Dinner in about fifteen minutes. Would you like something to drink, Kelly?"

"Oh, Vaughan, the stuff is in the car. Some wine and soda and juice. Can you grab it?" Kelly asked him.

He ran out quickly to retrieve the stuff, not wanting to leave them unsupervised for very long.

But when he came back inside, Kelly was offering

to help with dinner, an offer his mother declined, but it was a friendly response.

Ten minutes down. They could do this.

MICHAEL CAME IN, a child under each arm. He wore a big grin and was clearly happy to see Maddie and Kensey. This softened Kelly's heart toward the Hurleys every time.

They loved her girls. Even when they hadn't loved her, there had been a place for Maddie and Kensey. Kelly hadn't seen her grandparents since she was younger than Kensey was. But their daughters were surrounded by people who loved them and counted them as one of their own.

If Kelly screwed up everything else in her life, that would be something she'd be proud of still.

They sat and it was pretty clear Sharon was trying. Which was enough right at the moment.

It wasn't fixed immediately. It would take some time to get it back on track, but Kelly didn't feel like they watched her as if she were from another planet. Or worse, watched her as if she was planning on kicking a kitten or two after she'd harmed their precious baby boy.

Sharon clearly had wanted to say something privately a few times but it had been impossible with the girls and everyone else around.

The ham was all it had been cracked up to be; the rest was also delicious. Vaughan and his dad had looked a little nervous a few times, but Sharon and Kelly had gone out of their way to be pleasant. And the kids were there in any case. Even when Sharon had been at her absolute worst, she'd never exposed the kids to any negativity.

After dinner, they washed up. Sharon even let Kelly help. It was a little tense because everyone was trying so hard to be nice, but by the time everyone was ready to head down to the gallery opening, Kelly was glad they'd done it and survived and ready to see her friend's fantastic debut on their way back home.

They stopped by Vaughan's house for a few minutes. Kelly hadn't been inside it since the divorce, but it hadn't changed much. Half the furniture in the place was something she'd bought.

"Yes, that's the couch you bought. I'm still sleeping in our old bed."

All night long she'd been holding on. Because that was what she was supposed to do. She was a grown-up. She had dinner with her former in-laws and managed to even have a decent time. She'd agonized over what to wear, but that was okay, too.

She'd held on, trying to keep the fiction that everything was just fine when in all truth, she was excited and scared and worried she'd mess it all up.

What if she couldn't make this work? What if she tried her hardest and it still didn't work out? What would happen to their daughters? Had she been foolhardy? She should have gone slower maybe.

Kelly held the pudgy corgi, who seemed content to be exactly where she was, as her daughters gave her a tour of the house. Vaughan had tried to explain to them that Kelly had been there before, a long time ago. They were more about showing off and sharing something they knew than really giving her a tour.

"I'm not sure your mother is going to like it when I put this dog in the car and we run off with her."

Vaughan grinned. "I got the dog for the girls without asking you. Remember? Then my mom stole her when I was on tour. But she looks pretty darned happy with you. We'd need a dog door. Supplies."

"Make it so, Number One. I dig this little dog. Though I don't want to actually steal the dog from your mom. I'd be sad if someone stole Minnie from me."

"They weren't supposed to take her forever. Just until I got back from tour. And then I moved in with you. But I promise to clear it with her first."

"Well, talk to her about it first. Let's not make a thing if we can avoid it."

They took Minnie back to Sharon and Michael's. She tucked Minnie into her bed. "I think I'll be springing you soon. Mum's the word," Kelly whispered to the dog, who licked her before she tucked herself into a little ball and went to sleep.

EVERYONE THOUGHT PARENTING was pretty easy until they did it. Kelly didn't want to freak anyone out but Kensey had too much sugar and was way past cute and precocious and well into bratty territory by the time they'd arrived at the gallery opening.

As they'd arrived, some horrible scene had been breaking up between Tuesday and the parents of her dead husband. Vaughan, concerned, rushed off to get caught up to speed while Kelly shadowed their daughters, trying to keep their hands to themselves.

Art gallery openings and kids were things to mix very sparingly.

Maddie was more patient than her little sister due to age, but also temperament. Maddie was introspective. She thought hard about things. Kensey emoted. All the time. Usually while moving at seventy-five miles an hour.

And right then she wanted to touch. Everything.

Finally, Kelly took Kensey's hand. "We're going outside for a moment," she told Vaughan on their way past. "Maddie needs your supervision unless you want to buy everything in the store she breaks. Tuesday would probably prefer to sell them under different circumstances."

He snapped to attention and she led Kensey outside. They sat on a nearby planter.

"I know there's a lot of stuff you want to touch. You want to look at it up close and see how the light hits it. You want to see how heavy it is. If it's smooth or rough. I understand. But this is Tuesday's special night and if you broke something she'd be sad. Oh sure, she has good manners so she'd act like it was no big deal. But it would be and then you'd be sad because you would have hurt her feelings."

Kensey's bottom lip quivered a moment. "I don't want to make Tuesday sad. She's nice and pretty and she teases Uncle Ezra until his grumpy face goes away and he smiles. She would be mad at me, huh?"

Kelly let Kensey climb into her lap. "She would be sad. Which is worse than mad. Because you like her and respect her talent, you need to take care around her things. Like a big girl. I know you can do it. We'll go soon, but Tuesday is family and we want to celebrate with family. This is Tuesday's big night."

Kensey slid off Kelly's lap. Tuesday stood near the windows, talking to Vaughan and Ezra.

"Why don't you go in, tell her how much you like her work and then you can come out here with me. You can dance here in this courtyard until it's time to go. Okay?"

"Okay, Mommy." She kissed Kelly and then went back inside, heading straight to Tuesday.

Kelly gathered Kensey's sweater and her bag and turned, nearly running Sharon down.

"I'm sorry. I didn't see you there."

"I heard all that," Sharon said. "I remember what it was like having kids that age. So much energy. Hard to keep still."

"Kensey and *still* have a very tense relationship." Kelly smiled, watching her children through the window.

"I was an asshole for years. I'm sorry. I'm sorry for everything I've said that was cruel and hurtful. He told us the truth. But you could have many times. Why didn't you?"

Kelly, still stunned by the apology, worked to find her reply. "If I had, it would have been to hurt the father of my children. As hurtful as the cheating was, as being thrown away by him was, he loves Maddie and Kensey. And you. You're his mother. What could I have said? You knew he wasn't a choirboy. Long before I came around. And it was over. I didn't tell you because that's something my mother would have done."

"Her I will continue being an asshole to."

Kelly laughed. "Fine with me. But I'm hoping she never makes it out this way again."

"She hurt you, too."

She was not going to bare her past with her mother to Sharon. Baby steps were fine, but it was too much to simply lay it all out like that.

"I took it and made myself better. I'd rather be a good example as a result of this than let Maddie and Kensey ever see the dark side of my childhood."

"You're a good mother. Vaughan loves them, no doubt. He works hard, too. But they're amazing girls and you're the reason why."

Surprised, Kelly managed to find her words to thank Sharon for the compliment.

"I… Thank you for not telling me," Sharon said. "It was hard hearing it from him, but he needed to confess to us. I have no excuse for my crappy behavior. I could tell you I love my kids. But you do and you never used it to hurt me the way I did you. I was so wrong about you. I rose to a defense that was never necessary. I acted terribly. I'm embarrassed and I'm sorry."

"I…I wasn't expecting this." But it was important. And necessary and it made her feel like crying and laughing all at once. Ever since Vaughan had announced he was bringing Kelly home to meet his parents, she'd been so excited.

Had imagined Sharon would take her under her wing and help with things when Vaughan was out on the road.

But that never happened. That first meeting had been terrible and things hadn't improved after that.

It was time to put away all that disappointment. Neither of them had been what the other thought.

"I love Vaughan. I want him to be happy. And he can't be if we're at odds."

Sharon nodded. "He always has been a sweetie pie. I never thought you were good enough for him. But I was wrong. I hate being wrong."

Kelly laughed, despite herself. "Must be where Vaughan gets it."

"So their father always tells me whenever they mess up." Sharon held a hand out. "Will you give me another chance?"

Kelly paused a moment and then took the hand offered. "I think second chances are pretty important. Yes. We'll both do that."

## CHAPTER TWENTY-SEVEN

KELLY CAME DOWNSTAIRS after finishing her shower. Normally the girls would stay asleep for at least another hour or two, but the sun was up early at this time of year so she wanted to get her coffee and enjoy the silence while she could get it.

Vaughan waited there with their daughters, a birthday cake on the table along with presents and cards.

She didn't know what to say. And even if she had, chances were she would have cried anyway.

Her mother had always made birthdays a terrible thing. As far as Rebecca had been concerned, aging was something to be ashamed of. To dread and freak out over.

Kelly always made a big deal out of the girls' birthdays, but people rarely made one out of hers. Even Stacey knew and respected Kelly's lack of importance for her own birthdays.

"No one has ever thrown me a surprise birthday party before," she managed to say.

"What? That's crazy. Clearly I have my work cut out for me. Luckily, we've got lots more birthdays to work with. The girls have a present for you and then I have one for you, too."

"First cake and candles!" Kensey managed to do

some jazz hands that were totally appropriate for the situation. They sang "Happy Birthday," lit the candles on the cake and she blew them out after making a wish.

Maddie stood next to Vaughan, who had his guitar out. Kensey started to dance as Vaughan began to play the first chords from one of Kelly's favorite songs ever, Patty Griffin's "Let Him Fly."

That was enough to set the tears free, and then Maddie started to sing and there was no stopping the onslaught of messy, snotty mother tears. This child was something special. Her voice was a gift.

Kensey might have been a high-energy monkey, but she danced like she was born to. And Kelly had long felt she had been born to do just that.

Their daughters were all the best parts of Kelly and Vaughan. Threaded with their lack of patience, they also had incredible amounts of compassion, love and creativity.

Kelly clapped at the end, using paper towels to mop up her eyes.

"My turn." Vaughan sat and started to play a song she hadn't heard yet, but it was definitely part of the new material he'd been working on.

The song was about losing love. About having this wonderful thing but not taking care of it. Loss, so much loss and pain and then happiness. Connection.

It wouldn't have been a good Sweet Hollow Ranch song. But it was a beautiful song. A Vaughan Hurley song. About Kelly. About their relationship and the stumbles and failures along the way.

"It's called 'Salvation,'" he said when he finished up. "What do you think?"

*"Drown, drown in tears, salt salt it dries you out,"* she said, mainly to herself. "It's beautiful. I don't know what to say. How to even put into words how much I love the songs and the dance. And the cake, of course. This is my very favorite birthday ever."

And that was totally true.

They ate cake, and Kelly didn't let herself think about the calories. She'd work out longer tomorrow morning. But for then, she had no cares at all.

"Oh, this is yours." Vaughan handed her some cards and little packages and she opened them. Some were from Stacey. Some were hand drawn by the girls; there was one from each one of his brothers, even. And then there was one from Vaughan.

When she opened it, a ring fell out.

She held it up, blinking at him.

"Yeah. So that happened. I was thinking you should marry me. Again. This time for keeps. See, I had no freaking idea how hard you worked. How hard parenting every single day is. You did that for years and years on your own and I had no idea. No. Idea. I'm ashamed now that I do know how much of yourself you put into your business. Our kids. Your friends. Me. You tolerate my insane family. You make me happy, Kelly. Happier than I ever thought possible."

He went to one knee as their daughters excitedly hopped around making little girl squeeing sounds in the background.

"Kelly Hurley, would you marry me?"

Everyone got totally silent as they watched Kelly's face.

Could she do it? There was no willing herself not to

love him. It was impossible. She'd tried and failed for a long time. So maybe it was okay to let herself love him. Since she did already, that could be a good thing.

"It seems like it was always inevitable I be your wife."

He kissed her and then hugged her, pulling them both to the floor where the girls joined them, laughing and cheering. Already asking if they could be bridesmaids.

"Can Minnie be in it, too? Since she's coming here to live with us?" Maddie asked.

"Daddy hasn't asked your grandmother yet so let's keep it a secret until then. After that? I don't know why not. Yes, Vaughan Hurley, I'll marry you. Because you need someone like me and our daughters to keep you in line."

Vaughan kissed her a few more times. "How about tomorrow?"

"You can't even wait one day to start being unruly?" Kelly asked, a smile on her face.

"It seems like I've been making my way back to you for a really long time. The unruly part comes with the total package. That includes crazy parents, brothers who all love to punch one another bloody, some assorted girlfriends, wives and more babies by the day. We'll even make room at the table for your best friend, who also happens to be your divorce attorney."

"She'll be glad to know that."

The following day he'd been back in her life not quite two months and yet it felt like years. He'd asked her for another chance. Said he wanted to be a better dad and get to know the Kelly she was now.

She'd taken a chance then, mainly because she loved him so much she wasn't ready to totally give up.

"Thank goodness for second chances."

"Yeah. Thank goodness for 'em."

* * * * *

## *ACKNOWLEDGMENTS*

THIS WAS A really hard one for me. I scrapped tens of thousands of words on a book I'd nearly finished because it just wasn't right. I started again, wanting to get the balance really right because this is a different spin on a love story and I wanted to do right by my characters, my readers and my amazing editor Angela James.

When I sent it to her (so totally late) I hated it. I thought it was awful and I cringed to imagine what Angela would say. But there's a reason why she's so amazing.

She liked it! Yay! Not only that but she gave me so much great advice on how to fix the things I'd been worried about.

This book is in your hands because people never gave up on me. Missed deadlines because I've been so ill and yet, Harlequin continued to help me. Angela continued to be amazing and my family kept being crazy but amazing so I could believe in a second chance at love even after someone does something really awful.

I'd be remiss if I failed to mention the support of my agent, Laura Bradford, who never blinked even when I said, "I cannot have this conversation right now or I will have a breakdown."

My husband, who I thank in every book because he deserves it, continues to be supportive and my greatest cheerleader. I am loved and for that, I am very grateful.

**New York Times bestselling author**

# GENA SHOWALTER

**introduces *The Original Heartbreakers* series,
where three not-quite-reformed bad boys are about
to meet the women who will bring them to their knees**

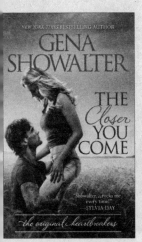

Just released from prison, Jase Hollister has only one goal: stay out of trouble. Strawberry Valley, Oklahoma, sounds like the perfect place for him and his two brothers-by-circumstance to settle down and live a nice, simple life. Model citizen isn't exactly this rugged bachelor's default setting—especially when it comes to a certain hot-blooded Southern beauty.

Brook Lynn Dillon has always been the responsible type. Not that it's done her much good. The down-on-her-luck waitress is broke, single and wouldn't know fun if it bit her. Or so she thinks. Jase makes bad look oh, so good. Dangerous, sexy and tempting as sin, he is everything she never knew she wanted.

## Pick up your copy today!

## Be sure to connect with us at:

Harlequin.com/Newsletters
Facebook.com/HarlequinBooks
Twitter.com/HQNBooks

**www.HQNBooks.com**

PHGS962R

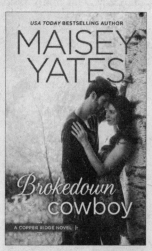

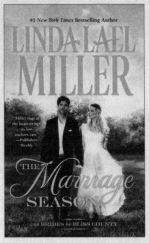

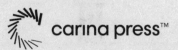

**From the creator of *The Originals*, the hit spin-off television show of *The Vampire Diaries*, come three never-before-released prequel stories featuring the Original vampire family, set in 18th century New Orleans.**

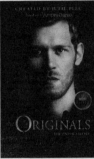

*Family is power. The Original vampire family swore it to each other a thousand years ago. They pledged to remain together always and forever. But even when you're immortal, promises are hard to keep.*

**Pick up your copies today and visit
www.TheOriginalsBooks.com**
to discover more!

**HQN**™
www.HQNBooks.com

# Get 2 Free Books,
## Plus 2 Free Gifts –

just for
trying the
**Reader
Service!**

**YES!** Please send me 2 FREE novels from the Essential Romance or Essential Suspense Collection and my 2 FREE gifts (gifts are worth about $10). After receiving them, if I don't wish to receive any more books, I can return the shipping statement marked "cancel." If I don't cancel, I will receive 4 brand-new novels every month and be billed just $6.49 per book. That's a savings of at least 19% off the cover price. It's quite a bargain! Shipping and handling is just 50¢. I understand that accepting the 2 free books and gifts places me under no obligation to buy anything. I can always return a shipment and cancel at any time. Even if I never buy another book, the two free books and gifts are mine to keep forever.

Please check one:   ☐ Essential Romance              ☐ Essential Suspense
                                    194 MDN GJAX                       191 MDN GJAX

Name                              (PLEASE PRINT)

Address                                                                        Apt. #

City                                      State                              Zip

Signature (if under 18, a parent or guardian must sign)

### Mail to the **Reader Service:**
P.O. Box 1867, Buffalo, NY 14240-1867

### Want to try two free books from another line?
### Call 1-800-873-8635 or visit www.ReaderService.com.

\* Terms and prices subject to change without notice. Prices do not include applicable taxes. Sales tax applicable in N.Y. This offer is limited to one order per household. Not valid for current subscribers to the Essential Romance or Essential Suspense Collection. All orders subject to credit approval. Credit or debit balances in a customer's account(s) may be offset by any other outstanding balance owed by or to the customer. Please allow 4 to 6 weeks for delivery. Offer available while quantities last. Offer only available in the U.S.A.

**Your Privacy**—The Reader Service is committed to protecting your privacy. Our Privacy Policy is available online at www.ReaderService.com or upon request from the Reader Service.

We make a portion of our mailing list available to reputable third parties that offer products we believe may interest you. If you prefer that we not exchange your name with third parties, or if you wish to clarify or modify your communication preferences, please visit us at www.ReaderService.com/consumerschoice or write to us at Reader Service Preference Service, P.O. Box 9062, Buffalo, NY 14240-9062. Include your complete name and address.

ROM15O

MAY 2 5 2015